Search for the Light

An Australian Saga

By Rosemary Noble

This is a work of fiction. Names, characters, businesses, places, events and incidents are either the products of the author's imagination or used in a fictitious manner. Any resemblance to actual living persons, or actual events is purely coincidental.

Dedicated to the men and women sent to Van Diemen's Land as convicts, but who stayed to build Australia, especially Ellen Fitzgerald (Henry 2)

With thanks to Arun Sribes U3A creative writing group also Jean Newman, Julie Moten, Bill Baxendale and my husband, Richard, for their support and encouragement.

Thanks to Karen Wells at Verité CM for the cover design. The cover photo was taken at the Richmond Convict Goal in Tasmania.

The London Convict Maid

Ye London maids attend to me
While I relate my misery
Through London streets I oft have strayed
But now I am a Convict Maid

In innocence I once did live
In all the joy that peace could give
But sin my youthful heart betrayed
And now I am a Convict Maid

Harry Gordon Hodges (c1830)

With thanks to the National Library of Australia

Prologue

April 1824 London

'For heaven's sake girl, can't you see the dirty mark? No, I'll not wear it.' Mrs Butler, more sour-faced than usual, threw the offending article back at her young maid in disgust.

Knowing that she had laundered the cap that morning and it was still damp, Nora shivered with anxiety. The mark in question was only a faint brownish smudge, most likely a tea stain. Mrs Butler was in the habit of dipping a biscuit into tea to soften it, on account of her teeth, rotting and broken as they were. No visitor would notice surely!

'Ma'am, there's been no visitors this week, and I will have the cap ready for you tomorrow.'

All she received was a sharp slap for her trouble.

'Who's to say there won't be visitors? I am expecting Lady Marchant at any time and I'll not receive her in a stained cap, do you hear? Go to Mrs Pocket's shop and find me a new one. I don't want rubbish mind. Ten shillings should be more than enough and be sharp about it. Twenty minutes I'll give you and no more. If you dawdle, there will be more than a ...'

Her maid didn't wait for the rest of the sentence but rushed from the room, her pale face crimson from the slap and her eyes smarting with tears. How she hated the old lady. God knew it was a rare occasion for anyone to visit, her being so spiteful and all. But perhaps she should not be so harsh after all, Mrs Butler complained daily about the pain in her joints. Her mother used to tell Nora always to look for the good in people and she did try. At times like these, it was so difficult.

Still, in her apron, Nora sped out of the servant's entrance of the modest Westminster residence. She dared not run in case Mrs Butler watched from the window. She was forever stressing how a maid should behave and running was one of the many things she despised.

How thrilled she had been to be made housemaid a year before. Even the frequent harsh words and occasional slap from the widowed Mrs Butler were better than scrubbing pans for hours in boiling water, getting up at five o'clock on a cold winter's morning to clean out hearths, light the fires and start preparing the other servants' breakfast. She had to keep telling herself that no job was worse than a skivvy's.

Out of sight at last, Nora ran across Portman Square. She did not pause to admire the newly budding trees or the few remaining daffodils dotted amongst the grass, but pressed onwards to Baker Street as a distant church bell rang the midday hour. Avoiding the muddy puddles from the morning's rain, the fresh horse manure and passing carts, she crossed over into Orchard Street.

She had never been inside the small bow fronted shop before but sometimes stopped on her Sundays off to look at the display of bonnets and lace handkerchiefs in the window. It rarely changed. There was a decayed air about the bonnets, un-admired, unwanted, gathering dust. Once Nora saw an abandoned cobweb hanging from a bonnet, but that, at least, had gone now. No one would describe the shop as fashionable, not even its elderly clientele.

Nora pushed at the door and a tiny bell rang above it. Tentative and nervous she entered the shop, adjusting her cap and tucking away loose, red curls that strayed down her neck. Inside it was poky and dark, a thick curtain dividing the shop from whatever lay behind. Nora caught a whiff of an unpleasant mixture of decay and cooked cabbage and wrinkled her nose. Shabby cupboards and drawers of blackened oak lined the wall next to the curtain.

The owner, Mrs Pocket, stood guard, owlish behind a narrow counter. She was a thin stringy sort of woman, whose lips pursed and then scowled. Nora, still breathless, asked her if she could see some lace caps. Begrudging, Mrs Pocket turned to the cupboards, and all the while watching Nora out of the corner of one eye, she brought out a tray and set it on the counter. As she began to show Nora some old-fashioned caps, the tinkling bell rang again and a gentleman entered the shop.

'Good day to you sir, and how may I help you,' fawned Mrs Pocket. Her sycophantic, shop owner's smile was immediate and fixed on the gentleman, like a hawk surveying its prey. He was hard of hearing and Mrs Pocket had to repeat herself, but with no sign of irritation. After the pleasantries, Mrs Pocket began to serve the gentleman, ignoring Nora, who was left looking through the choice of caps.

The shopkeeper had said not so much as a word to Nora, her distaste apparent in every movement and glance. Gone were the pursed, frowning lips, Mrs Pocket now wore a mask of friendliness and charm. The gentleman meant money, did she not realise that Nora also had money? She felt like getting the coins out of her pocket and waving them at her, but gritted her teeth and returned to her task.

She lifted each cap up to the only available light, the grimy window of the bonnet graveyard. Inwardly she chuckled at the thought. At last, she found a similar cap to the soiled one but worried about the quality, for the lace didn't look as fine as it should. If she bought it and Mrs Butler did not approve she would be in trouble, but would she be in more trouble if she went back empty handed? This was the first time she had been entrusted with such a duty and dare not get it wrong. She turned again to speak to Mrs Pocket who glared at Nora for attempting to interrupt.

The seconds ticked by and Nora was sure that more than fifteen minutes had passed. It looked as though the elderly gentleman was going to take an age in deciding which handkerchief to buy. Nora's heart began to beat a little faster as she tried gesturing to Mrs Pocket. She continued to ignore her. Nora heard the loud tick of a clock somewhere beyond the curtain and then a single quarter chime. Her heart began to hammer in her chest.

Frantic with worry Nora decided she could wait no longer. Grabbing the cap, she hurriedly made for the door and looking back towards Mrs Pocket as she opened it, she uttered 'Don't worry I will be back soon with the cap or the money.'

She sped down the street but before reaching Baker Street, Nora was surprised by a small boy tugging at her dress, telling her she must come back to Mrs Pocket's shop. She stopped dead, not knowing what to do. The boy grasped at her hand and with great reluctance Nora turned and followed the boy back to the shop. The boy pushed open the shop door and, in slow motion, Nora stepped on the mat inside the door. Her mouth dried with dread on seeing the malign expression on the shopkeeper's face. Mrs Pocket began a tirade of abuse, calling her thief and other dreadful names. The old gentleman turned and walked out without his handkerchief, further infuriating the shopkeeper. Nora tried to explain, but her words were drowned out by Mrs Pocket's venomous outburst, her face purple with fury, her eyes popping from their hooded sockets. Nora could not get beyond the word 'but'. By the time the constable arrived, brought once again by the small boy, she was in despair and could only think of Mrs Butler's anger at her tardiness.

Mrs Pocket took a deep breath and fixing her stare on Nora, she began her account of the girl's crime. She described how she knew the girl was up to no good as soon as she entered the shop. How she appeared nervous and fidgety and her flushed face showed she had not the appearance of an honest girl. She could tell by her colouring that she was Irish and everybody knew they were not to be trusted.

The constable, turning to Nora, asked her what she had to say for herself.

'But I can pay for the cap.' she said drawing the ten shillings from her pocket to show the constable.

'Would you look at that Constable.' screeched Mrs Pocket. 'That's even more despicable, to have the money and still steal the cap. I don't know what the world is coming to, really, I don't. Please lock the frightful wench up and throw away the key. That's all you deserve my girl.'

The constable brought out his cuffs and commanded Nora to hold out her hands. She looked at his stern, unyielding expression and suddenly her silly fears about Mrs Butler's anger turned into something far worse. She couldn't name it but she felt it spread through her whole body and it made her nauseous. The constable grabbed her hands, which unknowingly, she had raised towards him. Then clamping the cold, heavy iron around her wrists, he pushed the unprotesting Nora from the shop with Mrs Pocket's oaths still ringing in her ears.

Outside, the weak, April sunshine had disappeared, a fine rain taking its place. The constable shoved her down the street and her feet set to walking, while her eyes pricked with tears of humiliation. She cast them down, not wanting to see passers-by judge her, but she need not have worried as they were too intent on avoiding the rain, with caps pulled down low over brows or skirts drawn up to avoid the frequent puddles.

Suddenly she became aware that the constable was leading her south towards the river, away from Westminster and her mistress's house.

'Please sir,' she said 'My mistress lives in Portman Close. Take me to her and she will explain.'

Without bothering to look at her, he replied 'And why do I need to know that? You are going to Millbank, young lady and you will stay there until your trial.

He escorted the terrified girl blindly past Hyde Park and the great mansion of the Iron Duke. It was only when they passed Ebury Street, that she summoned all her remaining courage to plead with the constable to take her to her father, who would vouch for her honesty. He growled at her to stop delaying and walk faster. Nora screamed in the vain hope that someone, anyone would rescue her. The rain drowned out her cry but her upturned face received its second slap of the day, this one much harder than the first. Her green eyes widened with shock and she lost all further resistance.

The constable was more than irritated with the girl. 'Stupid chit,' he mumbled to himself, 'acting all innocent when she was caught in the act. I look forward to hearing how she tries to get out of this in court.' He was cold and wet and looked forward to a mug of ale and a hot pie in the White Swan, where a new barmaid had caught his fancy. Hastening to get out of the rain he hurried the girl along, ignoring her tears.

She could not believe what was happening until they turned left beside the Thames and saw the grim edifice of new Millbank Penitentiary looming over the river, dwarfing its neighbours. This fearsome five-sided fortress, with watch towers between, was only meant for the worst kind of villains surely; not for her, a sixteen-year-old housemaid, she thought in horror.

'No sir,' a final protest, 'it really has been a mistake. I shouldn't be coming here. My mistress will be wondering where I am,' she cried as he dragged her towards the prison.

'Stop struggling or you will be put in leg irons as well, girl.' He pushed her in the direction of the gates making her stumble, then hoiked her once more toward the entrance which swallowed her and her cries.

Chapter1

May 1824 London

Daring to lift her eyes, she glanced around. The kinder amongst those twelve good men would describe her glance as furtive, the less kind would say shifty. Had she been asked she would have said fearful; but no one did enquire. The judge asked his question a second time; this time with impatience.

'Have you anything to say on your behalf?'

What should she say to a judge? It was so beyond her experience, so she replied the only thing she could think of. 'Please sir, I am a housemaid and my family don't know where I am.'

She shivered uncontrollably, although the afternoon warmth made her stained, woollen dress stick damply to her skin. The huge courtroom overawed her. It was a room bigger and grander than she had ever seen or imagined was possible. The jury to her right stared intently at her, but she avoided their stare as she would avoid the look of any man. Instead, she hung her head and stared unseeing at her tight entwined hands, which made her look both sullen and guilty. It was of no consequence to them that she was young and pretty for she was just another girl, down on her luck. There were a thousand others, no ten thousand, others like her in London. Something must be done about it.

Nora felt unrehearsed for these legal proceedings. She had no money for a lawyer and found this whole experience terrifying. The stern appearance of the judge, in his scarlet robes and long horsehair wig, made her want to crawl into a hole somewhere. But here in this large courtroom, there was nowhere to hide, nowhere to escape. She was the main exhibit.

The horrors of the morning still tormented her. Chained to other prisoners at the ankle, she shuffled from Millbank to the Old Bailey. The journey taking a good hour, as they tried to avoid the rotting fruit thrown by ragamuffins, gleeful that there were some worse off than themselves. The shame of it sickened her. She felt tired and sore where the iron had bruised her ankle and, longing for home and her sisters to comfort her, Nora's mind began to wander again. But now the judge was speaking and she forced herself to try and take in what he was saying.

'Eleanora Nolan, you have been found guilty of grand larceny and will be transported beyond the seas for the term of seven years. Next case.'

A smirk of triumph appeared on Mrs Pocket's face, satisfaction on the constable's and boredom on the judge's. Nora listened to the judge but without understanding because the words made no sense to her.

'Please sir' she tried again 'when may I go back to my family?'

'Take her down,' was the terse instruction and the court official hastened to comply.

Her visit to the court of the Old Bailey was brief and forgettable. Who of the audience, other than Mrs Pocket, would remember her beyond the next case or a drink-befuddled sleep? What did she matter? After all, she was but another member of the poor and feckless class, so bedevilling London these years past. Good riddance. Let the colonies have her.

Nora tried asking the gruff constable, who had accompanied the prisoners to the Old Bailey, what the judge had meant, as he escorted her down to the waiting cell below. He informed Nora that she would not be returning to Milbank, but would go to Newgate Prison.

She opened her mouth to ask more, but he waved her away as he led another prisoner to the dock. Nora stood there confused and miserable. As she waited in the cell underneath the court, she had ample opportunity to wonder why she did not try to tell the judge and jury what had happened. However, she was so distraught not to see her father and so terrified by the court itself that she knew she would have been unable to get the words out to explain her actions that day. When Mrs Pocket described what happened she made it sound so bad that Nora herself felt guilty. She heard in evidence that Mrs Butler had sent the new skivvy to the shop to find out where her maid was. Mrs Pocket had told her that the girl was a thief and no doubt that message went back to Mrs Butler, who enquired no further.

With court over for the day, the convicted prisoners were either taken back to the prisons they came from or taken into Newgate Prison which was but a step away from the Old Bailey. Nora and some other men, women and children were led through a narrow brick passage adjoining the court. After a cursory medical examination by the prison surgeon, Nora soon found herself placed in an upstairs ward which held about twenty other women. Looking around she saw it was a light and airy room, with bare walls, but for some kind of text pinned above the fireplace, which she was unable to read. The whitewashed walls reflected the late afternoon sun glowing dimly through the oiled paper window panes. A large deal table stood before the empty fireplace, where some of the women sat sewing. They didn't spare her a glance as she entered. Around the room were hooks holding bed mats and above those, a shelf contained folded blankets. But after the stress of the trial and the last few weeks, Nora wished she could curl up and disappear.

'Well what have we here?' said a sudden loud voice beside her. 'Here's a pretty young miss come to join us, everyone. Tell the company your name sweetie?'

Nora looked up and saw a giantess, a full foot higher than herself, with skin the colour of milky chocolate. She was dressed in such a variety of vivid mismatching colours that Nora thought she might have come from a circus. A scarlet turban, from which a few jet-black curls escaped, covered her head. Her large round face was somewhat pock-marked but her teeth gleamed in a grin as wide as her face. Nora's mouth dropped open and yet again she lost the power of speech as she tried to take her in.

'Cat got your tongue, has it? Well, we shall have to call you Miss Mouse.'

'Let her be, Peg. You're enough to frighten anyone, let alone a young chit like her. See, she's shaking in her boots.' Another gaudy woman joined the one called Peg, but this one was much smaller and quite plump, especially her bosoms which were scarcely covered by her low-cut bodice. She also had a friendly face, though her smile showed crooked, gappy teeth.

'I'm Maudie, my love. Don't you fret! Well to be honest now, up close you do look like a little mouse. Tell us your name and we can get acquainted.'

'I'm Nora Ma'am.' Nora managed to whisper, looking around without success for a possible escape. Talking had been strictly forbidden at Milbank. Was it allowed here?

'Ma'am!' Peg hooted with laughter. 'Well Lordy, that's a first for you Maudie. Ain't you the polite young lady, Miss Nora Mouse.'

Nora's face flamed to the tips of her ears as the women smacked each other on their backs in mirth.

'It's first names in here, Nora, to us prisoners of course. You call the matron and the wardress Ma'am. But if you are going to be here for a while, you'll need to try and lose some of those nice manners or you'll be easy pickings,' said Maudie with a gentle tone to her voice, relaxing Nora a little. 'It's everyone for themselves in Newgate. Now me and Peg here, we've been in and out this place a few times, it's the nature of our work if you know what I mean?' Maudie winked and Nora blushed again as understanding dawned on her. 'So maybe we can give a little newcomer a few pointers to make things easier like. What do you reckon, Peg?'

'Well, it depends on whether she can give us anything in return, don't you think?' said Peg, giving Nora a long quizzical stare.

Not at all sure what she could give in return, Nora whispered as much. She didn't know what to make of Peg and Maudie, but she realised that she was going to need help from someone if she was going to understand what was happening to her. These women, although alarmingly dressed, appeared to be friendly and at this moment she craved any normal, human contact. During the day at Milbank, they had sewn endless canvas bags while listening to dreary religious and moral teachings. Not a word were the prisoners allowed to speak. They dare not even look at each other, not a smile nor a grimace, not so much as a look. At night, she was locked in to a cell with a stool and a washtub her only companions, while she thirsted for friendly talk and some little token of affection. It wasn't just her ankles which felt bruised.

'Don't worry Peg. I would like to bet that Nora, as young and innocent as she seems, has something that will prove useful.' Maudie put an arm around Nora and gave her cheek a quick pinch. 'In the meantime tell us your story, pet.' Maudie moved over to a bench and beckoned Nora and Peg to join her. 'Sit here and tell us about yourself.'

Nora looked at them both, still not sure about them but what other choice did she have? No one else was taking an interest and she longed for someone to confide in and comfort her. She took a deep breath and began her story, hoping she was not making yet another mistake.

'There's not much to tell, but I'll try,' she began.

'Speak up, said Peg, 'No need to whisper in here.'

Nora began again, her voice growing stronger as she told the story.

'My father and mother came to England, with their own parents, after the Irish Rebellion near thirty years ago. Da always said how there's only so much trouble and fear you can take, so even though they were Catholic they thought London would be safer. My Da trained to be a tailor and met my Mam, a seamstress, and they fell straight in love. He said it was like seeing the sunshine on Erin's green hills again; he loves the poetry and music. He often played the fiddle of an evening and Mammy would dance with us girls. Round and around we'd dance until we all fell to the floor. Dizzy, in fits of laughter.' Nora's face lit up at the memory of those happy times. She paused and then carried on.

'Well, I have two older sisters and three younger brothers. Perfect symmetry Da used to joke until the last babe.' She gulped and paused again, hating the remembrance of those dark painful days. 'Mam and the babe died before it could be born, a breech babe the midwife told him. Da couldn't speak for days, it was like a light had gone out and we crept around him not knowing what to do. But then Da's mammy came over and took charge.'

'My sister, Annie, was already a trained seamstress, so she took Mam's place in the workshop. My sister, Mary, is a fine cook and good with the little ones so Nan said she could take charge of the house and me, well I can sew and clean so Nan found a place for me with old Mrs Butler in Westminster at five guineas a year, which would come in handy to help feed and clothe the boys. I got one Sunday afternoon off every month and walked home to see them. Little Johnny is now thirteen and apprenticed to me Da. Annie is twenty-three and has a beau. If she marries I was hoping to take her place in the workshop. I love the sewing and....' At this point, Nora remembered where she was and started sobbing. 'I don't know what's going to happen now. I'm sure my family don't know that I'm here and I didn't understand what the judge said, it was something like seven years for larce... something and trans... something.'

Maudie and Peg looked at each other and grimaced, while Nora sobbed, her head resting in her hands on the table.

The wardress interrupted as she, and another woman, came into the room carrying what appeared to be supper and set it down on the table. The wardress, a thin, hard-faced woman, about fifty years of age, dressed in a sober skirt and blouse came over to Nora and said 'Come on girl, stop your snivelling and I'll show you which dishes are yours.'

Nora, trained to do what she was told, got up and followed the wardress to where a shelf contained tin plates, tankards and wooden spoons. 'These are yours' said the wardress pointing. 'I will expect them to be cleaned and put back after every meal.'

Nora wiped her eyes on her sleeve and returned to the table, with plate and tankard, to where there were hunks of bread, some small slabs of cheese and a large jug of weak tea. She ate and drank alone in silence. The light was beginning to go. After washing the supper things and visiting the privy, she was shown her bed mat and blanket by the wardress and fell into an exhausted sleep.

Peg and Maudie whispered together as they settled down for the night. 'That bastard judge! I'll bet it was a first offence. He's just seen a poor Irish, Catholic girl with none to speak out for her.'

'Yes, that's about the right of it.' replied Maudie. 'And she's just the type of girl they want out in Van Diemen's Land; strong, healthy and lots of breeding time. She's such a pretty thing. Don't you just love the colour of her hair? It's like burnished copper. And those bright green eyes, oh, they'll be queuing up for her alright. The judge wouldn't give a moment's thought to what he's done.'

'It makes me want to spit. Call it justice? Justice my arse.' declared Peg, her voice loud in indignation.

'Shut it you two, let a body get some peace.' growled the wardress from her bed.

Chapter 2

After first light, the prison began to wake. At first, Nora didn't know where she was. She watched as the other women began to stir until the wardress came over and told her to 'shake a leg'. Nora cleared her bed mat away and washed as well as she could in the single tub of lukewarm water shared by the ward's inhabitants. After visiting the privy, she went over to the table where a breakfast of thin gruel with tea and bread was spread out.

'You are lucky to be here now' said Maudie to Nora as they drank their tea. 'I was first here a dozen years ago. Gawd life here was bad then! We only got food if we could pay for it, beg for it or whore for it and no wardress to keep order. There were cat fights all the time with women screeching and tearing at each other for a bit of food. And if you think it smells now, well it's nothing compared to what it smelt like then. We didn't have bed mats but lay on the stone floor, in a dark room below here, and were fighting off men all the time, because they didn't take such trouble to keep us apart as they do now. Men, who said they had relatives here, could come in willy-nilly. I don't mind selling it but I'll not give it away if I can help it.'

'You're forgetting that we also had to pay the gaoler garnish before we could leave and there was only one way to earn money.' said Peg overhearing these last remarks. Maudie grimaced at the memory. 'Yes, and do you know who we have to thank for life's little improvements?'

'No,' said Nora horrified by what they told her.

'Mrs Fry and her friends, that's who. She first came here a few years ago and since then things have just got better and better. Not that I want to stay here you understand. I'd give anything for a comfy, warm bed, a roasted chicken leg or a drop of gin. Anyhow she's a blooming miracle worker and all she wants in return is for us to behave ourselves, learn our letters, listen to her God talks and sew. And that is how you can repay us, Nora. Me and Maudie we never learnt to sew at our mothers' knees, they spent too much time on their backs, if you get my drift?'

Nora did and blushed again. 'I'd love to help you sew if I am here long enough.' she agreed.

'Well, that would be sweet. If we can sew, we can make some money to buy a few luxuries like soap.'

'I could earn a little money to give to Da too' said Nora. 'I have none since I sent back the ten shilling to my mistress.'

'What did you want to go and do a thing like that for?' said Maudie and Peg in unison, horrified at the girl's honesty. 'Didn't the old woman owe you wages when you got nicked?'

Nora had never thought of that, but yes, she had been owed half a year's wages at the end of April, a full two and a half guineas.

'Why don't you tell us what happened and how you got here,' prompted Maudie.

Nora went back through the events of that April day, stopping from time to time to catch her breath and fight back the tears.

'Wasn't your mistress a character witness?' asked Peg. 'They should have told you about getting someone to speak of your good character at Millbank.'

'Yes, they did, but even though I sent her back the ten shillings she wouldn't speak for me. She was too respectable she told the constable and refused to have anything to do with prisoners.'

'That spiteful skinflint! She's saved herself your wages and not lifted a finger to help you.' Peg spat into the fireplace. 'And it sounds as if she didn't pay you much in the first place.'

'Well it's true she didn't raise my wages when she let me be a housemaid, but she said if I proved satisfactory I would get a rise when I turned eighteen.'

'Like I said, a spiteful skinflint!' Peg kicked the bench this time and received a warning glare from the wardress.

'I am so stupid. I was too scared to even summon up the words to tell the judge what happened. It was all a mistake really.' Nora said through her tears.

'Well nobody would believe you without a good character witness. Even if you had a lawyer, he could only question that Mrs Pocket and try and trip her up,' replied Maudie. 'I doubt that any of the women here could afford a lawyer. Once you're up before the judge and jury that's mostly it, I reckon. Guilty as charged.'

Nora was thankful to know there was nothing she could have said that would have made the outcome of the trial any different, but she still felt wretched.

'How can I let my father know what has happened? I should have gone to visit my family last Sunday and taken my wages. They'll think I am sick or even worse, dead.'

'Well that's an easy one,' said Maudie. 'We will ask one of Mrs Fry's ladies to write a letter to your Dad. He can then go to the skinflint's house and demand your wages. You will be able to talk to him yourself through the bars in the exercise yard if you fix a time.'

Nora clutched at Maudie's words, breaking down with relief this time; at last, some good news. The longing for her father's support and love had been unbearable. She felt a physical ache whenever she thought of her family. They meant everything to her and she felt sure her father wouldn't judge her harshly but think her only guilty of stupidity.

'Do you think she will write it today? Might I see my Da tomorrow? Oh, I forget he doesn't know his letters. Who's going read it for him?' These questions tumbled out amongst her tears.

'Don't worry; someone will read it to him. Let's ask the lady when she comes this afternoon.' said Maudie, patting Nora's hand while Peg gave Nora a ragged piece of cloth to dry her eyes. She accepted it gratefully and, after blowing her nose, asked the question they most dreaded.

'I must tell him how long I will be here? What did the judge mean?'

Her sentence ought to have been explained when Nora entered the prison. Perhaps they were too busy with the numbers of women sentenced after the court sessions. The wardress would explain it, but

Nora now trusted them and they had taken to her, so they decided to break it to her as gently as they could.

'Well did he say you must serve seven years for larceny and transportation?' asked Maudie.

'Yes, yes those were his words.' said Nora remembering them.

'Larceny is thieving, so he has given you seven years' punishment for that.'

'Does that mean I must spend seven years here?' asked Nora in dismay, that was near enough half her lifetime and she couldn't imagine it.

'No, I doubt that.' Maudie paused and sighed, knowing how the poor girl was going to react. 'Transportation means you'll be sent away from England, but not to a prison. They'll send you on a ship.'

'A ship, but where will I be going? I don't know anywhere other than England. I've never even left London.' Nora's dismay deepened further. She remembered walking with her older sister, Mary, to see dozens of sailing ships in the Thames by the great Tower. They made a fine sight and she and Mary would try to guess where they came from and what they carried. Not knowing the names of many countries, they would conjure up names, the more fantastical the better.

'Have you heard of a place called Van Diemen's Land?' asked Maudie.

'No, I don't think so.' Nora said and then she paused as a memory came back to her. 'Oh yes, I do remember, it was in one of my Da's songs, he sometimes sang a song about poachers and about them being transported to Van Diemen's Land. Where is it, do you know? Is it as far as Ireland?'

'Much, much further than that pet. They say it's on the other side of the world. The journey takes months,' sympathised Maud, while thinking it was a good job they were sitting down as she watched the colour drain from Nora's cheeks and her mouth open with shock as tears once again filled her eyes.

'How will I get back?' cried Nora. Neither Peg nor Maudie could bear to answer her. They knew people who were transported, none of them had ever come back as far as they were aware.

'Maybe you'll meet a fine young fellah there and not want to come back,' said Peg attempting to cheer her up.

Nora was not only shocked but utterly bewildered. 'But I'm not a poacher and I haven't done any thieving, it was all a mistake.' Maudie and Peg patted her hand again, tears of sympathy in their own eyes.

The longing for her mother threatened to overwhelm her. But this was impossible; not to see her family again was unthinkable. She glanced at the two women and saw tears glistening on their cheeks. Her mind refused to accept this disaster. She stared at them, were they joking?

Suddenly the room felt icy and she shivered, despite the warm sunlight lighting up the room. Realisation began to dawn. She sat dumbstruck, sick with fear, her limbs heavy and she swayed with shock. Peg grabbed her arm, worried that she would fall from her chair.

This was far worse than she ever imagined and she didn't know how to react. It was too difficult to think straight. Oh, what a fool she had been. How had she sleepwalked into this?

Several of the women in the ward were being led out for their own trials as both convicted and untried prisoners were assigned to the room. Nora found her voice to ask Peg and Maudie if they had been tried. They told her that they were convicted earlier in the week. Did their convictions mean transportation, she wondered? Her new friends both understood the unspoken question.

'They don't send women like us to Van Diemen's Land. Prostitution is not a transportable offence unless we'd pinched something as well and they don't want older women.' said Maudie.' We will be out of here in three months, until the next time, that is.'

Nora sat in silence, unbelieving and shivering in shock. After a few minutes, she noticed that several other women were sitting at the table preparing to work. Nora desperately needed time to take in what she had been told and sewing would at least calm her and make her see sense. She asked the women for some spare cloth and thread while Maudie and Peg drifted away to talk amongst themselves, understanding her need for quiet.

Nora had been living a nightmare for the past three weeks. She wished she could wake up and resume a normal life. But it wasn't going to happen. She saw that now. Although only sixteen, she was an adult in the eyes of the law. She could continue to try and ignore this news, but where would that get her other than even more misery? Or she could start to come to terms with the change her life was taking and force herself to bear it. No! Her family was all that mattered, she couldn't lose them! She sewed without seeing, her eyes screwed up against the tears which threatened to overwhelm her, her heart racing, memories spilling from all directions.

As thoughts tumbled around her brain Nora suddenly realised it was fear that had brought her to this point, the fear of losing her job; the fear of depriving her family of money; the fear of Mrs Butler's temper and her slaps. By letting fear win, Nora had brought far worse troubles on herself; troubles that were unimaginable. She ceased her sewing, looking bemused at the mess of stitches on the cloth. She forced herself to breathe slowly. Somehow, she must overcome this fear, if not she feared she would die.

Nora looked around the table at the subdued faces and then glanced towards Maudie and Peg who were laughing and joking, and yet their life was so much harder than hers. She would never want their life but she wished above all that she had some of their mettle. Nora prayed she could learn from them. How do you become brave, she wondered? She wished for a magic wand to be waved over her to fill her with courage.

The first thing she must do was to get a letter to her father; a letter showing she was resigned to her fate. The last thing she wanted to do was add to his troubles. Although in her head she knew this news may break his heart. She had to make him believe she could survive this horror. If not she knew this would kill them both. Guilt would send her mad. Nora started to plan the letter in her mind.

Later that morning the wardress told the women to take exercise outside. Maudie and Peg escorted Nora from the ward and down the bare stone stairs to a small yard where they walked around in the warm May sunshine. Women from other wards joined them as did half a dozen young boys, pleased to escape from the schoolroom.

'Now then, you just watch yourself with these ragamuffins, Nora. These boys are pick-pockets by trade, probably trained by Ikey Solomon himself. If you have anything they want they will slide it out of your pocket as soon as look at you, and you won't feel a thing.' said Peg.

Nora looked over at the boys, who were sullenly eyeing up the women. What a ragged group they were, with scarce a pair of boots amongst them. Although they tried hard to exhibit some bravado as any young woman passed close by. From their cold, blank stares she saw how unfeeling they were. She remembered the ragged, dirty children she had seen so often in London streets, skulking in doorways. Nora had never paid them much heed, but always hurried past them, eyes firmly to the front, as her parents always told her to do.

The cobbled yard was surrounded on three sides by scored brick walls where previous prisoners had carved their names and dates. On the fourth side was grating and beyond that bars separating the prison from the outside world. Nora watched one of the female prisoners talking to a young girl who stood beyond them both. The woman was clothed in a dirty, torn dress and the girl in something which no longer fitted her, her face pinched and thin from hunger and her unshod feet black from the grime of the streets. Nora supposed the girl was the prisoner's daughter and without support whilst her mother stayed in prison. Eventually, the girl turned away and left disconsolate through the gate to the street beyond.

'I will meet my father here.' Nora sighed. She imagined him beyond the bars and hated the image playing in her head. 'I may see him for the last time, with the bars between us. I may never feel his dear arms around me again.' In desperation, she forced herself to banish the thought to the back of her mind. If she started to cry now she did not think she could ever stop. The women were returning to the ward and she followed them with a weary heart.

Dinner was a stew of vegetables with gristly meat and dumplings. It was served with a hunk of coarse bread and tea again. Nora was relieved that it was not as inedible as the food at Milbank. Yet it was so much worse than food from the kitchen of her mistress or indeed of home, where Mary had a knack with herbs and could make even the commonest of vegetables, tasty.

'I wonder what they eat in Van Diemen's Land? Do they even have chickens and cows there?' she voiced her question aloud not realising her words were heard by everyone at the table.

'I heard tell that there are huge beasts that don't walk or run but jump around on just two legs.' said one woman at the table.

'And I've heard that there's a beast that looks and sounds just like the devil himself.' said another crossing herself.

'There are nekked, black savages roaming around with spears, I've seen pictures.' said a third.

'Aye, a terrible place.' agreed the first.

The wardress stepped in and told the women not to frighten young miss and to start clearing away the remains of the meal. As the women were washing their pots a young, soberly dressed woman entered the ward. Nora could see she was not a prisoner as the wardress bobbed a curtsey and her apparel, though plain, was of good quality. She had a gentle face underneath her bonnet and gave everyone a warm smile as she deposited a large bag on the table.

'How are thee today, ladies?' asked the soft-spoken woman.

The women stood, bobbed a curtsey too and replied in unison 'Well enough, thank you, Ma'am.'

'Ah, I can see we have a new face here today.' said the woman looking at Nora.

Yes Ma'am,' said the wardress. 'Tell her your name girl.'

'Nora Nolan, Ma'am,' she said shyly, bobbing yet again.

'Well Nora, my name is Mrs Barnard. I am a member of the Society of Friends. I come to offer solace to the women here and to bring God's word. Are you a Christian, Nora?'

'Aye Ma'am, my family is Catholic.'

'Good. But do you have the benefit of a priest?' Mrs Barnard asked.

'No Ma'am. The Spanish Church is a long walk from home and I worked three Sundays out of four. But it's where my parents married and we were baptised.'

'A chaplain holds services on Sundays here in the prison. I hope you will attend. His sermons will surely help you, child.'

Nora nodded and Mrs Barnard turned her attention to the women at the table who were by now sitting down and picking up their sewing. She carried a bundle of plain black cotton and as she unpacked it she said to Maudie and Peg, 'Here is cloth for more suitable dresses for you both. You have told me that you don't sew but will you not try and learn?'

Nora saw Maudie and Peg grimace as they looked at the cloth. She tried to imagine them in such plain garb and giggled to herself for the picture was too ridiculous.

'Nora has offered to teach us to sew Ma'am. She's a grand girl and needs a letter writing to her family, will you help her?' said Maudie.

'You don't read and write, Nora?' asked Mrs Barnard.

Nora struggled to regain her composure and answered 'No Ma'am, none of my family has had the opportunity to learn. My family don't know I am here. But who would read a letter to them?'

'There are members of our society throughout London. I daresay we can find one who lives close enough and who could read the letter. Come and sit by me and we'll work on it. Will you learn to read Nora? We can help you whilst you are in prison.'

Nora sat beside Mrs Barnard, pleased that she had thought what to say to her father before Mrs Barnard arrived. 'I'm not sure that reading and writing would be useful Ma'am. I have no one to write to and shouldn't want to put my family to the expense of finding a letter reader.'

'You could read the Bible, Nora, and the word of God will comfort thee,' replied Mrs Barnard, as she dug around to find paper, quill and ink in her capacious bag.

Nora didn't reply. Learning to read was for her of no consequence and she couldn't see how it would help her in Van Diemen's Land. Instead, she told Mrs Barnard what she wanted to say to her father and they began to write the letter.

Dearest Father

You must be wondering why I did not come to visit you last Sunday. Father, through a dreadful misunderstanding, I have been tried and convicted of stealing a lace cap and am in Newgate Prison. Please believe that I am in good spirits and people here are kind to me. You will take this news very badly, I know, and I wish that you don't think ill of me. I am prepared to take my punishment but only hope you might come and visit me. We take exercise in the yard between the hours of eleven o'clock. and midday, Please come, Father, I miss you so much.

Your loving and obedient daughter

Nora

'Do you not want to tell him of your punishment, child?' asked Mrs Barnard.

'No. I am to be sent to Van Diemen's Land and I must tell him that myself. I cannot imagine his distress if he were to read that in a letter,' said Nora with determination.

Mrs Barnard looked at the girl with pity. She has a sweet and gentle nature, she thought. She can't help but be corrupted by the degradations of the journey and the company she will keep. Even the influence of harlots such as Maudie and Peg, despite their clear affection for the girl, must start to have a malign effect on her. 'Nora, I will pray that God may forgive thy sins. As to this letter, I will send it to a friend this afternoon if you will let me know thy father's address.'

'I am very grateful to you Ma'am.' She told her the address. For the rest of the afternoon, Nora sat sewing a petticoat, while Mrs Barnard read passages from the Bible. Nora felt much calmer. Mrs Barnard's quiet voice soothed her soul. There was no judgement in her eyes. She was so thankful that someone was helping her, someone she could trust.

Not long after Mrs Barnard had left with Nora's letter, the door to the ward banged open and in came three new prisoners. Two strode in raucously. They were dishevelled and dirty, in their early twenties Nora guessed and could tell from their glowering faces that they were trouble. Maudie and Peg saw it too and each put a warning hand on Nora's arm. The third was a much younger, malnourished girl, dirty, shoeless and in rags. There was something desperate about her. Terrified, her glance darted around her new home.

'Would you look at those dirty tykes,' whispered one of the women at the table.

'Yeah, we don't want lice bringing in,' said another, 'This place was teeming with them last time I was here.'

'Ladies,' said the wardress 'you must wash yourselves at the pump in the yard. I will find out if there are any spare clothes; those will want burning.'

'Who are you to give us orders?' grunted the taller of the newcomers, scowling.' You're just a bleeding prisoner same as us.'

'I may be.' replied the wardress, coldly. 'But I am appointed as wardress and you will do as I say or I will have you down in a basement cell in irons.'

She sent one of the women to the matron to see if there were any spare clothes and led the cursing women and the silent, scrawny girl to the yard. The wardress stood over them while they stripped, reluctant to let the cold water of the pump splash over their skin. She found a tiny lump of soap and made them wash thoroughly. Each was given a coarse, scratchy blanket until the girl came back with petticoats, aprons and cotton bonnets for the three of them.

'They'll have to do. The Quaker lady may have spare clothes or you can make yourselves a skirt and top.' The wardress led them back to the ward where the two women vented their fury on everything that came into their minds. But the young girl shook and shivered on her own, standing as far from her companions as possible.

'Beware of those bullies. I have seen their type before.' said Peg. 'Take care Nora, you must stand up to them. If they are being transported, they will be on the same ship and will find ways to hurt you if you get on the wrong side of them.'

Nora nodded but inwardly was dismissive of Peg's warning. Why would the women pick on her? They did look most unsavoury to be sure. The taller one had a jagged scar up her left arm, thick matted dark hair and bushy eyebrows. The shorter one was a mass of flesh, podgy, Nora's sisters would say. She had a red disfiguring birthmark, the size of a guinea on her left cheek.

'They could be the ugly sisters,' Nora whispered to Peg who grinned and chuckled.

'Oh right, and do you think the waif is Cinderella? I don't think she'll see a handsome prince arriving anytime soon. Listen Nora, the like of us don't appear in fairy stories. Just make sure you look out for yourself.'

But Nora could not help being interested in the young girl who was doing her best to stay unnoticed. She was a poor little thing; her skin had the washed-out appearance of a girl who had never seen the sun. It was as though she were trying to blend into a corner of the ward, far away from everyone else. The girl's frightened eyes peeped warily through the damp, straggly curtain of hair, the rest of her features nondescript or obscured. Maybe I could befriend her, thought Nora, full of pity for the sad creature.

The evening passed without further incident and, as they settled down for the night, Nora wondered if she would see her father tomorrow. No, she decided it was too soon, and the day after was a Saturday, still a working day for him. She worked out the most likely day would be Sunday. She prayed to God that she would see him on Sunday and wished, not for the first time that she had her rosary to comfort her.

Chapter3

As they washed their breakfast dishes next morning, Nora managed to ask the young girl her name. Close to, she saw that the girl's face was marked by yellow bruised,

'Sarah. I'm Sarah Mawby.' Her hesitant, quiet voice was difficult to catch.

'How did you get those bruises?' Nora's eyes looked at her with sympathy.

Sarah looked frightened and tried to pull yet more of her lank hair over her face, but that only showed that her arms were a mass of different colours from vivid purple to a faded yellow.

'Who on earth did that to you?' cried Nora, her voice too loud, she later realised.

Sarah turned away shaking her head and she stumbled to the nearest seat, crouching into it, as though it might hide her; it did not.

'The slag got life; she killed a ponce,' laughed one of the new women walking towards Sarah. 'You'd never think she'd say boo to a goose let alone stick someone.' And as she drew near she shouted 'Boo!' and Sarah jumped in fright. Both women cackled and then shouted 'Boo!' again.

The wardress ordered them to stop, which they did, but both gave Sarah a sly pinch as they walked by.

Nora sat down by Sarah and tried to put her arm round her, but she flinched and tried to move away.

'Let her alone for a while,' advised Maudie, drawing her away. The girl has been abused; it's as plain as day. She will take some looking after and even then, with those two evil strumpets stirring it, she may not survive this. I have seen other girls like her. She may have escaped the hangman's noose but sometimes they top themselves later. The hurt eats away at them until they cannot bear it.'

Nora was shocked. She knew well enough that it was a sin and a crime to take your own life. She looked at Sarah who still sat at the table, her legs perched onto the bar below the seat, her shoulders hunched and her arms drawn tightly across her middle, her whole body tense, as though waiting for the next blow. It was instinctive for Nora to wonder how she might help her but the reality of her own situation made her pause.

I am being stupid again, thought Nora. I can try to be her friend if she will let me, but save her, no, that is down to God, only he can do that.

The morning passed as had the day before, but this time Maudie and Peg sat down to sew. Nora found them some old white material and she taught them how to hem, thinking it the easiest stitch, whilst willing the time to pass quickly. Was it at all possible her father would come today? The minutes ticked by. Maudie and Peg pricked their fingers so often that the white cotton was flecked with tiny spots of red but at last the wardress let them out for their exercise. In her head, Nora knew that her father would not have received the letter, but she couldn't help looking towards the bars at the end of the yard, only to be disappointed.

Nora stood against a wall and let the warmth of the sun soak into her body. For the past five-years what she would have given for an hour off to enjoy the sunshine. Turning her face upwards to enjoy the sensation of stillness and warmth, her eyes closed for a few seconds. She imagined, for a moment, that she was in a park, surrounded by flowers and singing birds and the noises of the yard receded. Nora remembered, with a jolt, an image from her childhood. It was her mother showing her bees hovering over a lavender bush, which had taken root beside her grandfather's grave, and explaining how bees made honey. Nora smiled at the memory of her sweet and gentle mother. Seconds later, she opened her eyes, looked around the colourless yard and wished she could recapture that moment.

The young boys were milling around outside again. Seeing the three women dressed just in their thin shifts and aprons, they made obscene gestures and harangued them with vile words. While Sarah tried to hide amongst the other female prisoners, the two older women caught two of the boys and whacked them so hard across the face that they fell to the floor. The other boys turned and ran off still shouting their obscenities and laughing. The two boys on the floor had bloody noses which they would wear for the rest of the day as a badge of honour.

Mrs Barnard arrived again after lunch and told Nora that she had sent the letter to a Friend who she was sure would deliver it that afternoon. On seeing Sarah, she drew from her bag, a plain grey dress and asked her to try it on. The dress covered her bare feet with inches to spare and fell loose over her childish chest but Mrs Barnard thought it could be altered. Nora offered to do it and gained a wan smile from Sarah. Nora took hold of the dress and was impressed at once by the quality and softness of the wool. She stroked it gently against her cheek and realised it must have been owned by someone with money. But why would you discard such a fine dress? There was not a single tear or stain to be seen and she thought Sarah would be lucky to own it.

'What about us?' demanded the two women who had arrived with Sarah.

'What are your names?' asked Mrs Barnard.

'Jane Smith.' said the shorter of the two.

'Lizzie Riley.' replied the taller one.

'Say Ma'am when you speak to Mrs Barnard.' instructed the wardress. The women, scowling and with reluctance, repeated their names and tacked on 'Ma'am.'

'Well Jane and Lizzie,' said Mrs Barnard, smiling at the women, 'Are you able to sew? If you are, I will bring in some cloth for a dress for you both.'

'No, we can't bleeding sew. How come she gets a dress and we don't?' Lizzie as an afterthought added on a sullen Ma'am to her reply.

'Mind, but you creatures have filthy manners,' said the wardress. 'Please excuse them, Ma'am.'

'Well, this dress would not fit either of you because it is meant for someone of a slighter build,' said Mrs Barnard, without any sign of annoyance at their rudeness. Nora heard sniggering around the table, as Jane was almost bursting out of her shift, while the same size shift drowned young Sarah.

Jane and Lizzie were unabashed and gave several of the women who had sniggered a gesture with their middle fingers. Nora was sure it was rude but Mrs Barnard ignored it and the wardress did not notice.

'Well, you can't go around dressed just in your shifts. You need a long skirt at least. I will bring in cloth next time I'm here. In the meantime, I suggest that learning to sew may prove a skill well worth pursuing. Sewing can provide a respectable income.' Mrs Barnard looked at them without judgement, but they shook their heads and scowled. 'So be it,' she said and turned back to the women around the table who wanted to learn.

The rest of the afternoon passed in peace until tea-time when Nora sat next to Sarah, by now dressed in her new grey robe which, even after altering hung, loose on her thin, child-like frame. As they ate their evening meal of bread and cheese, Nora chatted away to her, noticing how Sarah kept stroking the cloth of her new dress with two fingers. She tried to draw her out but Sarah said not a word and Nora remembered how quiet and numb she had been only two days ago. The kindness of Maudie, Peg and Mrs Barnard, had made a big difference to Nora and she was grateful to be at Newgate because the silence and regime at Milbank had left her feeling helpless. Imagine being there for months or even years, she thought, it would drive you mad.

Jane and Lizzie sat together grumbling, not liking the way that Sarah attached herself to Nora, who was protected by those two doxies. They had meant to have some fun by tormenting Sarah.

'There's time. We'll bide our time and soon we can have fun with both of them,' said Lizzie, smirking.

On Saturday, Nora was sad to think she would not see Mrs Barnard for two whole days. She realised how much the gentle lady had come to mean to her. She brought a sense of normality to the mad world she found herself in. However, the Society of Friends did not mean them to be unoccupied and had provided cleaning materials. The women set to cleaning the ward and then washing their petticoats and aprons. Most of the women had one shift, a single skirt and a top. The lucky ones with two petticoats could change theirs each week, but the others just wore their skirt and top for the day until their linen was dry again.

"Thank God, it's not winter," said Maudie. "I don't half feel the cold these days," she grumbled as she scrubbed her stockings.

Nora enjoyed the camaraderie of sweeping, washing and cleaning as the women loosened up and chatted as they worked. She noticed those two hard-faced newcomers appeared to do as little as possible and got away with it. That made her mad, used as she was to seventeen hours of skivvying a day.

Mrs Barnard had left some wool and knitting needles, so after the washing and cleaning were done, Nora decided to knit a shawl. She sat again with Maudie, Peg and Sarah starting them all out on making aprons. They tried their new skills in hemming and seam making. The morning sped by as she was often interrupted for help with the aprons. Fewer dots of blood that morning proved their needle skills were improving.

They left for their morning exercise arm in arm and giggling at their slow progress with the aprons. As they came outside Nora felt the coolness of the day and wished her shawl was finished so she could wrap it around herself. She had not been outside for more than fifteen seconds when Nora heard her name called by a familiar voice and looking up she saw him by the bars with a frantic arm waving at her.

He saw her standing there, his darling girl, the image of his wife at the age she had been when he fell in love with her. But Nora hadn't seen him yet. She was standing with two old doxies, to judge by their dress and demeanour and he felt sickened. When that kind lady came round yesterday evening and read the letter, at first there was relief to know that she was not lost or taken. For the life of him, he could not understand why she was in this awful place, but she was still alive and unharmed and for that he thanked God.

He called and waved and she looked up in surprise at his voice. She came towards him slowly at first and then started to run. Her dear face showing such joy until reaching the grating separating them, she cried in anguish. He stood behind the bars and cursed them for coming between him and his daughter. Neither could say a word at first. At last, he managed 'Cushla, cushla.' He wiped the tears from his eyes and managed a 'Why?'

It was the question she knew was coming but it was so difficult to reply. She dug her nails into her palms and forced herself to tell him the story of that awful day in April. She studied his face as she told her halting tale, accompanied by sobs and looks of entreaty, as she tried to gauge his anger. But she saw no anger directed towards her in his pale blue eyes. His dear face, lined with care and worry as it was, now appeared wan and his black hair newly shot through with grey.

But he was angry, no furious, not with her but with Mrs Butler and the shop owner who refused to listen to his daughter. How could they fail to understand what a good, honest girl Nora was? Sweet mother of God, they had only to look at her to see her innocence.

'Why that damned widow woman! I went around to her house when you didn't appear last Sunday and she told me you had left but knew not where. I was shocked because I never thought you would do such a thing. Yes, I shouted because she didn't send us a message when you left and I imagined something terrible had happened. But never, in a thousand years, this,' and his outstretched palm waved towards the prison despairingly. 'That Mrs Butler, she threatened me with the constable if I didn't leave.'

'Da, she owes me my wages. Please go back and get them. They are the last you'll have.

'Why do you say that? You will be out soon enough. Then you must come home and help with the sewing. I wish to God I had never agreed to you working for that besom in the first place.' How he wanted to hold her, stroke her hair and make everything better. But it would be alright. They gave three months for a first offence and one of those months was already almost past. He smiled to calm her.

'Da, I will not be coming home.' she stumbled over the words. 'They say I am being transported.'

At first, he didn't take in her words, how could he? It was as though the devil had taken hold of his heart, twisted it around and stopped his breath. He looked at her face and saw her torment and his world just crumbled to dust for the second time in five years. He banged his fists over and over against the bars. 'The English bastards, what have they done? We came to this God forsaken city so they could do this?' He didn't know that he was howling in pain and anger until he caught the horror in Nora's eyes.

'Da, Da. I have to bear it, please help me through this.'

He looked at her pale oval face, now wrecked with tear-washed, grimy streaks and her nose tipped with red where she had tried to rub away the tears on her sleeve Not close enough to see the finest dusting of freckles on her nose, he realised he might never be close enough again and the thought tore him apart once more.

'Please Da, make it easy for me to leave you. I can only be happy if you are going to be alright when I am not here. I doubt I will have the chance to return so I want to keep a picture of you all smiling, here, in my heart.' She pressed her palm to her bosom, attempting to smile at him.

Stunned by the new-found strength of his daughter he nodded. But then clutching at hope he said, 'Surely there must be something we can do; maybe I can persuade someone to look at the case again and shame Mrs Butler into writing a reference. I could go to the shop and speak to the owner about the mistake. Perhaps she will withdraw the complaint.'

She gave a brief smile. 'Yes, Da, that would be good, but I am not going to raise my hopes. It's unlikely they will change their minds and I need to prepare for the worst. Just as you left Ireland and made a home here I must be ready to do the same in this new country, Van Diemen's Land. If only it were not so far away.'

He felt the optimism drain away. 'When did you become so brave my sweet? At least I had my Mammy and Daddy when we came here. You have no one.' She was putting on this brave front for him and he found it too hard to bear.

'I promise to choose my friends with care. Listen, there are all sorts of people here. Some you would think are sluts but their strength and kindness have helped me. I will search for a man like you Da, someone who values their family, someone kind and hardworking. When I find him, pray God, we will make our own family. Think of that Da, your little Nora with sons and daughters. I'll name my first-born son, James, to remind me of you.'

Oh dear Lord, she was speaking to him as though she were the adult and he the child. He was astounded at the words she was saying. How could she have become this mature young lady, so sure of herself? When he saw Nora last, she was still a young girl, frightened of anything new or unfamiliar. He remembered his walks accompanying her back to her work on dark Sunday evenings and how she jumped at dogs barking or any other strange noise. He blamed himself now, of course. He should have prepared her to cope with life and its adversities. She left home to work at ten years of age and perhaps he had wanted her to remain a child when really, she was old enough to marry, old enough to have her own children. He had let her down, let her mother down, how could he ever forgive himself?

But Nora listened to herself with amazement; she had not practised what she would say, but now it seemed right. The words calmed them both and Nora realised that she could make them come true. In three short days, had she become someone who thought of the future and not of the past? Oh yes, it was going to be tough to get through the long voyage and whatever lay ahead in Van Diemen's Land. Now she must hold on to that hope of a husband and family of her own, whatever happened. The exercise hour was nearly up and she told him she must go as she saw the wardress beckoning her.

He promised he would send her sisters tomorrow and asked if there was anything she needed. She asked for soap and her comb and rosary. Leaving him was hard; she looked back every few steps until, reluctantly, she re-entered the prison.

He stood for a long time with tears flowing down his face, while hanging onto the bars for support. His body wanted to sink to the floor and stay there. The pain was the same as when his dearest wife had died and it had taken months to feel any normality. He wondered if he could ever recover from this. It was worse. His beloved daughter would be on the far side of the world where he could not take care of her, wouldn't even know if she were ill or if she married and bore children. Now he must go home and tell her brothers and sisters what was to happen, thanking the lord his Mammy was no longer alive to witness this, for she would surely blame herself.

James Nolan turned away and stumbled from the prison. He had one place to go before journeying home. He must deal with that harpy before he let his feelings overwhelm him. Later, people passing him on the street, remarked to each other about the poor man who must have been bereaved. He looked in so much distress.

As Nora sat on her own in the same distress for the midday meal, Sarah joined her. She took Nora's hand in her own reddened, cracked hand and gave her the briefest of smiles before starting to eat. Nora smiled wanly back.

Chapter 4

Sarah

My name is Sarah Mawby I told her, but I don't really know what my name is or even If my mother ever gave me one. Mawby was the name of the street where I was left. No, I don't know who my parents are. No one claimed me. Why would they? Just another wailing mouth to feed.

I don't know my age, about fourteen I think. I have never had a birthday. Some of us foundlings survived our childhood, but it was just luck, lots of children didn't. We were given a cot to share, as many as ten to a cot, a few patched second-hand clothes, a morsel of food, if it could be called that; much worse than in here it was.

When sickness came, whole cotfuls of babies succumbed in turn. They told us they had gone to live with God. God obviously didn't want me. I'm not surprised.

Yes, we were taught to read and count. They didn't teach us to write. Too dangerous, we might write and tell someone how we were treated. Sundays, we went twice to church and heard all about hellfire and damnation, whilst we shivered in our thin smocks. What else did we get? Oh yes, the stick. There was lots of that. Was there love? I didn't believe it existed. I'd heard of it but I never had any.

Then I watched Nora with her father today and saw love for the first time. It was the most beautiful thing I ever saw. I wanted it so badly I could taste it. It tasted like the honey I stole once, sweet and thick and flowery. Even their tears were beautiful. Their tears didn't mean hunger or cold or darkness and even pain, they meant love and tenderness and sorrow from being parted forever. I could live with that; I would die for that.

I'm going to watch again. It will fill me up like food has never filled my stomach.

Chapter 5

On Sundays, the wardress encouraged the prisoners to attend chapel. Nora rushed across the yard with Maudie, each trying to protect herself from the blustery rain that filled the dirty cracks in the cobbles with dark, oozing puddles. Peg and Sarah had refused to go with them. She asked them if they went to church but Peg laughed and said no, she doubted that she could ever be saved. Sarah mumbled something about churchmen frightening her but Nora couldn't get anything further from her.

The prison chapel was a square building set within the prison walls. The women were led upstairs to a gallery overlooking the men. Peering down Nora saw the tall, oak pulpit and a curious partitioned square in the middle of the floor below. As the women entered there were raucous calls from the male prisoners. Some of the women, including Jane and Lizzie, called back in response, their obscene gestures having the desired effect on men below, who shouted even more. Nora shivered in her damp dress as a thin, net curtain was drawn across the gallery, attempting to block the view of the men. It offered little defence. Maudie held her hand.

'Don't worry pet. You're safe here. Ignore them, pretend they don't exist.'

A few well-dressed men sat in a blocked off area underneath the gallery. Other men, in various states of dress, stood at the back, facing the pulpit. Maudie told Nora that the better-dressed men were those who could afford to pay for their keep and they were housed in a separate part of the prison with food brought in from nearby taverns.

'What is that bit in the middle where two men are standing?' asked Nora pointing below.

'They're condemned men. They might be up for a hanging tomorrow outside the prison. It always draws the crowds. There's nothing so popular as a good hanging. Nora gasped in horror and stared down at them with pity.

'When I was first here, at Newgate, they used to put a black coffin in front of the men, just to remind them what would happen on the next day, as if they needed any further reminder,' said Maudie.

Nora was unused to being in a church of any description as Catholics still had few rights in England. There were only a handful of priests and catholic churches in London and she had never been confirmed, so the service felt strange to her. She enjoyed the songs because she loved to sing, although she didn't know the words to these hymns and regretted not being able to join in apart from with the choruses. The chaplain's sermon on guilt and God's forgiveness for repentant sinners, she guessed was a familiar theme and aimed at the men who may not see another full day. However, many prisoners didn't bother to listen and carried on talking or yawning throughout the service; no one seemed to attempt to bring order. The chaplain spoke in a rushed monotone, as though he too could hardly wait for the service to finish.

'Does the chaplain visit the wards to give comfort to the prisoners? She asked Maudie.

'What him! He's the laziest, most good-for-nothing chaplain you will ever find. Takes his money for Sunday service, but that's the last you'll see of him all week.'

'It's not at all what I expected. There's nothing divine about this service. Why do people bother to turn up if they're not made to?'

'So, the men can see the women and harlots like that Jane and Lizzie can see the men.'

'So why do you come?'

'Well I don't as a rule, but I didn't want you coming on your own. You can hear why.'

What a friend she was and Nora was very grateful for her presence because as they left the chapel, the male prisoners turned to stare at them, and Nora felt distinctly uncomfortable at the obvious leers. It was worse once outside, as the leers were accompanied by catcalls and whistles, despite the ineffectual warnings of the turnkeys.

As Nora rushed to the exercise yard, she decided that she would not plan to attend chapel again, unless forced to. But she cheered up when she saw Annie and Mary waiting beyond the bars of the exercise yard. The rain had lessened to a fine drizzle and they looked cold as they stamped their feet trying to get some warmth back into them. Nora was overjoyed to see her sisters but sad that they looked so flustered and unsure of themselves and that it was all her fault.

'Oh Nora, you are looking much thinner; what are they feeding you?' said Mary even more concerned now that she caught sight of Nora. 'We've brought you a little food but you need much more I think.'

'Don't worry Mary. The food is better in here than it was at Milbank. Newgate is much nicer. You are allowed to talk and I've made friends. Oh goodness, it makes me so happy to see you. I worried that much about not visiting you all last Sunday.'

'Oh Lord, Nora, we've been frantic.' said Annie. 'Da has been beside himself and now with yesterday's news, well I don't know how he'll cope. He came home like a broken man yesterday. You remember what he was like when Mam died.'

'I'm so, so sorry, it was such a stupid mistake. If only I could turn the clock back a month.'

'We're not angry with you Sis. It's just a great shock. If you are going to the other side of the world we just wish that one of us could go with you. I have heard they sometimes allow relatives to go,' said Mary.

'Don't even consider that Mary. The family relies on you so much, and Annie, you will get married soon and I am content with that really I am. Please trust me.'

'We have a few things for you. Da said you wanted your rosary, comb and some soap. We also reckoned you'd need a change of stockings and another petticoat. He's sent you five shillings because he went and got your wages from that tight Mrs Butler right after you met yesterday. He shamed her into it. Even she blanched when told where you were going and he begged her to write to the courts and say you were a good girl. She told him that she thought you had taken the cap on purpose to keep the ten shillings. So now Da thinks she might write a letter.' said Annie.

'God, bless you all. I would happily bear prison here if I didn't have to go to the other side of the world. Surely if she writes they will take notice of it, don't you think?'

Mary and Annie could scarcely bear the pleading tone in her voice and Annie moved to the question of how they could pass their gifts to her.

'Maybe you can sweet talk the turnkey into letting you come this side of the bars. There's enough space between the bars and the grating.'

Annie and Mary went to find the turnkey and after a few minutes, he let them squeeze through a gap between the bars and the grating. A kiss each was all he asked. They did not let Nora see their disgust at his foul breath and wandering hands.

Annie passed a small scrunched up parcel through the grating. Mary got out a meat pie, still warm from the pie-man, and a slightly wizened apple and passed these through.

'We'll come every Saturday Nora. Da says he will come on Sundays and might bring John sometimes,' said Mary. 'He will not bring Jimmy and Patrick because he doesn't want them remembering you here. Let's hope the letter does the trick.'

'Thank you, both. I am so happy to have seen you and Da. I'd been worrying about you all so much. I understand about the boys, though it breaks my heart to think I might never see them again.' Nora started to cry and her sisters tried to comfort her until it was time to leave.

As she turned away Nora noticed the girl saying goodbye to her mother, the one she had seen on her first outing to the exercise yard. The girl looked even more pinched and exhausted than before. Nora brought out the apple and threw it over the grating and it fell just short of the bars near the girl. Both mother and daughter gawped at her and then the girl, understanding, poked her fingers through the bars and managed to grab it and bite into it ravenously. Nora turned back to her sisters and mouthed 'Sorry.'

"How's she going to cope? She's such an innocent. What are we going to do without her? Cried Mary, watching Nora re-enter the prison.

"God only knows," said her sister, wringing her hands "We'll tell Da she looked cheerful, though?" Mary nodded through her tears.

Nora went back to the ward to share the pie with Maudie, Peg and Sarah. She resolved to ask Mary if she had a spare dress that she had grown out of for the girl. Normally it would be passed on to Nora or cut down to make clothes for the boys, but she could hardly bear to see that girl in rags. Then again, the girl may sell it for food, which was likely a more pressing need. But any help for her would ease Nora's mind, so yes, she would ask Mary.

Chapter 6

Sarah

If I never set foot in a church ever again it would be too soon. Those churchmen with their high and mighty words looking down on us sinners, when did they ever try to make things better for us orphans? No, it was all harsh words about the punishments if we were naughty or disobeyed our betters and how we must be thankful for the meagre food and clothing we were given. Yet they didn't look cold and hungry, those churchmen, they were fat and sweaty and so satisfied with themselves, it made me want to puke.

I once saw a picture of Jesus with the words underneath 'Suffer the little children to come unto me.' It was such a beautiful picture. There was a man in a long white robe with shoulder length curly, dark hair and he had this golden light above his head. He smiled so sweetly at the children sitting around him. The children were plump and smiling too. He held his hands out to them, long lovely fingers he had, soft and clean they were. I asked the churchman how I could become one of those children and he glared at me and said it was unlikely that I would ever be brought to God being a child of sin and wickedness an' all. No, I should learn my place which was to labour and serve others so that my sins may be forgiven. Pah! I spit on all churchmen.

I think Nora was one of those children. She's not plump but she has the sweetest smile and see how she cares for others. She gave away her apple and shared her pie with me. Oh, it was delicious, that little piece I got, such tender meat and pastry so golden. Who would do that? I know I wouldn't ever do that. No, I'd hide in a corner somewhere and gobble it up as fast as I could in case someone stole it off me.

I worry that this place is a lot better than where we're going. I've known hell in London but are we going to a worse hell? Nora will need someone to look out for her. I have never looked out for anyone but me, but I reckon I will have to look out for her too.

Chapter 7

August 1824 London

As the summer months heated up the prison, Nora found the ward stifling. The persistent stench of barely washed bodies often made her want to retch. Most prisoners had no change of clothes and the limited washing facilities made little impact on the sour body smell. A few strange accents began to be heard as women were brought in chains from distant prisons for onward transportation. Once at Newgate, and with fetters removed, Nora was shocked to see their skin suppurating from weeks or even months of chafing on wrists and ankles.

Mrs Fry's Society of Friends and the women, sewing at the ward table, worked at full speed to make new skirts of serge or calico for the newcomers. The pump in the yard was used again and again to try and get rid of the filth and to clean their oozing, stinking sores.

The mood became gloomy and fractious. Jane and Lizzie were even louder and more quarrelsome, but threats from the wardress kept them from doing much harm and they spent a lot of time playing cards. At first, they bet just for buttons, but one day they had money. Nora was sure they had filched money from her belongings, as the five shillings, given by her sisters, was missing. The two women had looked slyly at her the day before the money disappeared. She complained to the wardress, who just shrugged her shoulders when told of it. There was no proof of course. She did not dare tell Peg or Maudie because they would not be able to protect her for much longer.

That summer was one of the wettest anyone could remember, but it was often still too hot to sleep at night and Nora became increasingly tired and listless. Her bright green eyes looked dull with dark semi-circles visible underneath. Her father and sisters noticed how she grew thinner as the weeks progressed. Her coppery hair, usually well combed and gleaming, appeared greasy and lifeless, beneath her cap. She was diminishing before their eyes, and yet what could they do about it, other than to bring small gifts of food to tempt her.

The rain didn't help. Often, they met with the water streaming down their faces and backs, making a sad, bedraggled sight as they attempted to talk through the bars and grating, unable to touch let alone hold each other. She still smiled when they visited and tried her best to be positive and she was always grateful for the small items of food they brought, but they knew she suffered. It was not the weather that unsettled Nora the most, but the growing realisation that time with her family would end soon. It broke her heart. Before long she would neither see them nor talk with them ever again.

Nora shed many tears during sleepless nights tossing around on the thin mattress. The days passed much the same, sewing, some chatting and walking around the yard, whatever the weather. Sarah stuck close to Nora, as would a shadow, but scarce a word was ever uttered from her mouth. Nora, now used to her silence, accepted it and thought little more about it. One day Sarah might speak but until then Nora let her be.

Nora's father tried to get his daughter's sentence reviewed. The Quaker lady, who had delivered that first letter, helped him compose the letter of appeal. The weeks passed with no response to his entreaty and Nora lost that tiny glimmer of hope she had clung to when told of Mrs Butler's willingness to write to the authorities.

To compound her growing distress Peg and Maudie had finished their three-month sentence and were leaving the prison. Nora and Sarah were upset and troubled to see them go because they had both given them a measure of protection during their stay at Newgate. The two women were, as ever, dressed in their multicoloured finery as somehow, they could never summon up any enthusiasm for black cotton or brown serge.

'I really don't know how I would have managed without your help when I arrived. You taught me so much as well. I think I am less of a 'mouse' now,' joked Nora.

'That you are,' replied Peg, laughing. Then she looked at the two girls and her expression became serious. 'But you mind, once you get to that place they're sending you to, find someone else who will look out for you. I have heard tell that there are ten men for every one woman out there. You will need a strong man to protect you or I wouldn't like to think how you'll fight them off. Remember what we showed you?'

Nora drew her knee up sharply and Maudie and Peg laughed. 'Yes, that and use your teeth to bite and your thumbs to gouge their eyes. It may help to carry a small knife around with you too. Best of all, avoid being alone; there's safety in numbers.'

Nora listened to Peg but doubted she could defend herself in any of those ways. Surely the best way would be to deport herself as a modest young maid and not attract the eye of any villain.

Sarah also listened and knew from experience how Peg spoke the truth of it. She'd heard women talking in Newgate about being brought up on the streets and surviving only because they had developed the necessary skills of finding enough to eat, by stealing or scavenging and defending themselves in any way they could. Would it be the same in Van Diemen's Land? Her heart sank and she found herself shivering.

To lighten the mood Maudie said, 'And we want to thank you for teaching us to sew, Nora. We will now be able to make ourselves a new apron, or even a petticoat!'

Nora laughed because Maudie and Peg were not the best or fastest of seamstresses. In three months they had managed to make just the simplest of garments and earned the princely sum of one shilling each. It would not have been that much, had Nora not redone much of their work before it could possibly be sold in the prison shop.

'But we have made you these bags, one for you Nora and another for you Sarah.' Maudie brought two simple hessian bags from behind her back. 'You will be able to take these with you to store all your worldly possessions.'

The stitching wasn't neat but each had done their best and both Sarah and Nora were moved beyond words. Nora hugged both the women fiercely. They were so generous with their affection and had taught her not to judge by appearance alone.

Both Maudie and Peg then opened their arms to Sarah, Sarah, who had never been hugged nor even liked people to touch her. Flinching at first, then allowing herself to be gently enveloped in their arms she held her breath, not daring to break this spell. Both touched their lips fleetingly to Sarah's cheek and Sarah trembled with the shock and pleasure of it. As the women composed themselves, Nora dared to ask what would happen after they left prison.

'It'll be back to scratching a living on the town. Peg sighed. 'We're not getting any younger and as time goes on, it just gets more difficult. We had a few regulars, maybe we won't now but there ain't any other work for us. Perhaps we'll end up selling flowers for a few pence if the gin or the pox don't get us first. But we never mind being in here these days, at least we get a dry bed and enough food 'til they kick us out.

Maudie, ever the optimist, gave Peg a playful thump and said 'Cheer up, we've always got each other and we don't need that much food. Perhaps if we stole something they might be kind and send us to this Van Diemen's Land too, and we can then see how you two misses are getting on.'

At this point, the wardress called to those who were leaving and several of the women walked to the door waving goodbye to their own particular friends. Nora and Sarah watched them go with sadness and returned silently to the table to pick up their sewing.

It would be good to say the days passed much as they had before but just seemed that bit longer, without Maudie or Peg to lighten the time by sharing a joke and story. The truth of it was that only the next day the sly pinches started. This was followed by the foot which managed to trip one of them up and send her sprawling in the dirt of the yard and the hot tea spilt over sewing only recently completed and being admired. Nora was never sure how they managed to take them by surprise, as they both now kept a constant eye on Jane and Lizzie. Each time it was a different insult, a new hurt and always when others weren't looking. Nora saw Sarah retreating more into herself and longed to hit the bullies, but she knew she could not win at that game, although it was probably the only thing they understood. Why were they like that, why take so much pleasure from hurting them? She didn't understand.

Neither Jane nor Lizzie ever talked about why they liked to torment others and if asked they would have just said, 'Why not?' They were like those boys who enjoy pulling the wings off flies or drowning a cat in a sack. No one had ever shown them another way of life so they took their pleasure where they could.

They had been partners for as long as they could remember, both with mothers who drank themselves senseless to forget the beatings of their husbands. Jane and Lizzie dragged themselves up, united against a world which taught them only pain, hunger and cold. By the time, they were ten, they lived permanently on the streets of Southwark, using any strategy they could to stay alive. They learnt cunning from those that tricked and duped them. They learnt how to steal from those that stole from them. By the age of eighteen they had teamed up with two footpads who would lay in wait with cudgels in a darkened alley for men lured there by Jane and Lizzie. When the footpads were caught and hung, Jane and Lizzie hid out in a cellar, knowing they were hunted. At last desperate for food, they ventured into street-walking only to be attacked by the prostitutes whose turf they had dared enter. They travelled further out towards Wapping and the narrow lanes where sailors came ashore with a bag of coins and a thirst for drink and women. It was a battle to survive but they did until a group of sailors ambushed them to get their stolen coins back and then handed them over to the constable. They refused to be cowed by anything and they had learned to care for no one but themselves.

Chapter 8

The women waiting for transportation were called to the chapel one Monday after midday dinner to be addressed by the governor. As they filed into the chapel and up to the gallery speculation was rife and worried glances flew back and forth amongst the prisoners. Nora sat between Sarah and a new arrival, Helen Fitzgerald, a girl around the same age as her sister Mary. Helen nursed a tiny infant, which made soft sucking and mewling sounds, and she reminded Nora of how her mother loved to have babies at her breast. But Helen didn't have that soft bloom of motherhood, she appeared tough and wiry. Nora guessed that her body had never been replete with food. She was thin and small in height. However, she could see strength in her rough hands and weathered complexion, and in her face, she saw grim determination.

Helen told the other two, while they waited, that she had been held at Nottingham Gaol. She had stolen a few yards of cloth from a market stall to make herself a dress. 'I was in rags and winter was coming on. The previous winter was so cold and I dreaded going through that again. My family tramp around the country, looking for any work and we live in fields or barns when we are allowed to. I just knew I couldn't survive the winter without something warmer to wear. Well, I suppose I have survived just, though it's a mystery to me because at first, that gaol was foul and full of fever. By the time I left, it got better. They told us we should be grateful. You wouldn't keep an animal the way we were kept at first, apart from rats, and there were plenty of those.'

Nora detected a familiar accent and asked her if she were Irish.

'Yes, I was born in Cork but we came over after old Boney was defeated and the soldiers all drifted back. The work just dried up. Life there was too hard, not that it's any easier in England, worse really because they hate us, so they do. We struggled to live off the land and we lost two of my younger brothers to hunger and cold before they were six.' Helen crossed herself.

Nora thought it very strange that here was a girl so much like herself in background and with almost the same Christian name. Not that anyone in her family had called her Eleanora since she could first remember. It felt almost that she had gained a sister, and for some reason, she found it brought cheer to her. But how sad it was for Helen, whose brothers had died of starvation. She couldn't imagine how terrible that would be. She thanked God for her family's good fortune. There was little money spare but they never went hungry.

The governor, Mr Newman, entered the chapel and the chatter of the women subsided. Helen removed the baby from her breast and covered herself. The women had seen Mr Newman before as he regularly walked around the prison inspecting the wards and asking if there were any problems. Nora found him a decent man, but he looked more serious than usual.

'Ladies' he began, looking up at the women and young children in the gallery. 'I have had word that a ship, by the name of Henry, is being prepared to take you to Van Diemen's Land. It should be ready within the month and will set sail before the end of September so that you miss the worst of the winter storms. The journey will take about five months, possibly a little less, depending on the weather. Be assured that the government has arranged for adequate rations for your journey and a surgeon will be on board to ensure your health.

When you arrive at your destination you will be assigned duties, either as servants for officers and settlers or work in the female factories. I would urge you to behave demurely both during the journey and when you reach your destination. It should be possible to find husbands when your sentence ends, or possibly earlier with the permission of the authorities. If you do not behave, the ship's surgeon has authority to punish you and it goes without saying that, once on land, you will be subject to the full force of the law.

I know that you will be concerned about leaving your friends and family and, if possible, we will allow you to bring in two female friends into the prison to take tea with you in the week before you depart for the ship.'

Mr Newman didn't wait for any reaction from the women and left as suddenly as he arrived. He had given them news they were bound to find difficult and it was best now for them to have time to digest it on their own.

As he left the hubbub began with the women reacting to the news. A few cried, one said that it was about bloody time and it couldn't be worse than here. Others were subdued and yet more seemed excited by the prospect of a new land and a new start. Those, like Nora, with close families, were the most upset by the news. Tearfully Nora asked Helen when she had last seen her family.

'My Da was at the trial, but I haven't seen my Mam since I was arrested. He told me she dreaded the sentence, it being my second time an' all. I reckon she knew what would happen. They'll be working on the harvest now, probably at Mr Dodd's farm in Lincolnshire. That's where they normally go in August. I wish I could send them a message with some kind of keepsake.'

'What do you mean by keepsake?' asked Nora.

'Oh, just a small token, so they would remember me,' replied Helen sadly.

In a quiet, shy voice Sarah said, 'Why not make a pincushion and stitch a message on it.'

Both of the other girls stared at Sarah in surprise. It was the most Nora had ever heard Sarah say. She was so used to Sarah's silence that her soft rasping voice almost came as a surprise.

'Goodness what a wonderful idea. But how would I write a message?' asked Helen.

'I ..I could do it.' Sarah replied.

'Can you read and write Sarah? Lord, aren't you clever!' Nora exclaimed. Sarah nodded and her eyes lit up at Nora's praise.

'Will you help me as well because I want to make a pincushion too, for my family.' She would give it to her sisters when they came to tea. 'What do you think we should write?' Her spirits rose as she thought of their pleasure in the little gift.

As Nora, Sarah and Helen walked back to the ward they tried to suggest words that would mean something but also fit on an item as small as a pincushion. They settled on 'When this you see, think of me.' No one in Nora's or Helen's family could read so they believed the simple rhyme once heard wouldn't be forgotten.

They had been dawdling and as they reached the stairwell up to the ward Nora found that Jane and Lizzie stood smirking front of them, arms akimbo, barring their way. No one else was about. Nora's heart sank, she was sure that they were all going to get a beating.

'Give us your boots,' said Lizzie pointing to Nora's well-shod feet.

'No I need them. They wouldn't fit you anyway,' Nora tried to say this bravely, but her heart was hammering in her chest.

'Stupid cow! We ain't going to wear 'em but sell 'em. Hand 'em over now and don't snitch to the wardress cos soon enough there'll be just you, us and the sea. Can you swim?''

'Can she swim! Ooh, that's hilarious, that is, said Jane.

The two bullies turned towards each other and snorted with laughter. Lizzie turned back to raise a threatening hand at Nora. But before she could land a blow, Lizzie's arm was twisted hard round her back, and she was screaming in pain, as jagged nails raked her skin. Jane lumbered towards her friend to help, but her shins were kicked hard from behind and she fell heavily to the floor, her forehead banging against the stair.

'Don't mess with my friends. I always fight dirty and I never lose.'

Nora at first stood in shock then looked back at Sarah who was open-mouthed and holding Helen's baby. Then she turned towards Helen, who stood behind the women daring either of them to move. To make the point again, she shoved Lizzie's arm further back and landed another kick at Jane, with her wooden clog connecting loudly with flesh and bone.

'Come on, let's leave them. They best not come near you again if they want to live.' This pointed barb thrown at the bullying women, who were now both nursing cuts and bruises and casting malevolent glances at the retreating girls. Jane was attempting to sit up, whilst nursing her bruised temple. 'Sarah, you go in front with Davy.' The trio made the short journey back to the ward with Helen bringing up the rear and keeping a watchful eye out for her back.

'Wherever did you learn to fight like that?' breathed Nora in admiration and relief, her heart still pounding with fright.

'Daddy taught us. He said the English hated us Irish so much that we needed to protect ourselves and he was right. I have lost count of the times we had to fight or get a walloping. My Mam and sister are good scrappers too. Listen, don't tell anybody about it, alright. I don't want trouble.'

The door to the ward flew open and Mrs Barnard, looking up from the table, where she was helping a young girl sew a buttonhole, saw Nora, Sarah and one of the newcomers, rush in. Sarah was carrying a tiny bundle which was now starting to cry, a cry veering between angry and forlorn. The girls rushed to the table and clamoured for plain cloth. Nora and the new girl talking with such animation, that she had difficulty in understanding what they were saying.

'Slow down please and tell me calmly what you want and please introduce yourself.' She nodded towards the newcomer.

'This is Helen Ma'am and we want to make a keepsake to send to our families and Sarah has agreed to help us write a message and will you help Helen send it because she can't read and write the same as me.' Nora still spoke too quickly but Mrs Barnard began to understand what they wanted.

'Welcome Helen and is that your babe being held by Sarah?'

The baby was now screaming his displeasure and Sarah held him out to Helen with a beseeching look on her face. Helen took him back, opened her dress and Davy soon settled, snuffling with pleasure, his earlier feed, interrupted by the governor, now forgotten. Yes, the baby was Helen's, no need for further answer. The girl sitting beside her was coping with the buttonhole, so Mrs Barnard sought out two scraps of plain blue cloth for pincushions as well as some scraps of wool for stuffing and gave them to Nora.

'Now Sarah,' she said 'come and sit with me awhile. No don't shrink away you know that I will not hurt you, don't you? I just want to ask thee about thy reading.'

A tremulous Sarah came and sat on the edge of a seat, not daring to make herself comfortable, in case she might need to escape even from the gentle Mrs Barnard.

'Please read me for me my dear; just a sentence or two. Which is thy favourite bible story? '

Her reassuring tone persuaded Sarah to whisper, 'Suffer the little children.'

'Oh, what a good choice! Now let me find the passage in the Bible and we can read it together. Here it is in the gospel of Matthew. Shall we start?'

As Mrs Barnard began to read the passage, she patted Sarah's hand encouraging her and, after a false beginning, Sarah began to read. She was hesitant at first, but then her voice, though still quiet, grew stronger. Mrs Barnard stopped reading and let Sarah carry on until the end of the short passage. Mrs Barnard was astounded for Sarah read, not only with confidence but also with feeling and understanding. For the three months, Sarah had been in the ward, she had shown no sign of intelligence. She answered questions with a gesture. Her eyes had been dull, without expression and her face, a mask of incomprehension. What a waste of precious time with this girl. She had believed her simple-minded, but that was not the case at all. She must beg forgiveness from God for her foolishness and lack of understanding. How could she have made such a mistake? There may be little time left, but she would work to put it right.

Her eyes moistened and Sarah looking at her, noticed this and her grey eyes grew round with surprise. Her mind had refused to trust this woman. She was just a do-gooder like the others who visited the foundling home. They did not really care.

'You read most beautifully Sarah. I do hope thee will consent to read to the other ladies. Will thee think on it?'

Chapter 9

Sarah

They gave me a button when I left, said it was attached to the rag they found me in. It was the only kindness I ever got from that place. That button is my token, the only thing I have from my mother. I used to smell it hoping it would give me a scent of her. Then I'd keep it in my mouth and taste it. If it wasn't in my mouth I kept it in my hand or in the straw of my bedding. I'll never let it go. It's sewn it into my dress now so that I can touch it whenever I want.

I used to imagine her, my mother. She'd be pretty and kind. There were visitors; smart ladies walking around in their fancy dresses and bonnets. The matron or the beadle was always with them, and I thought maybe my mother was one of the ladies and had come to take me home. I was little then, I soon learnt. They would say, 'Oh, the poor darlings, how good you are to look after them. What a Christian act of charity and so forth. Blah, blah blah.' Not once did they ever ask one of us were we warm, had we enough to eat? They never come too near, or they might catch something.

Reading was my only fond memory of that place. I loved the stories in the Bible like the three wise men and the one about the prodigal son. Some of the little children asked me to help them with their reading. It felt good to help them and I dreamt I might be a reading monitor there, helping to teach the younger children.

They wouldn't let us write, but I learnt as best I could. At night, I would see the letters in my mind and trace them in the air until I fell asleep. Then I found a feather. It was so soft and grey, like the material of this dress. I found that if I dipped it in the soot of the fire and then spat on it I could trace letters on the floor. I had to be careful. If they caught me I knew I would be whipped. When the other children were asleep I crept out of bed and wrote letters on the floor next to it. I couldn't see of course, but I imagined the letters in my mind. The next morning, I rubbed them away, the soot mixing with the rest of the dirt. How I longed to write on a slate or better still on paper. I don't reckon I'll ever have the chance to write on paper.

Then one day the beast came into the room where we laboured and said 'I'll have that'un.' pointing at me with his filthy, calloused hand. I knew my dreams were over and misery would be all I'd get.

Until today, no one in my world has ever said a nice thing to me. Nora is always friendly, but today she called me 'clever' and Mrs Barnard told me I read well. And Helen, well she hit back at those bullies and defended us. Us, who she has known a bare thirty minutes. I don't know what to say about her. We'll surely stick close by. We may need her again.

That's three good things inside an hour. This is the best day of my life.

Chapter 10

Sarah marked out the letters for their pincushions with a thin sliver of wood she found in the log basket in the fireplace. She dipped it in some old soot from the chimney and with painstaking care drew tiny lines on the cloth which Nora and Helen cross-stitched over. Both girls wanted their names to appear on the pincushions and Nora had been fascinated to see her name and the shape it made.

'Do you think I might learn to read and write after all?' She asked Mrs Barnard later that afternoon.

'Certainly, we can make a start now and Sarah will continue to teach you on the ship.' She looked questioningly at Sarah, who nodded her agreement. 'Why Inside of six months you should be able to read quite well. Sarah I will find you a slate to write on to practise your writing while you are here,' replied Mrs Barnard. 'How about you Helen, do you want to learn?'

'I don't think I can Ma'am. These marks that Sarah has drawn are just swimming around on the cloth. My eyes can't seem to pin them down. I don't believe my brain is up to it.' Helen looked downcast.

'It could be your eyesight, Helen. Do you see things better when they are far off or quite near to you?'

Helen puzzled over this and at last said 'I was always the first to see a rabbit or a hare in the field for my Da to kill with his slingshot. Then I kept a look out for the gamekeeper.'

'That means you are probably long sighted. I will see what I can do.'

Mrs Barnard noticed their confusion. She decided not to say anything further in case she was not able to fulfil her half-promise. The girls remained mystified by what she said, but none had the courage to ask. How could she alter Helen's sight? It didn't make any sense. Nora helped to embroider the tricky bits of Helen's keepsake and by the next day, it was ready.

'I will send this for you, care of the farmer, but you do know that it will take time, maybe a few weeks to get to him. I doubt there will be any reply before you leave here,' said Mrs Barnard, trying not to raise any hopes Helen might have.

'Oh yes, Ma'am. They may not get it for a year or more if they changed their harvest work. Please ask the farmer to keep it for them should they come his way again. I will just be so happy to think they may get it one day and remember me. Oh, and can you tell them about my baby, please. My family don't know that I have little Davy.' Helen rocked and kissed her baby as she held out the pincushion. He gurgled his pleasure at his mother's ministrations.

Mrs Barnard took the keepsake from Helen's rough hands. This sturdy girl with her chestnut hair and steady, blue eyes was remarkably sanguine. Of the three friends, Helen, she felt, was the one who would bear what lay ahead most easily. She worried about Sarah, so damaged and yet she had read a small passage of the Bible with great feeling to the other women this afternoon. Despite the early tremor in her voice, she grew with confidence as the other women listened and even gave half a smile when she saw their nods of approval. If only she had more time to help her or might find a way for someone else to help her, on the voyage.

And Nora, how would she fare, away from her loving family? It might go either way. She may sink under the great loss of her family, or come to accept it and grow to be a very decent addition to the colony. Mrs Barnard prayed for the latter. What an iniquitous system to send poor young women many thousands of miles away from their family and friends. All three of these girls were basically good, well behaved and modest in behaviour, yet they must see great evil, mixing with those who were irredeemable and corrupted. She had heard dreadful stories about the behaviour of loose, abandoned women in Van Diemen's Land and New South Wales. Pray God one day there would be a Society of Friends there to help these women.

Chapter 11

September 1824 London

It was just after four o'clock in the afternoon on a cool, autumnal Thursday when the door to the ward opened. Nora had been sewing throughout the afternoon and her back ached. She arched it to stretch the knotted muscles and watched as the matron entered and talked quietly to the wardress, who nodded and grimaced. Once the matron had departed, the wardress moved around the ward talking individually to certain women. Nora nudged Helen. Something was up and as they watched the certainty grew that it was to do with those being transported. The reaction to her words, hands flying to mouths, a face turned away or an involuntary moan told its own story.

The wardress came towards Nora and her friends. Her face was frowning, and yet there was sympathy in her eyes as she told them that the women were to be moved to the ship, Henry, in the morning. There would be no time for the women to say goodbye to loved ones, and despite the promise, they would miss the chance to invite friends in for a farewell tea.

Nora's blood drained from her face. She had never looked forward to saying goodbye to her family, but now, even that painful duty was denied her. Hot tears formed at her eyes. She looked wildly at Helen and Sarah for comfort and seeing their own shocked faces she started to sob uncontrollably. How could she bear not to see her family again? It wasn't possible to live through the pain of it. Nora's chest tightened and her breathing became shallow as she gasped for air, but it did not reach her lungs. She grew panicky as Helen and Sarah tried to give her comfort but her sobs just grew louder and her breathing more ragged. Helen shook her and told her to breathe slowly and calmly, stroking her back until her breathing became easier.

Mrs Barnard, aware that the women were becoming more and more distressed, sought to regain order by offering calm, soothing words and commiseration. She asked that the women pray for forbearance and

God's help in their hour of need. How she hated these moments. No matter how much notice the women had, it always came as a shock, and she felt their pain and sorrow keenly. But this time it was harder to reach the women. They were angry as well as upset. Instinctively she dropped to her knees on the hard, wooden floor and began to pray, not in silence as was her practice, but in a clear, moderated voice she recited Psalm twenty-three.

'The lord is my shepherd,
I shall not want
He maketh me to lie down in green pastures.
He leadeth me beside still waters.
He restoreth my soul.
He leadeth me in the paths of righteousness
for his name's sake.'

Now some of the women were joining her on their knees and she carried on, willing the others to follow, and gradually they began to. She continued with the psalm and, after a few seconds, only her voice was heard. She watched the women comfort each other, some subdued and silent in their own thoughts, some still quietly weeping. As they rose from the floor they held each other's hands and once upright hugged and kissed each other with great gentleness. 'Sweet Jesus,' she prayed silently again. 'Guide and comfort these women, for they have great need of thee.'

Standing once again Mrs Barnard passed amongst the women wishing them well in their new lives and asking that they live by God's word. When she came to Sarah she grasped her hand and looking deep into her eyes told Sarah that she must search inside herself to find the inner light.

'Sarah, God is within you and if you listen to your inner soul you can find peace and calm. It will help overcome whatever has befallen you. Find the teacher within you when you are troubled and let it guide you to the right path. Trust God and he will deliver you from evil. I will pray for you daily.'

Sarah listened to her and acknowledged her instruction, with just the briefest nod and the tiniest pressure of her fingers, as her hand slipped out of Mrs Barnard's grasp. Yes, thought Mrs Barnard, she would pray for this girl above any of the others. Coming to Nora, Mrs Barnard told her that she would let her father know of the departure.

'Please, can you send him this keepsake,' said Nora, still very distressed. 'I was going to give it to my sisters when they came for tea on Sunday.' She handed her the tear-stained pincushion.

'Of course, I'd be delighted to do that for you, my dear. Stay strong Nora, things will work out because you are a good girl. Find a respectable husband and raise a family. Keep up with your reading lessons and if you send a letter to your family one of the Friends will read it to them.'

Nora bobbed a curtsey to Mrs Barnard and tried to smile her gratitude, though it was still difficult for her to summon up anything but grief.

After Mrs Barnard left the ward the grumblings of the women resurfaced, and when the evening meal was being cleared away the atmosphere began to turn very angry. The sound of pots and pans banging together began to permeate the prison. Several of the women in their own ward began to shout and bang their wooden plates and tankards. The sound of glass smashing somewhere raised the shrieks of the women ever higher. By now all three of the women's wards were in uproar. Nora, in her misery, got caught up in the anger and she found it helped to scream and shout. It was the first time in her life she felt able to let herself go and it was liberating. Sarah joined her and the two girls banged their plates and tankards together and screamed at the top of their voices. They screamed their protest at the callous system which forced young women to be sent away from their homeland and loved ones, never to return. They screamed their anger and their hurt. The governor was called and he spoke to the women from the courtyard below.

'Ladies,' he began. At this, some of the women began to shout obscenities. 'Ladies, please.' he began again. 'I am afraid there has been an unfortunate misunderstanding. We try to give you fair notice of your removal to the ship but in this case, it has not been possible. I told you that you would be embarking within the month and that is still so. I am sorry that not all of you have had your visitors, but we can do nothing about that now. Please now go back to your beds and get some sleep. You will be leaving at five o'clock tomorrow morning.' He was a decent and compassionate man who hated this part of his job and tried to make it easier for the women. In his heart, he cursed the authorities who had caused this problem. There should have been another week in which to prepare the women.

Still grumbling, the women began to drift away from the window. Jane and Lizzie still swearing loudly, but most started to settle down. Nora could not sleep that night as her thoughts were racing around her head. She had to leave her beloved family. She had no expectations that she would ever see her dearest family again. How was it to be borne? By the time, she had to rise and prepare to leave, she like all the women, who had created such noise the previous evening, was exhausted and submissive.

Chapter 12

Sarah

It was as if something broke in me tonight. It felt so good to scream and shout. Nora and me, we screamed and screamed till we were hoarse and our throats couldn't find another sound. I screamed for the loneliness, for the hunger and for the pain I had endured for the fourteen years of my short life. The memories bottled up inside of me and I let them go tonight. Memories of those long, long days since I was four and put to work spinning wool and then knitting stockings as soon as I could hold the needles; my eyes so sore and my shoulders aching all the time. Unless you were at death's door you worked all day and there was no respite. After I left that place there was another kind of torture with the beast and his wife, I don't want to think of that.

But tonight, something lifted. Where I had seen blackness I now saw a tiny glimmer of light. Is that what Mrs Barnard meant? She said to search deep inside to find my inner soul. Maybe there's a chance for me of something better than this filthy midden, which, until now, has been the only life I've known.

Chapter 13

Nora, Sarah, Helen and the other women walked down to the yard, whilst it was still dark that Friday, early in September. Once outside, in the damp, cool air of the early autumnal morning, they saw the horses attached to the barred prison vans and were so thankful not to be sent in open carts, to be the butt and scorn of all passers-by. They pleaded not to be handcuffed, but apart from Helen who had a baby to hold this was denied. But for Helen, who wore no handcuffs, leg irons were found.

This is the end of one life thought Nora. From now on I will have a different existence, one not planned, nor intended and the result of my own foolishness. But I must try to make the best of it and make my father proud of me.

Part Two-The Henry

Part 2 - Chapter 1

The vans set off from Newgate yard, each with a guard and driver sitting up front. The clip-clopping of horses' hooves on the cobbled streets, joined the sounds of a city waking in the half-light, signalling dawn is on its way. Nora slumped against Sarah. There was not so much as a friendly wave farewell, just this furtive and shabby departure. Despairing and exhausted she dozed as they made their way towards the Thames crossing at Blackfriars Bridge.

Helen had slept well. The previous day's emotion had scarcely touched her; she felt ready for this journey and, while little Davy slept in her arms, she watched as more of London revealed itself to her unfamiliar eyes. The gloomy bulk of Saint Paul's Cathedral dominated the skyline. Helen wondered aloud what it was and a woman sitting next to her told her and then gave a running commentary about the sights of her own childhood as they passed over Blackfriars Bridge. But Helen saw tears in her eyes as the woman breathed her silent goodbye to all that she had known and the people she loved.

Carrying on south, at first and then eastwards towards the newly risen sun, they soon reached open fields where the untidy stubble showed harvest underway. She caught sight of a few hardy men and women in their smocks, grappling with scythes and making stooks of corn. They reminded her of her own family's harvest time labours. As they passed by it was as if these labourers knew where they were going for they stood and leant on their tools and waved a desultory farewell. Helen felt her eyes dampen with unshed tears and she waved forlornly back. Her stomach grumbled loudly for lack of food and drink since the evening before. What she wouldn't give for a cup of warming tea and a hunk of bread. Davy was becoming restive and she knew he needed a feed before long, so she put him to her breast but he was still too sleepy to latch on. Helen looked at his tiny body with adoration, he was her future and she would do everything in her power to keep him safe.

Ordered off the carriages at Woolwich they clambered down holding on to their few possessions. Nora, still half asleep, shook her skirts and would have offered to hold Davy while Helen got down, but for her handcuffs. Helen had to wait, in any case, for her leg irons to be unlocked. At last, she dismounted and peered around seeing several ships in the river and wondered which was theirs.

The women were told to form a line, where a clerk checked them off against his list. If this were any later convict ship, more details other than their name would be checked, but as it was, Helen was back waiting with her friends just a few seconds later. They watched as the tender plied to and fro between the pier and the brig, moored and waiting in the river. Nora told her that she had seen these small boats in the Thames often enough, but had never been in one.

Stepping warily into the tender, Helen almost lost balance as the small boat rocked beneath her. She found herself grabbing on to Sarah in front, while a sailor held on to Davy. It had turned blustery and the little boat bounced through the waves until they came alongside a two-masted brig, far smaller than many of the East Indiamen, moored further up in the Thames. It was tricky to climb out of the boat onto a rope ladder but impossible with handcuffs on. Nora rubbed her wrists when the cuffs were removed; even after only a couple of hours she was complaining how sore and chafed they felt. Helen did not bother to tell her friend of her journey from Nottingham to London, in leg irons all the way. She still bore the marks.

Davy, now wide awake and screaming in hunger, was placed in a basket to be hoisted up to the ship above. Helen held tightly onto Nora's hand for comfort as she watched the basket swinging around in mid air. Her mouth dried with fear as she imagined him falling into the river and saw herself plunging after him to certain death. But he soon disappeared over the side of the ship and a sailor signalled her to follow.

Helen reached out to grab the ladder but found the rowing boat moving backwards as the brig moved up and down in the swell of the river. At last her hands found purchase and she forced her feet to start climbing, trying not to let her skirts trip her. She was all too aware of her nakedness under her petticoat, should she fall back, into the boat. Helen did not let herself think of falling into the murky river.

Surgeon Superintendent Carlyle watched as the women lined up in front of him. They looked a healthy lot, for the most part. He put their average age at around twenty-two or three, just what the colony needed. There was one thin, scrawny looking girl, no more than fourteen, and he saw a woman next to her with a babe in arms, which she was desperately trying to pacify; he tutted to himself and hoped the mother had plenty of milk. He had read the condemnatory report of a woman sent from Chester where warders stopped her from breastfeeding her baby in prison, knowing it would die for lack of milk soon after they had set sail. He really didn't approve of cruelty. But now he had a job to do.

He checked them for signs of fever, asked them if they felt well and looked in their mouths and ears. Without reasonable teeth, they could not cope with tough, salt meat or ship's biscuit and dried peas that never softened even if they were boiled for a week or more. He would have no compunction about returning them to prison if unfit for the voyage ahead.

As they waited in turn for their examinations Nora looked around in wonder. The two wooden masts soared above the deck, bare of sails, but fitted with a complex array of ropes and pulleys, attached to the side of the ship and to the deck. There was a spar at the bow leaning out at forty-five degrees above the water, with yet more ropes attached. Around the side of the ship were thinner ropes holding up the hatchways, cut into the side to bring air and light into the first deck below. In the centre of the deck was a row boat, similar to the one they had travelled in from the shore. An open hatchway sat off centre, below a smaller raised deck at the stern of the ship, close to where the rear mast stood. Everywhere she looked there were neat coils and loops of ropes, ready for the business of sailing. Nora liked the open feel of the ship and wondered how it all worked. She felt Sarah's hand slip into hers and glanced at her. Sarah was pointing to the hatchway.

'Will we have to sleep down there? She whispered. Her face looked paler than ever.

'I suppose. But we will be together, so don't worry.' Her reply did little to comfort Sarah.

Once the girls had finished with the surgeon, they were handed two sets of clothing and bedding for the journey, followed by a numbered tag, to put round their necks. Each item had the same crude numbers marked on the cloth. They were told to remember the shape of the numbers if they could not read. Nora offered to carry Helen's load but a sailor took Davy and led them to the hatchway.

He descended easily, with Davy nestled under his arm, but Helen wondered how she would manage as there was no handrail. She supposed she would get used to negotiating the steps whilst carrying David, but for now, it felt awkward. Her long skirt, clothes and bedding, required her to feel for each step. She was grateful to reach the firm wooden deck below. Helen rewarded the sailor with a smile of thanks as he led them to a further hatchway and yet more steps. She noticed before descending once more that this deck was divided in two by a wooden partition in which sat a door. There was a little light filtering in from two of the open hatches, she had seen in the ship's side, whilst climbing the rope ladder. The rest of the deck was made up of small rooms with a passageway in between.

The darkness of the prison below reminded her of the gloom of Nottingham prison, and it was a while before her eyes adjusted. There were no openings in the sides of the ship here. The only light came from the hatch above and a few candle lights hanging on chains suspended from the deck above. A line of barred, metal cages lined both sides of the deck, in between stood tables, benches and cooking pots. Sarah shrank back against Helen and she wished she could hold her hand, but her arms were still full of clothing and blankets. Instead, Sarah somehow managed to grip Helen's skirt, her breathing ragged and shallow. She did not see the tears forming in Sarah's eyes but she felt her fear. They gagged at the sour smell, permeating the deck. It was the smell of privies, unwashed bodies and stale food.

Each cage held two tiers of sleeping berths, three abreast, jutting out from the side of the ship. Walking through the passageway between the cells the sailor pointed to a cage which contained two women and indicated they should enter. He handed Davy over to Helen as she put down her load on the table next to the cage. Then he left to repeat the process with the next batch of prisoners.

Part 2 - Chapter 2

The newcomers looked at each other for a moment then glanced around at their surroundings and nodded to the two other women in the cage. Nora plucked up courage and asked them 'How long have you been here?'

One of the women replied 'Two days; we was brought here from Worcester. Bloody terrible journey it were. We got soaked on us furst day and they kept us in irons all the way. It's not as if we could go anywhere cos we had no money. They gev us dry clothes when we got 'ere but just look at the quality, they won't last five weeks let alone five months. I see yo've got yours, so yo had best change into 'em. They'll tek all your belongings to stow somewhere and tell yo you'll get them back sometime after yo land. I hope they don't bloody steal 'em. I'm Anne Farrow and this here is Patsy Fowler.' pointing to a tall, thin woman with grey hair, whose face was marked with red splotches. They looked like old burn marks.

Both women were older, more the age of Maudie and Peg but without the warmth or humour, Nora guessed. Anne was stout with heavy jowls and a sour expression; one of her front teeth was missing and her others looked grey in the gloom of the deck.

'How old is the littlun?' asked the one called Patsy.

'Ten weeks,' replied Helen.

'We 'ave six children each,' said Patsy.

The girls gasped in disbelief. Who would be so cruel as to send mothers away from any child, let alone six? It didn't bear thinking of.

Helen asked 'Who is looking after them?'

'Us husbands of course,' snarled Anne. Patsy nodded, but she looked upset.

'I ain't seen mine for three years now. They live in Staffordshire, so it were too far for 'em to visit the prison.' Her eyes filled with tears. 'Do you reckon I might hold your littlun? I do so miss mine. The youngest'll be five years old be now.'

Nora changed her mind about Patsy and realised that she was unhappy and not cold hearted. Anne reminded her of Jane and Lizzie and her heart sank, but best to try and make friends, so she introduced herself and the other two girls followed suit.

'When do we get to eat and where is the privy?' asked Helen, by now bursting and crossing her legs in desperation. Anne pointed across the deck.

'There's a privy on the other side of the deck. It's going to smell to high heaven in here with even more women and especially with a babbie puking and what not,' she grumbled.

Helen let Patsy hold Davy, who was now ravenous and beside himself with fury, while she went to made herself more comfortable. The water closet, although just a small wooden cupboard, at least gave some privacy. She had often had to use fields, but there was more often than not a bush or a tree to hide behind, but everyone here was in earshot and could hear and smell bodily functions. She grimaced and got on with the job, making her way quickly back to her Davy, who was sobbing, his first real tears falling down his soft cheeks. his dark blue eyes, wide open, accusing. Patsy was doing her best to pacify him, cooing and gently patting his bottom but Helen took him back as only milk would quieten him.

Anne had delayed answering Helen's first question until she returned from the privy but her expression showed little friendship. 'As to food, I don't know. Yesterday some was brought round at midday but with all yo lot coming on board, who knows? We get rations each day and have to cook it on those stoves. Can yo cook?'

Only Helen admitted to cooking, but her experience was limited to what could be caught or filched not the kind of rations they would have here.

'Oh, don't take any notice of Anne, er's always a moody cow,' said Patsy.

Nora sensed that this voyage may be difficult living in such close quarters with Anne and others like her. In the meantime, they had to change into these dresses for the journey and she exclaimed at the thinness of the brown serge and the poor stitching, loose in some parts. The clothes they had on their backs were far better.

Once all the Newgate women had been assigned their dormitories or cages, as the women thought of them, and had changed into their ship dresses, they were called to go back to the deck for an address by the surgeon. Helen was pleased to see the sailor who had helped them before, and he took hold of Davy again for her while she negotiated the steps. One by one, they climbed through the hatch, blinking in the sudden light again. Helen's stomach audibly groaned and she knew that if she didn't get some food soon she might very well pass out. They were made to stand in rows, guarded by sailors, who eyed the women up and down, one or two making lecherous gestures, out of sight of the surgeon. Here we go, thought Helen to herself.

The surgeon waited for hush and took mental note of those women who took the most time or winked at the sailors.

'Welcome aboard the Henry ladies. You have been shown your berths. You will find eating utensils there and one lady out of each dormitory will be appointed to collect your food every day. The food is plentiful, but will not be fresh. Once we set sail we will be making only one stop on the journey, so it has to last. I expect you to keep the dormitories clean and will arrange a rota so that you each take turns.' Wry laughter was heard as he said the word dormitories, but he ignored it.

'As we get underway you will be able to come up to this deck for exercise, and we will leave your prison unlocked during the day. However, I stress that you must behave decorously. A small number of lady passengers will be travelling to meet their husbands in Van Diemen's Land. They will not want to observe any wanton behaviour so expect severe punishment, if you attempt indecent relations with any of the sailors.

You will attend church services on Sunday and we have the good fortune to have a reverend sailing with us. There will be a school for children, so they can learn reading and writing. If any of you fall ill, or have an accident requiring medical treatment, see me as soon as possible. At the journey's end, we will be reporting on your behaviour, which will affect your work assignment, so make sure you behave yourselves. You will be asked to comment on how you were treated on the voyage, and if you had enough food, so there will be a chance to raise any complaints then.'

As the surgeon finished talking and prepared to leave one woman asked, 'Will we be sailing tomorrow sir?'

'No indeed,' he replied. 'More women and cargo are yet to arrive. It could be two or three weeks before we set sail.'

Most of the women groaned. This news meant living up to three weeks below in a dark and poorly ventilated space. Nora was doubly upset, as she thought of the tea she had been denied with her sisters. Why had it been necessary to move the women to the ship from Newgate so early? But neither she nor any other, dared to voice this, as obvious as it seemed.

Helen dared to ask a question 'Sir, will there be fresh milk for my baby if my milk dries up?'

'No, I'm sorry. We have to hope that your baby won't need cow's milk, as there will be none on board. We have some livestock to slaughter during the journey, but no milk cow.'

Helen's heart sank and she offered a prayer to God to allow her milk to keep flowing.

With no more questions, the women returned to their dormitories. Back on the prison deck, Nora grumbled to Helen about the delay in sailing. Other Newgate women were doing the same until several prisoners turned on them. In graphic terms, they told them they were fortunate not to have had the journeys they had endured, from such far distant places as Liverpool or Newcastle. There was no shelter from the elements for them, just straw to sleep on and little food unless an innkeeper felt sorry for them. Other women spoke up in a language that no one understood until someone realised they were Scottish.

'It's not Gaelic.' said Nora, 'I'd recognise the sound of that because my grandparents used to speak Irish to each other. No, they're most likely speaking English, but not so you could tell.'

'Dear God I'm hungry, when do we get to eat?' cried Helen. Feeding her son made her ravenous, so Patsy offered her a crust of bread that she had saved from her own breakfast rations and Helen accepted it gratefully. But before long a woman was called from each dormitory to collect food for them all. Patsy agreed to go and came back some minutes later with enough rations to make a vegetable and beef soup. As it bubbled in the pot, their mouths started to water and they could scarcely wait until it was ready, so great was their hunger. When the time came to share it out, the Newgate girls grabbed the plates and each ate with undisguised relish.

'It's not at all bad,' said Nora relieved.

'Yo wait.' said Anne. 'Once we get to sea, there won't be any fresh food. It's bound to get worse. I wouldn't be surprised if we don't end up eyeing each other up,' and she laughed at their horror as they realised what Anne meant. Helen grasped Davy tight to her chest and he squealed his displeasure, but that just made Helen rock him more vigorously while eyeing Anne with patent dislike.

'We have to go and wash us dishes now. There's a tub of water out in the corridor.' said Patsy trying to break the mood. As they filed out Nora whispered to Helen not to take any notice of Anne.

'She's the kind of woman who enjoys tormenting you. Once we are at sea I hope we'll not see too much of her in the daytime, but let's stay close you, me and Sarah. We need to protect each other and try not to get noticed by troublemakers.'

'And there are a few sailors to avoid as well. I saw one or two of them eying you up earlier. We must go around together at all times, safety in numbers,' replied Helen. Nora was one of the prettiest girls on the ship, and in these circumstances, that was not a desirable asset.

With lunch over, the hatch was closed from above, plunging the deck into darkness. The only light on prison deck came from a barred ventilation shaft, some distance away, and the candle lamps. Sarah screamed in fear and Nora had to put her arms around her and whisper soothing words into her ear. Eventually, Sarah stopped shaking and let Nora lead her to her bed.

All of them dozed in the afternoon. Most of the Newgate women felt exhausted from lack of sleep the night before, and the dark allowed few other activities. Nora still found it difficult to sleep whilst worrying about her family. Would they know yet that she had left the prison? They might be standing outside the bars wondering why she had not shown up in the exercise yard. Would somebody think to tell them?

'It is going to be so tedious waiting for the ship to leave with nothing to do other than clean.' she sighed.

The older children suffered most from the unremitting gloom of the prison deck, their mothers at their wit's end, tried to occupy them. But they whimpered or grizzled for much of the time. A few women had packs of cards, but even these could not be seen unless close to a lamp. What would it be like, Nora wondered when the openings on the deck above were closed because they were at sea? There would be so little air, it would start to smell even more awful than it already did.

Part 2 - Chapter 3

By dawn the next day Nora knew the answer. The stench of the privy mingled with the smell of dozens of women, packed in the confined space. Although each of the openings on decks above had remained open throughout the night, the hatchway from the prison deck remained closed. As the women queued for the privy they held cloths to their noses, in the vain hope it would help lessen the stink.

Patsy went off to collect their breakfast. But Nora could not stomach the thought of food, whilst breathing in the foul air, and longed to be back at Newgate, anywhere but here. Helen encouraged her to chew some bread and drink the sweetened milky tea. She dreaded the next three weeks if it meant being kept below deck without the chance of fresh air. Nora returned to the cage and curled up in her bed hoping to sleep away the time. She noticed Sarah had done the same and realised that she had not heard her speak since they came onboard.

They were not left to sleep for long. Sailors carried rags and buckets of water down to the deck and told the women to clean. They stood around to watch, remarking about this woman or that, while the women got down on their knees to scrub. Norah's face flamed as she overheard the sailors talk about her. She didn't mistake it because no one else had coppery hair, and they asked each other whether they thought her hair was the same colour elsewhere. She felt ashamed and sick with humiliation, along with other victims of their crude quips.

'Shut your filthy gobs,' said one woman.

'Aye for two pins I'd thump 'em.' Nora thought it was Anne's voice this time. She dared not look and kept her eyes towards the floor.

The surgeon overheard the comments as he clambered down to the prison deck to inspect the cleaning. What could you expect with men and women such as this? There was bound to be banter, but he did not want it to get out of hand. He shooed the men away and decided to ask Captain Ferrier for his most reputable sailor to be surgeon's assistant for the voyage.

After his inspection, the surgeon left and the hatch was closed. And so the day went on, interminable. Helen crooned at Davy and she let Nora, Patsy and even Sarah hold him from time to time, which they enjoyed until he started to squeal for his mother and food. Anne left the dormitory and went to find other company and they soon heard bawdy jokes and then raucous laughter coming from her direction. Helen started to sing little rhymes to Davy and soon Nora and Patsy joined in with her singing 'Hush a bye baby' and 'Twinkle, twinkle, little star.'

'Come on Sarah, why not join in?' asked Nora after a while. Sarah shook her head.

'Did your Ma ne'er sing to yo?' asked Patsy.

'I never had no Ma,' Sarah said, blushing unseen in the gloom.

'Sarah, why not tell your story? You never said anything about why you're here. If we're to share this tiny space for weeks on end we should spend our time talking and comforting each other.' Nora reached out and took Sarah's hand squeezing it with concern. 'We wouldn't do or say anything to hurt you.'

Sarah didn't answer. Did she have the strength to say the words out loud to others? And trust, who could she trust? She, who had never trusted a soul. Nora perhaps, but Patsy she didn't know at all and Helen? Helen was a good mother. She watched her and Davy with a quiet hunger, longing for a mother of her own. Yes, Helen, she had trusted ever since that first day when she stood up to Jane and Lizzie.

'Perhaps it'd help yo if I told yo my story.' said Patsy. 'Why don't we all speak in turn? Not while Anne's around of course. We won't tell her anything or speak when she's nearby. We can hear one story a day and yo can go last Sarah, so yo'll have plenty of time to think on it. It'll help to pass the time an' all.'

Sarah thought about this. She let the idea spin around her head for several seconds and then lightly squeezed Nora's hand back. She nodded faintly and Patsy took this slight movement as a yes and said.

'It's nearly dinner time. Why don't we leave it until this afternoon to get started and I'll start the stories off.'

As Patsy spoke the hatch cover came off and weak sunshine lit a square yard of the prison deck. How Nora hungered to go up the steps and out into the fresh air and stay there. Just to stand in sunshine, free of shackles, maybe walk around the ship would be blissful. She looked around her cell and saw the same yearning in all their faces.

However, far from the women going up the steps more newcomers descended and were shown into any dormitories with spaces. One woman was directed into their cell. She was youngish, no more than thirty years of age, guessed Nora and she had a strong, handsome face framed by dark hair and an old bonnet, which may have been cream, once upon a time, but now was a dirty grey. You could not call her pretty but the woman's features were striking. She had high cheekbones and clear grey eyes beneath thick, arched eyebrows. She wore a torn brown dress and her filthy petticoat showed through the material. She carried her prison issue dresses and petticoats. The woman smiled broadly and introduced herself.

'I'm Jooanna from Norfo'. How do?'

'From where?' they asked.

'Norfo', yew know, East Coost, Great Yarmouth.'

Nora didn't know. Living in London, you got used to different accents, but this was a new one to her and she marvelled at how could English be spoken in so many different ways?

The women made space for Joanna and showed her which bed was free and then each, in turn, gave their name. Joanna greeted them and then took off her old, tattered clothes, which smelt faintly of fish, to change into the ship's replacement clothes. She didn't shimmy out of her dress, trying to hide her body as Norah had done. She held it proudly, unashamed of her nakedness, her body statuesque under the dirt and grime of the journey.

'What I doon't understand,' she said, 'is yew get sent to prison and then sent half way round the world for stealing cloothes, but they're happy to give yew cloothes for the journey. If they gev us 'em afore we had to steal them, they'd save themselves a deal of trouble.'

'You are so right.' Helen said laughing. 'I never thought of that. Perhaps we should suggest it.'

'But who to? They never listen to the likes of us,' replied Joanna as she fastened up her dress. 'If they did, they might find it worth their while. There wouldn't be so many poor people, tha's for sure.'

Anne returned to the dormitory as dinner was due. Frowning at Joanna she couldn't help herself blurting out 'Oh God, not another body, we'll be so bleeding cramped in here.'

'This is Joanna.' said Patsy, 'and mind your manners. I have had enough your moods for the last year so it's high time yo mended yo ways.'

After a couple of minutes of strained silence Anne stamped off to fetch dinner and the others told Joanna that she shouldn't take no mind of Anne, as she was always rude and in a temper.

A subdued dinner over, dishes washed and privy visited, Anne left to join her new friends and Patsy told Joanna of their plan to tell their stories. She stressed the need not to let Anne in on it as she would use their stories against them. Joanna was more than happy with this idea and they all settled down to listen to Patsy begin her tale.

Part 2 - Chapter 4

Patsy's story

I was born in Catshill near Bromsgrove, it would be the year 1780, maybe the year before. Mam never did remember detail. We was nailers, Dad, Mam and us children, we all worked as soon as we was strong enough. We lived in a cottage, just one room downstairs with a tiny window, where we cooked, ate and us children slept, and one upstairs where Mam and Dad slept with the babby. There always seemed to be a babby, but several died before they got to sleep downstairs with us. Out back was a small forge and the nail master sold us the iron. We'd get it red hot in the forge and then shape it into nails on the anvil. How could I ever forget the searing heat and how it almost burnt your lungs, if you weren't careful. It were that cramped and dark, we fell over each other trying to work. We were often burnt by the cinders blazing red through the air.' Patsy drew up her sleeves so they could see the red and white puckered marks. They had to peer closely in the dim light, but that explained the marks on her face.

'The smoke clogged up our lungs and it was filthy, filthy work from seven in the morning 'til sundown, with a couple of breaks for food and drink. But it never paid much, all that work. Dad would go to the foggers with the nails and they'd weigh 'em, but he often came back with less money than he wanted and tell us that he'd been cheated again. How Mam fretted and cursed when he came home with so little money. Them foggers used to rig the scales, Dad was sure o' it, but could never prove nothing.

We didn't get much free time, just a visit to the fair in June and October. We only had a penny to spend, so most of the time we would just watch the tumblers and clog dancers. I remember the hours I spent just thinking how to spend my penny. Oh, the first taste of barley sugar, and how yo mouth fills with sweetness! Oh, it was bostin!' she saw the puzzlement in their faces. 'Wonderful, I mean. Once I saw something called chocolate there and wondered what that tasted of but it was far too expensive for the likes of us.'

'I have had chocolate.' interrupted Nora. 'My mistress had some that she didn't finish and I pinched it while taking the plate back to the kitchen. It's smooth like velvet, rich and sweet and if you let it melt in your mouth you could swoon with the delight of it. I never tasted anything better.'

'Well, I can't see any of us getting the chance to taste it where we are going, mores the pity.' and Patsy continued her story. 'I suppose I would be about seventeen when I met my Charles. Mam had sent me to the Tuesday market to buy food for the week, as she was laid up yet again with a new littlun. I dawdled if truth be told, cos it was such a treat for me to be out of the forge. The air was smoky with all the furnaces going, but it was so good to be out in the daylight. It was about forty- minutes' walk to the market. I took a shortcut across a field and the sun was shining, birds were singing and I was just enjoying myself. I bought everything Mam wanted and was struggling back home with the sack. It was mostly potatoes, turnips and a slab of fat bacon. We had a patch of garden but it wouldn't keep us in vegetables for a whole year. Well, there was I, walking back down the lane, when I heard a man's voice singing a merry tune behind me. I turned around and saw him driving his horse and cart. He stopped and smiled. My oh my, I tell you, my heart immediately flew into my mouth, cos he was so handsome, even though he was a fair bit older than me. I was that glad that I'd scrubbed myself hard in cold water that morning, though my dress was old and patched. Anyways 'e says to me 'Would the pretty miss like a lift in my wagon. I can see you're struggling with your heavy sack.'

I looked hard at him, not answering at first, but then he smiled again and said 'don't you worry about me I'm as harmless as yon butterfly on that honeysuckle. The name's Charles, by the by.' So, I gets up into his cart and we trot along and he tells me that he's a carter, born and brought up in Staffordshire, but comes this way quite often, carrying goods back and forth. I thought what a wonderful life he must have out in the open air, not breathing in the smoke and dust of a furnace all day. He smelled so clean and fresh and the hair below his cap shone where the sunlight glinted on it. I told him a little about my family and by the time we got back to my lane we were laughing and joking and I didn't want the journey to end. I offered him a jug of ale and he smiled and said perhaps next time, but he was late getting to his next stop. So I climbed down from the cart, thinking I would never see him again. I turned to look back before I went inside and he was still there. I waved and he waved back before he flicked the reins and the horse moved off taking him out of sight.

Two months later, on a Sunday he stood outside with a handful of wildflowers and asked my Dad if he could take me for a walk. We were wed by the next spring, and so I moved to Staffordshire, with only the clothes on my back. We lived with his widowed mother, Ada, who was the most welcoming woman I ever met, and I loved her straight away. I found work in a laundry. It was hard work, but nowhere as bad as working in a foundry, and it was clean too. As the babbies started to come, I took in washing, helped by Ada, and once a year Charles would take me with him on one of his trips. We'd call into Catshill to see my family and show off our children. How I loved those trips! We'd camp in the open air, cook on a campfire and watch the stars. Some nights there'd even be shooting stars. Charles knew the names of groups of stars and he'd point out the Plough and the Polestar and such like. By the second night, we'd be camped on a hill, overlooking Dudley, and it was like gazing into the mouth of hell. Chimneys, hundreds of 'em, belching out orange flames, smoke and soot; you could hear the clanging and the screeching way up on the hillside. I was so thankful I'd escaped, and didn't have to live down amongst them again. What if I had not met Charles that day? He's such a good man and I miss him so much.' Patsy stumbled over her story and swallowed down tears. After a few seconds, she wiped her eyes on her sleeve and began again.

'About three years ago, we took a trip again to Catshill. I had my youngest with me and old Ada was looking after the other youngsters, not my Phyllis. She's married and got babbies of her own.

Dad was dead, and my brother Bill was working the foundry with his family. Mam was old and worn out by work and childbearing. She slept downstairs with the children, but while I was there, she took a turn for the worst, dying in my arms. Bill says, there's just enough money for a pine box. When I came to lay her out, all she wore was a filthy, ragged petticoat. She'd not got out of bed for month or two and her only dress had been cut up for clothes for the grandchildren. I just couldn't see my mother sent to her grave like that, for no amount of washing would have made it better. I wanted to give her my petticoat but 'er body was so swollen it wouldn't fit 'er. I asked my sister-in-law for a winding sheet but she didn't have a spare sheet, they were all in use.

Charles wasn't due back for three days and I had only a few pennies, so I walked into Bromsgrove to look for a clean, second-hand petticoat or dress. I found one in a shop but my pennies wouldn't stretch that far so I took it. I know it was stupid, but I was grieving and not thinking straight. Of course, they caught me and threw me into the lockup. By the time Charles found me, my mother was in the ground in her old petticoat, so it was all for nought. He wanted to pay the shopkeeper but it were too late and they sent me to Worcester Gaol to wait for the assizes.

After I was sentenced I was in that gaol three years waiting for this ship. My Charles visited me every three months, but wouldn't bring the children. He thought it would upset them too much to see me in prison and it was too far. Ada died while I was there. She must have been eighty years old, but my poor Charles said her heart was broke. I was like a daughter to her, and she never had any daughters, just four sons. He never blamed me, and always said he loved me no matter what, he called me his daft ha'porth. Oh yes, he wrote asking for mercy, but never got a reply. I thank God that most of my children have grown and will look after little Flo. I fear Charles won't live much longer, once I'm gone. He's over sixty years old now and that careworn with worry about me. I thank the dear Lord he has our family to look after him, but who will care for me in my old age? I'll not have children or grandchildren in this Demon's Land, or whatever they call it. No, it'll be the poor house for me.'

Patsy sighed as she came to the end of her story, her tears flowing freely. Helen leant over, stroking her back and murmured words to soothe her. Even Davy joined in by gurgling and grinning at her until she smiled weakly.

'Can you write to your husband?' asked Nora after the tears ceased.

'Yes, that I can. The three years spent in Worcester gave me the chance to learn. I can also weave which I couldn't do before either, so that's some consolation.'

'How come you spent three years there waiting for this ship?' asked Helen.

'I suppose it weren't worth sending me, so when Anne was tried last October there were two of us and worth someone's time to organise the journey. Of course, I was in no hurry to go, because I still was getting visits from Charles. I hoped after three years they'd decide not to bother. He tells me he will save every bit of money, so he can to pay my fare back. It won't happen. He or I will be dead by then cos it'll take years and years to save up.'

They fell into silence brooding over the story and the pure shame of a large family being split apart.

'I'll tell you my story tomorrow.' volunteered Helen breaking the silence.

Part 2 - Chapter 5

On Sunday, there was no chance for Helen to tell her story. Divine service at ten in the morning meant that all the women were called on deck to take part. No one was allowed to miss it. Sarah was so relieved to be up on deck again. The dark prison deck brought back such awful memories, ones that she tried to put to the back of her mind, but they kept resurfacing. Would telling her story be a good thing or make her nightmares worse? She, along with all the other women, concentrated on gulping in huge lung-fulls of fresh air to try and take away the stench of the fetid air below.

The Surgeon led the service and he was pleasantly surprised by the gusto with which the women joined in the prayers and singing.

Helen would have happily stayed there for a two-hour service rather than the half hour it lasted. She hated being shut up below with Davy who needed as much fresh air as he could get. She worried about him catching a fever stuck down there.

At the end of the service and with the majority of the women now on board, the surgeon told them that It was not only his role to ensure the women were delivered to Van Diemen's land fit and healthy enough to work, but also to provide some measure of training in cleanliness and moral rectitude.

'In each of the dormitories, I will choose a leader whose job it is to fetch the rations and read from the scriptures. Obviously being proficient at reading is a prerequisite. She will also encourage your good behaviour and report any problems to me.'

The women looked puzzled for a moment until realisation dawned that someone in each dormitory was to spy on them.

'A payment of one sovereign will be given to the leader at the end of the journey. I will now call out the names of those I have chosen and you other women can go back down below, while I give the chosen women more instructions about their duties.'

He read through a list of names from the sheet, fluttering in his hand. When each name was called, there were either smiles from the women around them or groans. When Patsy's name was called all those in her dormitory cheered, apart from Anne, Anne stamped towards the hatch muttering under her breath and by the time Patsy returned she was beside herself with rage.

'That sovereign should be mine. I can read too. If yo think I am going to listen to yo reading those snivelling Bible stories, yo have another think coming yo big lummock,' and she shoved Patsy back against her bed.

Patsy stumbled, cracking her head on the bed above, but Helen and Joanna helped her up and stood either side of her. Anne took a swipe at Patsy again, but Joanna caught her arm and held on tight. Anne retaliated by catching hold of Joanna's ear with her free hand, twisting hard. Helen, seeing this but still holding on to Davy stamped as hard as she could on Anne's left foot with her wooden clog. Anne screamed in pain, hopping on her right foot while using her other hand to scratch at Helen's unprotected face.

The door to the cell opened. It was the same sailor who helped with Davy earlier. He picked up Anne by the waist and hauled her outside, fastening her hands to the bars with handcuffs. He left to fetch the Surgeon whilst Anne screamed the foulest obscenities that Nora had ever heard. Anne's friends from other cells shouted their support.

The Surgeon clambered nimbly down the hatchway steps and walked over towards Anne and she began pointing towards Helen and Joanna saying how they had attacked her.

'That is not what the sailor told me,' he began.

'Well, 'e didn't see what those two cows did to me.'

'What did they do, are you injured?' he asked.

'It's my foot, I think 'er broke it,' pointing towards Helen.

'You got your own back judging by those scratches on her face. George, bring both of the women to the hospital for examination please.' With that, he turned heel and left.

George, the sailor, opened the cell door and escorted Helen out. Reluctantly she had to leave Davy behind with Patsy. Although she was angry she was also frightened. Would she be punished in some way? She bit on her lip while he unlocked Anne's handcuffs. The woman was still muttering and scowling. George pushed her in the direction he wanted her to go and Helen followed behind. They climbed to the deck above and then waited for George to unlock a door in the partition. Helen's mouth felt dry with worry as George chivvied her through. On the other side of the door lay the hospital. Passing a room with empty beds she followed George and Anne into the Surgeon's room. He sat at a desk, with a chest of small coloured bottles beside him, each labelled and containing potions of some kind or another. Helen relaxed a little.

'Let me look at your foot,' he demanded of Anne. As she pointed it at him he said. 'No, no take off your boot and stocking.' This she did and he took it in his hands, grimacing at the dirt, but feeling it all over. Anne groaned and said 'Ouch' several times as he pressed down.

'Nothing broken, just bruised I should think. You can go back and don't waste my time in future. I will not have fighting, do you hear? If there is a next time you will both be in irons. Understood?' George led Anne out and the surgeon attended to Helen's scratches, cleaning them with iodine from one of his bottles. She flinched as it smarted.

'You have a baby,' he said whilst dabbing at her face. 'They assured me there would be no nursing mothers aboard because I don't believe babies should be brought on the ship until weaned. I should not want to put you on short rations if you get into more mischief.' Helen said nothing she was too frightened by the veiled threat. When George returned, the surgeon dismissed her and the sailor led her back to the dormitory.

George said to Helen 'I saw what happened and I'm sure the surgeon will believe me, so don't worry too much about what he said. It's not an easy job looking after you women, but it'll make his life easier if all of you behave. He's laying down a marker.'

Helen looked up at George, who was a good ten inches taller than her. His expression was friendly but not overly so. He looked as though you could trust him not to take advantage, but she wouldn't allow herself to fall into that trap. After all, men were men and on this ship, they were in total control of the women. If they wished to take advantage, there would be ample opportunity.

Back in the cell, the atmosphere was strained. Anne told them that Helen was in danger of being put in irons, so the others were relieved when she returned. It was almost dinner time and they hoped that after dinner Anne might disappear to join her companions. But before dinner, the hatch opened once again and Nora's name called out. Nora wondered if the surgeon wanted her to ask for further details about the fight, but when she got to the top of the upper hatchway, unbelievably she could see her father and sisters across the other side of the deck.

Nora almost collapsed in shock but was caught by George who led her across the deck to her family, where they hugged each other, wordless, their eyes bleary with tears.

'I never thought to see you again,' she sobbed as they still hung on to her.

'Aye when that lady came again yesterday and gave us your keepsake, she told us that it was unlikely that the ship would sail straight away. So, this morning we put on our boots and set off to walk as soon as we had broken fast. She told us what the writing said on the pincushion and don't doubt my darling girl that we will look at it every day of our lives and remember you.' Her father clutched at her, his shoulders heaving.

'Oh Da, Da, what am I going to do without you?' He swallowed hard and took her hand, gripping it tight.

'Remember what you told me outside the prison on that first visit, Nora. You will find the strength and you will have your own family. I just wish we could hear from you to know you are alright.'

'You will Da, I am learning to read and write. My friend Sarah is teaching me and I can write my name now. By the time, I get to Van Diemen's Land she said I'd be up to writing a letter to you.'

'Then we will learn too. I'm not sure how, but If I can send little Patrick to school somehow, he can teach us as he learns himself.'

'Ask the Quaker lady if she knows of a school that will take him. Here Da, take this money for his first lessons.' Nora reached into her pocket and handed him five of the shillings she had earned whilst at Newgate. He didn't want to take her money but she insisted.

'They are going to take my money off me and I don't know when I will get it back. I've still got ten shillings and I'd be so happy to think we can keep in touch by writing.'

Annie told her the news that she was to be married in the spring of next year. 'I do wish that you could be there. I wanted you for my bridesmaid along with Mary.'

'Oh, I'd love that, Annie. I'll be thinking of you. Your Thomas is so kind and I am sure you will be truly happy.'

'We have a present for you. We want you to feel part of the wedding. I have been making the dresses and sewn one for you. Maybe you can wear it for your own wedding, as we pray you'll find someone as good as my Tom.'

Annie and Mary gave Nora a box and, lifting the lid, Nora drew out a fashionable high-waisted, striped dress in brown and beige cotton, with decorative buttons of the same material down the front of the blouse, a scalloped collar and leg of mutton sleeves.

'It's so beautiful,' breathed Nora. 'I'll be so proud to wear this and will miss you and Mary so much, you know that, don't you?'

'And there is one more thing I want to give you,' said her father drawing some delicate, rosary beads from his pocket.

'But they were mother's,' whispered Nora.

'Take them, we all want you to have them and we pray they bring you comfort.'

'Oh yes, they surely will. Thank you so much. I will treasure them always.' Nora took the glass beads with reverence and kissed them. Her eyes shone with gratitude.

They spent another hour together talking and hugging until George approached them and said it was time they should leave. It took a further ten minutes before they could tear themselves apart. George led a weeping Nora to the hatchway. Her family waved and blew kisses until she disappeared.

'Shall I take your box miss? I can store it in the hold where it will be safe.' suggested George.

Nora was reluctant to let it go and shook her head.

'Really miss, it will be safer. We can put your name and tag number on the box. It won't get damaged, nor will it go missing, I promise. You know it won't be safe to keep any possessions below.'

Nora thought some more and reluctantly agreed, as it might prove too much of a temptation to a few she could think of. But it was heart rending to be given the dress and then to let go. Who knew when she would see it again?

Nora had missed dinner, but Sarah saved her a bowl of vegetable stew, now cold and congealed, together with a chunk of bread. Nora thought she would gladly miss a hundred dinners if it meant she got to see her family again. But exhausted, and emotional she was in no mood for a story. She asked Helen to put hers off for another day and Helen, still shocked by the fight with Anne, readily agreed.

The wooden boxes were distributed that afternoon and it didn't take long to pack them, as few women had brought much with them. Nora kept her rosary beads to use them on the journey, and she gave a grateful Helen the old wooden beads her father had rescued from Mrs Butler's house. The boxes were marked with their name and number on one side and taken down to the hold. Many doubted that they would see them or the contents again.

The women were subdued for the rest of that first Sunday, especially after Anne came back to the dormitory. No one knew what to say or how to lighten the frosty atmosphere.

Part 2 - Chapter 6

Nora woke late on Monday. Breakfast was underway by the time she roused herself. Her mouth felt dry and sour and she accepted a mug of sweet tea from Phyllis with thanks. After the meal and washing up were done, the hatchway opened for visitors to the prison. This time it was the great Mrs Fry herself accompanied by Mrs Barnard. Mrs Fry visited every female convict ship, leaving from London, to inspect the accommodation, speak to the women and to hand out useful items for the journey. Word soon flew around the prison deck; most of the women had heard of Mrs Fry, a friend and saviour to Newgate's female prisoners, and they were curious to meet her.

After an hour or so, they arrived at Nora's dormitory. The women dropped a respectful curtsey. Mrs Barnard introduced Nora, Sarah and Helen to Mrs Fry. Nora shyly looked at the great woman dressed in similar plain garb as Mrs Barnard wore. Her bonnet covered her hair, but Nora saw greying, blonde hair above a serious but kind face. She was much taller and older than Mrs Barnard with a matronly figure.

'I have good hopes of these girls.' said Mrs Barnard to her mentor. 'Sarah reads the Bible beautifully and is helping to teach Nora and Helen to read. Nora is a competent seamstress and dutiful daughter and Helen is a good mother to little Davy here.'

'That is very good to know, girls. Who else do we have here?'

Patsy introduced Joanna and Anne to Mrs Fry, who asked which prisons they had come from and about their experience there.

'Anne and I were at Worcester prison, Ma'am. I stayed there for over three years and it did get better in the last two years. We were separated from the men, had employment and learnt to read, so I have no complaints.'

'I was in the Tollhouse prison, Ma'am.' said Joanna.

'Ah yes, Great Yarmouth,' she said recognising Joanna's accent. 'I was born in Norwich and lived at Earlham Hall until I married,' replied

Mrs Fry. 'I have read bad reports on Great Yarmouth prison and I remember it of old. How did thee find it, Joanna?'

'It were terrible, Ma'am. I hardly dare tell yew, for it were shocking bad.'

'I have been shocked very often, Joanna, which is why I do this work. Please tell me as much as thee can.'

'I be there since April this year, Ma'am. It's a real, old broken down building and small. There was one tiny day room and exercise yard for us prisoners and some of the male prisoners were real villains, Ma'am and would take advantage of me, if I weren't careful. There wuzn't any clothing to be had either, so a few men wuz in rags and I can't repeat what I saw. The only privy was fearful bad, so filthy and rank, I can't describe the smell. The sleeping cell was dark and windowless. I wuz that afraid at night because I wuz there on my own, with men just a few yards away.'

'Did thee have a chaplain, matron or employment?'

'Oh no, Ma'am, nothing like that.'

'Very well, that is another prison that needs to go into my letter to the Home Secretary, Mr Peel.' Now, ladies, I bring essential items to take on this journey. Here are Bibles and combs for each of thee and a book of sermons for thee, Patsy, which can be read out to the other ladies. I truly hope that God will bring thee to the path of righteousness by taking note of the wise words in the book. Here are material, straw and wool to occupy thee on the journey; and Helen, I have spectacles for thee to try. Mrs Barnard said thee had trouble sewing and reading, so hopefully, these may help. They may not be perfect, of course, we had to take what was available.'

Helen was overwhelmed. She tried on the wire-rimmed spectacles and then was asked to thread a needle. Mrs Barnard dug around in her bag for a needle and cotton and while Patsy held Davy. Helen held up the needle to the dim light and was astounded when she could see the hole to thread the cotton through.

'Oh Ma'am, what can I say. I have never seen such things. No one I knew had spectacles even though their eyes were bad.' She put the needle down and took Davy back.

'Take good care of them, they break easily, no sitting on them mind. Thee will only need to use them for close work. Oh, and be careful with young Davy there.' Davy seeing his mother with something strange on her face made a grab for them and almost got them, which had them all laughing. 'I must move on ladies, but I wish thee a good journey, and pray that thee learn, through God's mercy, to be good, virtuous women. May God be with thee.'

They each bobbed a curtsey again and watched her move to the next cell. For a while no one said much, Sarah was stroking her Bible, overcome with a present that offered hours of pleasure. Helen let Nora and Joanna try on her spectacles, but all they saw were blurred images, so they quickly handed them back. Patsy was looking through the book of sermons.

'If 'er were going to bring stuff to improve our journey then a pack of cards and some baccy would be better,' grumbled Anne. 'I couldn't half use a pipe of the stuff right now to take away the stink of that babby.'

'When Mrs Fry has left, we should do our washing.' Patsy said. Everyone now, including Anne after her initial outburst, accepted her as the leader of their dormitory. Nora and the others agreed to wash their meagre supply of linens but were stuck with how to dry them, as there was no real place below deck to dry anything. It would be much easier once they had set sail as they could take things up to dry in the fresh air. In the meantime, they hung things around the bars and hoped they would dry in a day or two. After the midday meal, Anne went off to another dormitory and Patsy asked Helen to tell her story.

Part 2 - Chapter 7

Helen's Story

'We left Ireland when I was nine and my sister, Fanny, just six years old. There was no work but lots of trouble and we couldn't pay the rent to the landlord. Da asked the land agent to reduce the rent, but he wouldn't, so Da said we had no choice but to leave. None of us wanted to leave our tiny cabin and potato patch, but we'd have starved else. The twins were two years old. I remember the journey. It took weeks of walking to catch a boat to Liverpool. The twins had to be carried on our parents' backs, and we made frequent stops to try and gather food from the hedgerows after we had eaten what we were able to carry. By the time, we got to Liverpool we were starving.

Da heard there were jobs in the mills in Lancashire but he tried one for a few weeks and said no way could he work in those conditions, all noise and dust, he said. It was bad for his lungs and I remember him coughing most of the night when he came back to that room we shared with another family. They had four children too, so there were twelve of us in a room about twice the size of two of these dormitories. But their eldest two worked in the mills from five in the morning 'til nine at night. So did their mother, while Mam looked after all us little 'uns. I woke when they came home, white with tiredness and covered in fluff. Da wouldn't let me work when I got to ten, though I wanted to. He said that he saw a child scalped when her hair got caught in a machine. It made him sick to think of it.

Then he got a job on the canals. They were building the Leeds to Liverpool canal and that was good work while it lasted. Afterwards, he tried to get work on a farm. We heard there was a hiring fair coming up and walked to a Yorkshire town, I forget which, but as soon as they heard his Irish accent the farmers turned away. God knows the English hate the Irish. They called us lazy papists and other worse names. Since then we've tramped all over Derbyshire, Nottinghamshire and

Lincolnshire looking for work. My Da could turn his hand to most things like ploughing and harvesting. Fanny and I started out scaring birds but then we'd do any job as came our way.

Some winters we barely stayed alive and the boys didn't. They both died one really cold winter. First, they started coughing and over a few weeks just faded away. It broke my mother's heart. I don't think she was ever the same after that. We couldn't get any parish relief, so there was no choice but to keep walking and find any work going.

We all found work in the coalfields in Nottinghamshire. That was terrible, hard graft. Da worked on his back, chipping coal away from the face. Mam hauled wagons of coal on all fours through narrow passageways and us girls carried it on our backs up to the surface. But the dust started playing Da's lungs up again. As soon as he started coughing Mam would make him stop work and we'd be off on our travels. She was terrified he would die on us for then we would surely starve with no family to take us in.

Come May there was always something that paid a bit, right through to October. If we hadn't anything to eat we found an odd rabbit or two, even a straying chicken and maybe a turnip or potato to nick. The best was when Da tickled river trout and we'd smoke them over a fire, so we could take some with us. We had to keep a careful look out for the gamekeepers. Da said if they caught you taking even firewood, let alone a rabbit, you could be hung and used to recite this ditty whenever we were hungry and he was so mad to see us so.

> The law locks up the man or woman
>
> Who steals the goose from the common
>
> But leaves the greater villain loose
>
> Who steals the common from the goose'

'I know that one.' said Joanna. 'How true is that?

Helen smiled at her and then continued.' 'Harvest time was the best, Da scything the barley or wheat and us raking it up to make sheaves. We worked from dawn to dusk but it was outside, so we didn't care. The sun would make us thirsty and there'd be plenty of cider to quench it.

Then there was the harvest supper; everyone having a grand old feast with ale to drink, and dancing and a bit of a tumble in the hay. Lots of bairns were born nine months after harvest time. But a bairn born in June has a better chance than one born in December when a woman's milk dries up because there's no food, save a mouldy bit of bread or rotten potato.

Last year Bobby Smith and me we had a bit of fun in the hay. He said he was sweet on me, and maybe this year he'd have asked me Da for me. That's one reason I took that pretty bit of cloth, so Bobby could see me in a dress this year and not that raggedy old skirt and petticoat. He's a fine strong lad and said he expected the farmer to let him have a cottage when he wed. I thought once Bobby knew I had his bairn, he'd do the decent thing and we'd be wed before the end of harvest.

I don't remember now what it would be like to live in one place and always under a roof. I reckon I'd miss living outdoors and the hum of the bees in the meadows and the blackbird's song. Mind anyone would crave the smell of new cut hay in Derby gaol, where the straw on the floor was alive with vermin and filth. They only cleaned it out twice a year and you were lucky not to get gaol fever. Oh, I forgot to mention that. I spent six months in Derby when I was sixteen, for stealing clogs that time. Mine pinched my toes and Fanny needed 'em, so I took some second-hand ones from a market stall. Luckily Da was standing in the street when they let me out of prison and took me off to join Fanny and Ma where they were living. They'd found a big hollow tree in a forest and managed to live in it that winter.

The second time I got caught was in Nottingham at the lace market. I'm not saying it was the second time I'd pinched anything, we'd never have a stitch to wear otherwise. Mostly we took from washing lines, just a pair of stockings from one and a petticoat from another. We only did it when we were passing through somewhere, else we'd have been chased out a village for sure and anyway we had to try and avoid that village the next year, in case they remembered.

Nottingham Goal is in a huge, grand building. But us prisoners, men and women, we were shoved underground in a deep cave at first, but after a couple of months they moved us to a day room with a tiny yard to walk around and no men to hassle us other than that turnkey. He was a nasty character. It was best to stay clear of him as much as possible. I told him I had the pox and he let me alone, but I know he took his pleasure with others, men and women. They did it for a few extra rations.'

Nora gasped at this for she had never heard that men lusted after men.

'Yes, it happens lots in prisons and on ships, they say, where men are thrown together and there aren't any women.' Helen, understanding Nora's shock, patted her hand.

'Oh, but it was so cold and damp most of the time. I suppose the Gaol Act, that Mrs Fry talked about yesterday, had something to do with things getting better. To be sure nothing could have been worse than that cave. I heard that in the old days they used to shove men into a deeper cave and then leave them. Just throw a few bits of food down once in a while, if they ever remembered, or felt a bit kind. They always died in those holes, never saw the light of day again, poor souls.

The matron they appointed, had us washing clothes in the morning and finishing off lace breadths in the afternoon. It was really difficult work because I couldn't see what I was supposed to be doing and I got into lots of trouble for that. At least we had food, just bread and potatoes, sometimes another vegetable, never any meat but I have lived off worse rations. In Ireland, all we ever ate was potatoes, the same as our neighbours. I worried when little Davy was born. He seemed so puny, but I seem to have enough milk and since I got to Newgate we ate better food and even had milky tea to drink, so he's putting on weight at last. God help him on this ship if my milk dries up. I daren't think about it.

I wondered what people missed in Newgate because London was one big stinking mess. When we were brought down on the top of the stagecoach I never saw such a place, endless streets, full of manure and so many people. I wonder how the coachman drove through the crowds. And the noise, well, I couldn't imagine so much noise. I would hate to live there and that's a fact. If I can't go back to my parents Van Diemen's Land will do. I hope it has good farming land.'

'Yes, so do I.' said Joanna. 'We passed through some large places on the journey from the gaol. I didn't like the look of any of them. Give me a good Norfo' village and farmland any day.'

Nora was shocked when Helen talked about stealing clothes, quite casually, as though not really a crime. Then she remembered the poor girl waiting outside Newgate for her mother, and how ill she always looked. One day neither the mother nor the girl was there and she often wondered what had happened to them.

It must have been a real struggle for Helen's family to stay alive at all, so what would she have done in Helen's place? Nora began again to admire Helen's toughness. It was all very well for Mrs Fry and Mrs Barnard to expect them to live righteously, but would that mean starving or freezing to death rather than steal whatever was needed to survive? How she wished she could talk with her father about this. She pondered over it that night before falling asleep without an answer.

Part 2 - Chapter 8

The next morning the hatch opened early and it stayed open. When Patsy went to fetch the rations, she asked one of the sailors dishing them out why the hatch was open.

'You can have it open all day for you're not in danger of escaping,' was the answer. 'That Mrs Fry who came aboard yesterday suggested it and the Surgeon and Captain agreed. This ship was used for male convicts last year, but they don't reckon you women are a risk.'

The word quickly spread from dormitory to dormitory and a rousing cheer went up for Mrs Fry. And when wooden lids were fitted to cover the privies and vinegar for cleaning them handed out the cheer rose higher.

Nora felt somewhat guilty that she had questioned Mrs Fry's view on righteousness in the face of such care and kindness that she had shown them. It was her turn to tell her story today. After the last two stories, she thought she had little to say, her own life being so ordinary, in comparison to Helen and Patsy.

Patsy, again taking the lead, said that now they had more light they could knit stockings with the wool they were given yesterday. Most of them could knit blindfold, in any case, knitting being something taught to most girls from an early age. There was still too little light to read or sew by, but knitting was a good way of passing time.

The surgeon inspected the dormitories for cleanliness that morning. If they wanted to avoid illness he knew it was imperative that lice were kept at bay. He also looked for evidence of rats. If the women dropped food and did not clear it up it would only encourage them. He found several women were suffering with their bowels, being unused to the change of diet. Their diet on board ship was better than in the county prisons and including bread, meat, fresh vegetables and fruit. This would change once they set sail and they reverted to a poorer diet, which would bring its own set of problems.

Surgeon Carlyle looked at Helen's face and satisfied that the scratches were not infected and beginning to heal, he dismissed her. He gave instructions, to George, his newly appointed assistant, to bring the women with bowel complaints to his medical room, where he would give them emetics to purge the digestive system. After admonishing some of the women over the cleanliness of their dormitories he finished his inspection and left.

Following the midday meal and Anne's departure from the dormitory, it was time for Nora's story and she more or less repeated what she had told Maudie and Peg, that first afternoon in Newgate. Patsy asked what tunes her father played on his fiddle and did she remember any songs?

Nora thought for a minute and said, 'The one we all loved to sing was about a girl, Molly Malone.'

'Oh, I know that one, to be sure,' said Helen. 'Do sing it.' Nora started to sing but so quiet it was almost a whisper.

'No, no, sing up,' they clamoured. Nora demurred in shyness, but her friends insisted and she began again, closing her eyes and letting her mind return to the most joyful evenings spent with her family. Her voice now strong, clear and tuneful crept throughout the deck as the noise of chattering women subsided from other dormitories. At first, they listened to the well-known song and then other women joined in. The chorus grew louder and louder and after one or two verses everyone sang with gusto.

'Alive alive oo
Alive alive oo,
Crying cockles and mussels alive alive o.'

'Again,' someone cried as she finished, and Nora obliged. After she finished the song for the second time, she broke into the sad, haunting song 'Barbara Allen,' her mother's favourite, but which none of the family could bear to sing after she died. Somewhere deep inside Nora could almost hear her mother's insistence that she sing. It was as if her mother had taken over her body and she was left unable to resist. The words of the song poured out with such emotion that by the end she felt drained and weepy. In the ensuing silence, Nora was sure she heard her mother's voice promising to guide her through the next stage of her punishment. She felt close to her, so close that her spirits lifted and she looked around at her friends and saw they were now clapping.

'How beautiful was that! You have a wonderful voice,' said Helen.

'Let's have a cheerful one,' shouted a voice from another dormitory, 'How about the Saucy Sailor Boy?' a Portsmouth woman suggested. 'Aye.' And several of the most notorious women amongst their company began a rousing version which had some of the sailors above joining in.

The afternoon proceeded cheerfully as the women vied with each other to sing their own favourite songs from Scotland, and from the far north of England to the south.

Surgeon Carlyle, on hearing the women told George 'I think we are in for a pleasant voyage. The women are settling down well.'

George, preoccupied, mumbled an answer. He was bewitched by a voice so pure and plaintive that he could not rest until he knew the girl it belonged to. It had made the hairs stand on his neck. He felt sure that sound would be with him until his last breath.

Part 2 - Chapter 9

The women soon fell into a routine. Patsy fetched the rations, after breakfast, they cleaned the dormitories and washed up their plates and mugs. Surgeon Carlyle came down to inspect the convict deck and asked if there were any problems or complaints. Then clothes were washed and hung around the bars before Nora and her cell mates sat down to chat and knit until twelve o'clock. It's amazing what you can get used to Nora thought. The deck still stank, the darkness was mildly helped by the open hatch, but they were finding ways of making the hours pass with songs and stories and she found herself looking forward to Joanna's tale.

That afternoon a few more women and children arrived, this time from Devon. George showed them to an empty dormitory and the women around them explained everything they needed to know. Then another woman arrived but no one had a clue where she came from as she spoke not a word of English and was visibly shaking with fright.

'The poor thing,' women exclaimed in every cell as word travelled. When George came by with another prisoner, this time from York, someone asked about the woman who didn't speak English.

'She's Welsh,' he answered. 'She'll have to learn English otherwise God knows what will happen to her. No one will want a servant who doesn't understand a word they say.'

Nora thought about this. They were all afraid of the future and what would happen, but how terrifying if you didn't understand anything and had no one to ask or comfort you. She was so grateful that she had Helen and Sarah to share the journey.

Later that afternoon the women in Nora's dormitory settled down to hear Joanna's story.

Part 2 - Chapter 10

Joanna's Story

'I had a lovely childhood. We lived not far from the sea in Norfo' in a small village where my grandparents and their grandparents lived afore 'hem. My faither had a cottage and a strip o' land where he grew vegetables. We owned a cow, a pig and a few geese which grazed on the common land. We always had plenty t'eat. Dad worked two or three days a week fo' the local farmers and so we there was money for fish and bread an' all. I loved huntin' for goose eggs on the common and helping Maw cook and sew an' whatnot. Some days we went down to the seashore to net shrimps and backend there were plenty o' blackberries to be found in the hedgerows. Like Helen at harvest time, we gleaned and kept the wheat we found to make bread; there was orfen enough for the whole year. My two elder brothers, Samuel and Joseph, were right good to me and we played together until they turned thirteen and started to work for the farmer, as well as helping dad on his land.

Then one Sund'y, we went to church as usual, and there was this notice pinned up on the door. None of the men could read it so they had to ax the vicar what it said. He told 'em that an inclosure bill was to be heard in parliament for the village land round about. Of course, my dad knew of inclosure but never thought it might affect him. I guess the villagers trusted too much in the old ways to believe it would all come to an end, after all, we'd lived this way as far back as anyone could remember. Some of the villagers wanted to petition parliament but the vicar told them they would have to produce evidence of ownership of the land. They'd lived and worked the land for generations but none had a legal paper that said they had ownership of it. There'd be the expense of a lawyer and the journey t' London t' present a brief. So they just waited and hoped for the best.

About two or three months went by and then three furriners turned up in the village, commissioners, they wuz called. The land was inclosed they told us. We no longer had rights 'o the common, the Earl and Bishop were tekin' them to grow more food cos o' the war with Boney. We could hev our strip o' land but we must pay for it to be fenced plus the cost of fencin' the common. Well, the villagers couldn't afford the fencin' o' the common. So, we had to sell the cow, the pig and the geese because there was no land for 'em anymore. We sold our strip next because we couldn't pay for the fencin' o' that either. Dad was left with six pounds for a life's work.

Then because our cottage was built on our strip, they came and knocked it down. Can you imagine what that did to Maw, to see her hem pulled down in front of her? She stood there a howlin' and it whoolly frooze our blood to hear ut. The boys helped Dad build a shack on scrubland by the edge of a road. But we had no food and firewood; we used to gather wood from the common, but now we'd have to walk to the beach and hope to find driftwood along w' everybody else. The only means of making money was to work for the farmers and the Lord or the Bishop. There were so many villagers in the same straights that wages dropped and we only earned enough money for a few taters each week. We couldn't buy milk or bread or meat. Who had money for that?

Dad fared badly after. He gev the boys three pounds from the sale of the land and told 'em to walk to Norwich to find work. Joseph didn't want to leave, he had a girl in the village he was sweet on, but her father wouldn't consider a match between 'em now, so Samuel and Joseph left. We never saw or heard from 'em again. They said that they would get someone to send a message when they were straight and hopefully we could go and live with them. But I can only fear the worst.

I wuz nine when it happened, and it felt as though my life had ended. I wuz allus hungry, cowld and lonely. When I wuz ten years old, Maw walked to the miller's house and begged the mistress to take me as a skivvy. She didn't really want me but Maw worked there before she wed and the old lady had a soft spot for 'er. I didn't get much in the way of wages, but I got fed and that was wonderful enough after months of hunger.

It only took a year. With nothing further to live fer, Dad and Maw took to booze and drank what little wages they got. At eleven, I wuz on my own. No parents, no brothers.

Other villagers left the area to find work, but I never understood why it had to happen that way. We had us a perfec' life and they destroyed ut so quickly. I once asked Dad why the men didn't do anything. He said they'd talked about protesting and burning a few hayricks and such, but knew the militia would be sent fer and they'd be hung or transported. No one would or could speak up for 'em. The Lord didn't even live in the county, so he never cared about the village, and it was happening everywhere, all over the country.

I spent the next six years with the miller's wife but then I got wed to John Harrison, a good and kindly fisherman and we moved into our own little cottage by the seashore. I can't tell you how happy it made me, to have my own cottage; the second chance I'd dreamed of and vowed to make the most of it. It didn't last beyond the next tempest. John set off in bright sunlight, but the wind suddenly got up and then rain and lightning and waves, like you never imagined. The sea fairly boiled that day and the women stood wrapped tight in their shawls on the beach praying for their menfolk and I stood with 'em. Three fishermen died that day. And, still sixteen, I was a widow, who couldn't pay the rent. The other fisher folk shunned me, said I had brought John bad luck. I tried the miller's wife again, but she said she'd done her duty to my mother and I wuz now on my own.

So, I put my few possessions in a sack and walked to Great Yarmouth. I hev spent the last twelve years trying to live any way I can. I've done laundry and tavern work, cleaning, gutting the silver darlings when the herring arrive in the autumn, anything but whoring, like some of them kittywitches. One or two rascals offered to marry me but they owned nothing, not land nor even a cottage and I'll not fall into that trap again.

I stole sometimes, who hasn't? When you're in need, you do what must be done. This time I got done for stealing a pelisse. You might think it daft of me because which pauper would own a fur-lined pelisse? When I saw the coat I just had to hev ut, fer it wuz so bootiful, blue as the sky and the sea on a bright summer's day. It didn't even fit me, but I never cared. Just to look at it was enough. Of course, I copped it and they flung me into gaol. But perhaps I'd had enough of the life I was leading and wanted it to happen after all a grand larceny charge is an automatic ticket to a new land.

Plenty of sailors talked about this far away Van Diemen's Land, where you can get an allotment given free by the governor, and no lords to take it all away before you can count to three. I tell you I can't wait to leave England fer I've had enough of living hand to mouth. Once I get there I'll snaffle up a man as quick as you can blink and I won't let him go. Give me a landowner with a piece of paper in his hand that can't never be taken away. I don't care what 'e looks like, an' tha's a fact! But I will work so 'ard to keep that land and bring up a family to hand it down to, for my faither never had that chance.

He wus a good old boy and so were my brothers and I am so raw at those who took ut away. I hate 'em that are put in charge o' us; the bishops, the lords and their ladies, the members of parliament and all those who allowed the inclosure to happen. I spit on 'em all. They stole our land but it's us who get transported for stealing a silly piece of clothing. They stole our livelihoods, even our lives, and are rewarded fer ut.'

'What about Mrs Fry and the ladies who work with her, do you hate them as well?' asked Nora, shocked at the injustice in the tale she had heard.

'No not really. She maybe has a good heart, from what y' say, and is trying her best to make life better for the likes of us. But when I have seen such terrible things, it is difficult to believe any rich folk care about us. I want to make sure my children can read and write because without that you are without any means to defend y'selves, so ut seems to me.

Do you know I have never really thought about all this afore? Fer so many years all my effort has been put t' staying alive and keeping a little honour. Begging for food, which I have done more than once, soon reduces most of yer honour, but I never went to the next step down. I listened to your stories and then in telling mine ut was like a veil lifted and I began t' see for the furst time.'

Joanna stared into the gloom of the prison deck lost in her thoughts. Her handsome face, now free of the grime of her journey, frowned as she picked at her thoughts. The others were silent. This tale opened up questions that none had answers to. Patsy, Helen and Nora had accepted their lives as they had been, the rough with the smooth, the hardship which was the lot of most families they knew. That was what was taught by their betters, each to know their place in society. What Joanna said made them uncomfortable and confused.

Sarah, who had retreated to her own world, since the time the hatch had first descended and shut out the light, suddenly broke into their reveries.

'Joanna, perhaps you're right. Those that hold sway over us, no matter what their position, never answer for their actions. We ought not to accept, what is not right. For we read the word of God but do not understand his message - Love thy neighbour as you love yourself.'

'Sarah, whenever you speak, you surprise us with your good sense,' exclaimed Nora in awe. 'I wish Mrs Barnard were here so that we could ask for her guidance. '

'Perhaps this reverend who is ailing with us, will make it clear,' said Patsy firmly. She had been very grateful for the religious teaching she had had at Worcester Gaol and was not inclined to start questioning it. Surely in her position as dormitory leader, she should dissuade others from questioning it too. These young girls - what did they know of life? Nora was obviously sheltered from all evil by her caring family. Helen and Joanna had known only hardship over recent years, so they may have a jaundiced view of society and that Sarah, well, who knew what went on in her head?

They were saved from further thought by the increasing wails of a hungry baby.

Part 2 - Chapter 11

Nora and her friends had been on board the Henry for a week now. They were sick of their enforced idleness and dark, smelly quarters; the brief cheer provided by the opened hatch was short lived. Only the older children had been allowed on deck for an hour of supervised exercise each day, one of the free women on board having been given the task of watching over them. The convict mothers were grateful for this brief respite and they used the threat of withdrawing this privilege to keep their children's cries of boredom under control.

When the Surgeon next visited his charges, he heard the women's grumbles and complaints with a degree of sympathy and was pleased to give them some good news. So far, their behaviour had been better than he was led to expect, there being so many stories of the dire character of female convicts bound for Van Diemen's Land. Loading was going to plan so why not give them a little cheer. He stood in the middle of the prison deck and commanded them all to pay attention. Eventually, the hubbub diminished as women shushed each other.

'Well, ladies, I have news for you. We will be leaving this mooring and moving further out into the channel. This means that as from tomorrow you will be allowed up on deck all day unless the weather is inclement. We are only waiting for our final passengers and then we can set sail for Van Diemen's Land. This may still take a couple of weeks. I will be issuing a duty roster so that you take turns in cleaning your dormitories every day. The bedrolls should be taken up to the deck each day to air; there is room for them in the nets. When we finally set sail you will just need to stay in your quarters for a day or two, as the sailors will be busy on deck manoeuvring the ship safely down the river.'

The women cheered this news and then he went on to say.

'Remember my instructions earlier. Do not engage in any kind of relationship with the men on board, nor behave raucously or immodestly. Infringements will be treated with utmost severity. Please keep an eye on children because I do not want to lose any overboard. A year ago, a boy was sadly lost by playing too near the bow of a ship.'

Those who were mothers shivered in horror and drew their children closer.

'Let me know if you have any problems or complaints. Do not go to anyone else for I am in sole charge of your wellbeing.'

Nora liked this plain-speaking surgeon. He had a faint accent, most likely Scottish. She guessed his age as mid- thirties, not handsome, his face was too weather-beaten for that, but warm brown eyes softened his manner and sometimes she thought she could detect a hint of a smile. She hoped that he would take good care of them.

Amidst the chatter, following the surgeon's departure, Nora asked Sarah if she was ready to tell her story. Sarah nodded but did not look too happy with the prospect. 'Only tell what you feel able to. If it gets too much you can stop and we will understand.'

That afternoon, optimistic about the following day and with fresh air beckoning they settled down to hear the last story.

Part 2 - Chapter 12

Sarah's Story

'This is going to be very hard. I am not used to talking. I listened to your stories and you are all so brave; not me. You each had a choice in your lives but not me. I learnt to accept everything that was done to me, even though it was often painful. To survive I learnt not to care, not to feel, not to live. I don't have Joanna's anger, or Nora's love, just nothing, emptiness. The three months spent in Newgate were the best of my life. I had enough food and I had friendship.' She paused and smiled briefly at Nora. 'Now I will try to tell you my story.' Nora grasped her hand and kept hold of it, hoping to pass on some courage.

Sarah sighed and for a few seconds attempted to find some inner strength that would allow her to continue. Closing her eyes, she imagined talking to herself, not wanting to see their expressions, their pity, their disgust.

'Someone found me on the street with nothing but a scrap of old cloth around me. Whoever it was, took me to a place for foundlings and I stayed for about twelve years. We were not allowed out unless to go to the church across the street. So, that place was all I knew.'

Sarah told them of her life in the foundling home in a monotone. She had practised the story in her head but refused to let it mean anything to her. It could just as well be a story about someone else. She allowed no emotion to cloud her face. Her voice didn't waver and she spoke without once opening her eyes, but inside her heart was racing and her mouth felt dry. Getting to the point where she left the foundling home, she opened her eyes and asked for water. Patsy went off to find fetch it and Nora said.

'There, there. You did really well, Sarah. What an awful place to be sure. How sad for women leave their children to be brought up in such a home?'

'Do you think they have any choice? What if they live on the streets themselves and turn a trick or two to make money enough to eat or to drown their sorrows. They probably grew up themselves in such places and left with nothing,' admonished Joanna, who knew how easy it would have been for her to drift down the path to being a cheap streetwalker.

Patsy came back with water and Sarah grasped the cup to her and taking tiny sips she attempted to give herself more time. But then she said quietly. 'That is not the end of my story.'

'What! Oh, of course not. You haven't told us how you got to Newgate. How stupid of me,' said Nora. 'Do you want to go on?'

Sarah took a deep breath and nodded. 'When I was about twelve this man came to the foundling home. He pointed to me and they told me I must go with him. He was my master and I must do what he says. I didn't like the look of him. He was a very big man. Fat round the middle and a great balding head attached to his body, with no neck to speak of. His clothes stank of beer and his breath of rotting teeth. I remember crying when he pulled me out of the door. Then he shoved me forward and I stumbled into the gutter, so he pulled me up and dragged me down the street. All the while I was crying and screaming, but no one took any notice. After a minute, he got fed up with the noise I was making so he swiped me across the face with his rough, meaty hand and told me to shut up.' Sarah took another drink to calm her nerves.

'I don't like to remember this, let alone talk about it.' Nora heard the tremor in her voice.

'Don't tell us any more, it hurts you too much.' Nora put her arm around Sarah and squeezed her gently.

'I need to. If I can get the words out perhaps he will lose his hold on me.' She paused and took another deep breath. 'Well, in a few minutes we got to a tavern. He was an innkeeper. He showed me to his wife, who was equally fat and also drunk. I had never seen anyone drunk before, but she slurred her words and stood so unsteady on her feet, that she looked as though she were doing an awkward little dance. She led me to the kitchen and showed me a mound of potatoes to peel, then told me I must wash all the dishes. Not bad, I thought, a job I could do. There was an elderly cook who was also very deaf. She didn't talk much, which suited me. I kept on peeling and washing for hours, way after my normal bedtime. I was exhausted and cut myself several times with the knife not being used to peeling vegetables. It might have been the early hours of the morning when we finished. The innkeeper's wife came back to the kitchen, grabbed me by the arm and led me to a door, opened it and said. 'Sleep in there.' I fell down several steps in the dark and ended up on the cellar floor. Behind me, the door closed and then locked.' Sarah stopped and gasped and gasped again.

'Here, drink more water. Yo look proper poorly. Take time until yo feel better.' murmured Patsy. After a few minutes, Sarah nodded her head and continued. She was determined to finish this.

'It was pitch black in the cellar, and very cold. It took time for my eyes to adjust so I felt around and found some sacks full of something or other and a couple of empty sacks, which I used for bedding. I was lying there, shivering and trying to get to sleep but then this rustling started and I saw tiny little eyes. I just screamed and screamed, but no one came and I didn't dare fall asleep on my own. I was too used to being in a room full of children and hearing their noises, coughing, snoring, even shouting. But those eyes, they unnerved me. After what seemed like hours I heard the door unlock and a voice saying, 'Get out here now.'

'It was her, the innkeeper's wife. I was blubbing about the eyes and she laughed and said 'It's only rats! Throw summat at 'em. If they get too bad, I'll find a cat to go in and catch a few.'

She showed me the pump, where I could wash, and told me to clean up the public bar, then get on with peeling another mound of potatoes. That's how my days went. I slept in the cellar for two years and worked all day and most of the night in the kitchen. Ate the scraps left on the plates, rarely meat, just gravy and potatoes. I got no wages. They said they had to pay the foundling home for me. I never had a chance to leave the tavern, for I had no time off, just eighteen hour days, seven days a week, until I could scarcely stand up with tiredness.

I got plenty of slaps and the odd boot in my shin. She whipped me as well if I broke anything or she didn't think I was working quickly enough or if her husband paid me any attention. When his wife wasn't watching, he would grab my chest and pinch it or try and put his hand on my bottom. The wife mostly was watching and I tried never to be alone with that man. The only person who had a kind word was John, the tapman. He told me he had a daughter about my age and felt sorry for me. I didn't have time to feel sorry for me, it was the only life I knew. I never stopped being terrified when the cellar door shut. Exhaustion meant I slept in spite of the rats.

The wife got drunker and drunker every day but one day she didn't let me out of the cellar. The old cook found me after I banged on the door for what seemed like hours. She couldn't hear my banging of course, but she knew where I slept. The wife kept the key hidden from her husband so the cook had to go and ask her where it was. The mistress had taken to her bed, that day and was scarcely sensible the cook said, but, after much coaxing, she was able to tell her where to find the key.

Cook always finished before me at night and it was my job to clear up. While I was at the sink I sensed the innkeeper come and stand behind me. I could smell him, a mixture of strong drink, tobacco and filth. His hand crept around my waist and he said that his wife was out for the count so I would do instead. I froze but he grabbed me, turning me around to face him, and I remember screaming. He started to tear at my clothes and forced me to the floor and then was on top of me, crushing me and pawing under my petticoat. I was still screaming so he slapped me and punched me hard a few times until I passed out. When I came around, John was kneeling beside me saying. 'Tell them you did it. Please tell them you did it. I have a daughter that needs me. They will hang me but not a scrap of a girl like you. Don't worry Sarah, I will tell them it was self-defense.' So, that's what I did. John had heard my screaming and run to the kitchen and hit the innkeeper really hard over the head with a heavy pan and he was dead. John had saved me so I now had to save him. It was fair.

They took me off to prison and found me guilty of manslaughter. The innkeeper's wife was too drunk to attend, so only John was a witness. He told the court how he'd heard screams and found me on the floor with the innkeeper dead on top of me. He said I had been badly treated, and they saw my black eye and other bruises so they were lenient. I got transportation for life.

I don't expect much will change. What I have seen of most men doesn't make me want to marry, unlike Joanna. Neither do I want children if they have to go through this kind of life. We will work there, in Van Diemen's Land, and be at the mercy of whoever is in charge of us. My only hope is that the winters are warmer.' Sarah was silent and drained, but she asked herself did she feel better for having gone through her story? Was the pain any less?

'Yo were right to take the blame.' said Patsy. 'A family needs a father or they'll end up on the streets.'

'How harsh, Patsy! But you are right. Sarah, you don't know what love is. Not all men are like that and you shouldn't shun the idea of marriage. A family will be the saving of you.'

'Oh Joanna, how would I ever know how to bring up a child? I have never looked after anything. I have only ever known fear.'

'We've all had hard times, struggled to survive, worked long hours, but the rest of us have known love and someone else has been there to share the pain. You need a family, Sarah.' said Helen.

'Sarah, let us be your family. We will teach you how to love. Learn from Helen and how she looks after and loves little Davy there.' said Nora trying to soothe her.

Sarah said nothing more. These women did not understand and how could they. She felt nothing, she was nothing. Perhaps she should not have let them into her life by telling her story. It would take more than a few kind words to change her. She wished she knew what it would take, for then she might have a future worth living.

Part 2 - Chapter 13

Nora heard a plaintive cry some distance away and an anxious mother trying to soothe her child. The cries went on and on before someone went to the prison gate and shouted for the surgeon, who arrived a minute or two later. He took the child and his mother to the hospital and after a while, she returned alone. Word passed around that the boy, having felt unwell since they arrived from Devon, was now feverish. The surgeon suspected smallpox, as the mother explained there were several cases in Exeter before they left.

Helen's heart pounded with fear. Smallpox was a killer, especially of small children. In this overcrowded space, surely Davy would succumb. Her terror made it difficult to breathe, but she didn't dare speak out loud, in case she wished this new calamity on herself. Taking up her wooden beads, she clicked them through her fingers relentlessly, mouthing her prayers, praying God would hear her plea.

An hour or so later the surgeon appeared on the prison deck and asked which women and children had ever had either smallpox or cowpox.

'Don't worry please,' the surgeon said. 'There is a vaccine which may stop you from catching it. If you never had one of those diseases, then you should take the vaccination.' He hoped the tone of his voice would calm them; the last thing he wanted was women panicking.

Many of the women did not understand what he meant by a vaccine and were as afraid of that as they were of the disease. But a few women and several mothers of children spoke up, requesting the vaccine. The surgeon left to fetch it, reassuring them that all would be well.

'What do you reckon I should do?' cried Helen. 'Davy is only a few weeks old. I'm so scared. If he catches smallpox he's bound to die.'

'The surgeon wouldn't suggest it if he thought it was dangerous,' said Patsy trying to comfort her but was very unsure herself.

Joanna said that she'd caught the cowpox when only six or seven and that it wasn't too bad.

'What about yo Sarah?' asked Patsy.

'I don't know if I ever had it. There were plenty of children in the foundling home who died from it. If I didn't catch it then, I don't think I will catch it now. Nora, have you had it?'

'No I am sure not. I think I will have this vaccine, whatever it is. But I am afraid too.'

The surgeon returned with a black medical bag and asked that women and children line up for the vaccine. Both Helen and Nora queued up with a few others. He asked them to bare their left arms and proceeded to scratch them with a needle dipped in a phial of cowpox-infected material.

'I am giving you a dose of cowpox which should stop you getting smallpox. Expect to see a red lesion or angry looking spot come up in a few days. If it's there the vaccination has worked.

'Please sir, is it safe for my baby to have this?' asked Helen anxiously.

'It's safer than catching smallpox. I will keep an eye on him, don't worry too much.'

She watched the surgeon scratch the skin of Davy's arm with the needle. The baby's eyes opened wide in surprise and then he opened his mouth soundlessly for a moment or two then howled in angry tearful gulps. Helen smothered his face with kisses, scarcely noticing the surgeon perform his vaccination on her own arm.

For the rest of the afternoon and evening, Helen worried about every snuffle and cry from Davy. She kept feeling his forehead to see if he had a temperature, smiling in relief every time it felt cool to the touch. The danger of smallpox was all she could think about. At best, Davy could be scarred for life and at worst dead. She knew they wouldn't be allowed to leave the ship but must stay cooped up surrounded by infection. Her fingers continued clicking her beads and her mouth moved silently in prayer; God now her only hope.

At six o'clock the next morning the women were called up on deck with their bedrolls and shown where to stow them in the nets. The ship had moved further from the shore. There was a gentle swell so Helen had a little more trouble keeping her balance. She held on to Davy tightly.

The surgeon reported that his patient, William Lugg, was as well as could be expected and there was no doubt that he had smallpox. He instructed the women not to approach the hospital, to avoid infection. But, if they or their children became feverish, were very thirsty, or spots erupted on their bodies, they must call him immediately, day or night.

'It is doubly important that we have high standards of cleanliness, so after breakfast, I need you to go and clean every inch of the prison decks. I am going to give you holystone to use after the deck is washed and dry.

Wash clothing on Fridays and Tuesdays and hang it to dry on the nets. This being Friday you may wash clothes after breakfast. Every one of you must wash yourselves thoroughly at least once a week. There is an area set aside for this on the deck, it is quite private.

As the weather is dry and fine you can spend all day on deck but use the time profitably. I want to see you walking about and taking exercise, but reading or sewing are also valuable pastimes. You will do well to take time doing some of each.'

Sailors drew up water from the murky Thames in buckets and the women set to and soon had the prison decks washed and clean. The sailors no longer stood around to watch and comment. They had their own tasks.

Nora was happy to have work to do, even this menial task which she had once been so glad to hand over. The prospect of all that fresh air kept her spirits up, despite the worry of smallpox.

Helen cleaned as though Davy's life depended on it. Each scrub was like a prayer or a promise to God, should he spare her darling boy.

The surgeon inspected the work and he was pleased to see the women working in a spirit of co-operation and gentle teasing. It was time for him to go to the lowest deck and break open casks of flour, suet, sugar, rice, oatmeal and salt pork for the cooks. The ship's steward would ensure each dormitory was provided with sufficient rations. The surgeon hoped this ship's steward was honest or the women brave enough to complain if they were being short changed. Somehow, he thought these women would be. To drink they would have black tea, boiled from cask water, gallons of which had been loaded and must last them until they reached their destination.

Helen felt her terror recede as the days passed. Surely there would be signs by now if Davy were going to catch this pox? She started to relax and enjoy the companionship of the ship now that they were allowed on deck during the day. All the women enjoyed the balmy and sunny September days. Occasionally it became overcast but with no rain to send them scurrying below.

The women formed into small groups, the three Welsh speakers found each other with great relief. The Scots were already a close-knit group, have sailed together from Leith. Those who liked to play cards and enjoyed bawdy talk sat together, but if the surgeon happened to be passing by, sewing came out to cover the cards soon enough.

Sarah spent time teaching Nora more words and gained a new pupil in Joanna. Helen was disappointed that even with her new spectacles the words still swam around. Often, she mistook bs for ds and ps for qs. In the end gave up on reading. Sewing was much easier now and she happily devoted her time to that.

When they wanted a break the girls set off around the deck, trying not to get in the way of any working sailors. Helen and Sarah stood amazed at the river traffic. So many sailing boats came by, heavily laden with merchandise for London - straw, hay and vegetables from Essex farms, or hops and fruit from Kentish ones. Joanna recognised Great Yarmouth boats bringing smoked herring to London and waved frantically. She received friendly waves back. She wondered if she had been able to swim, would she have been tempted to hurl herself into the river. Probably not, she had left that life behind.

The sunshine glinted on the river and the brightly coloured sails made a colourful picture tacking to and fro. In grim contrast, the prison hulk, Retribution, sat squat in the water, its own cargo of male convicts awaiting their inevitable removal to Van Diemen's Land.

Once or twice a row boat came alongside and women and children boarded. These free passengers were mainly wives of convicts who had been granted permission to join their husbands on account of their good conduct. They looked sympathetically at the prisoners, unlike the few free settlers who looked at the convict women in their uniform brown dresses with disdain.

'They draw in their nostrils as though we stink.' Helen commented to Nora who, still feeling shame, cast her eyes down, rather than see their condemnation.

No one reported sick during the week and, according to his mother, William was out of danger so the women thought the danger of smallpox had passed.

The surgeon inspected those that had been vaccinated and privately he was disturbed by the results. Few had the expected lesions. He revaccinated, telling the women it was best to be on the safe side and prayed fervently that the vaccine had not lost its potency. It was too late to send for more.

Part 2 - Chapter 14

A tender drew alongside the ship carrying Mrs Barnard and another lady, Mrs Pryor. The surgeon came on deck to greet them, first warning that he had a case of smallpox on board. Both of these indomitable ladies continued their climb on board, saying they had been vaccinated previously because of their daily dealings with the poor and unfortunates of London. They had brought more things to distribute to the women, this time aprons, straw for plaiting hats and patchwork pieces.

'Ladies I have a favour to ask of you because you know many of the women better than I. We are likely to get more cases of smallpox by next week, and I will need nurses. I am looking for intelligent women or girls who will obey orders. I need ones who can read and write, but more importantly, ones who will not be too disturbed by very sick children. They must not be at any risk of getting smallpox themselves, nor should they have children accompanying them. Most of the women on board declined the vaccine and I cannot believe that all the rest had smallpox or cowpox in childhood. Can you give me a few names so I can choose two to assist me?

'We will most certainly give it our earnest thought Surgeon Carlyle. Above all we will pray for these women and children whom God has seen fit to put in even greater peril,' replied Mrs Pryor.

'Surgeon Carlyle, forgive my ignorance, but would it not be better for the women and children to be taken off the ship until the danger is past?' asked Mrs Barnard.

'No Ma'am, it is a valid question, but wrong for two reasons. Firstly, the ship must sail within a few days to take advantage of the fine weather. It would be a grave mistake to delay as autumn gales set in. Secondly, we must try to contain the infection from the general population, and a ship is a perfect place to do that. For that reason, I recommend that you destroy any clothes you are wearing once you get home, also please wash thoroughly before greeting your families. I beg you do not go below deck to the prison and take care not to touch any of the prisoners, especially the children.

'Thank you for explaining it, Sir. We will do our best to follow your instructions.' With that both women started to walk around the deck talking to the convicts, enquiring after their health and handing out the supplies they had brought with them. It was difficult not to touch them, especially those that they knew well. It felt awkward, ungenerous, even ungodly.

Helen was sewing when Mrs Barnard came to speak to her. She sat down opposite Helen.

'Oh, Mrs Barnard, I am so pleased to see you. Please tell Mrs Fry that these spectacles are just wonderful. Look at the size of stitches I can now do.'

'I am so glad to hear it, Helen. How is little Davy?'

'He's doing fine, Ma'am, and enjoying being outside on that blanket rather than all swaddled up in my arms. See how strongly he is trying to kick his legs?'

Mrs Barnard smiled at Helen and Davy and drew something from her capacious bag. Helen gasped in delight, a letter; she could not believe a reply had come so quickly.

'It came yesterday, Helen. Shall I read it?'

Helen nodded in excitement and Mrs Barnard drew a letter opener from her bag, cut through the seal, opened it out and smoothed it down. As she did so something bright fell to the deck, she bent to pick it up, set it to one side and then began to read.

My Dearest Helen

Your family were so overjoyed to get news of you and receive the keepsake you sent. I could not believe the news that you were to be transported to the far side of the world. It broke my heart because I had so wanted us to marry this harvest time. I have a cottage now and everything was waiting for you. I regret we did not seal the knot last year when we had the chance, all the more when I read you have a son, named after my beloved father. Thank you for remembering. As I write this I weep that I will never see David or come to know him. You will both be in my prayers constantly.

Helen, I pray you will understand what I have done. When you did not come back and your parents told me the reason I sought a way to make amends. Therefore, I asked your sister, Fanny, to be my wife. In that way, I can provide her with a home and know that she will be safe from harm. Your parents agreed and Fanny became my wife one week ago. I shall cherish her and any children that God chooses to give us.

Your parents send you their love and good wishes for the future. They pray you will find a husband to look after you and David. Your father and I have fashioned a memento for you. Please remember us with fondness when you look at it.

Your loving brother Bobby

Helen was sobbing by the time the letter ended. Mrs Barnard desperately wanted to hug her, but dare not, remembering the surgeon's instructions.

'I am not weeping in sadness, Ma'am, but in happiness. I long ago gave up hope of Bobby as a husband, but it pleases me so much to know that Fanny has a fine husband who will take care of her. Could you write and tell him that, please. There is nothing to forgive as I truly do understand and approve.'

'Yes, of course, my dear. Will you look at this engraved penny they have sent you.'

Helen took the shiny penny and saw that instead of its usual markings it had a tiny sailing ship and some words engraved upon on one side. There was also a hole above the lettering. 'What do the letters say Ma'am?'

'It says *Helen always and forever.*'

'Oh, that's just lovely Ma'am. I can wear it around my neck if I put some thread in it. I will always treasure it and thank you most earnestly for bringing it to me.' Helen's eyes filled up again as she struggled not to weep in front of Mrs Barnard.

Mrs Barnard left Helen to her tears and thoughts of her loved ones and moved on to find Sarah teaching Nora.

'I know all my letters now Mrs Barnard. I can read some words from the Bible, but many are very difficult. Sarah is so patient and a good teacher.'

'Well done, Nora. By the end of the voyage, you will learn enough to be a credit to your new mistress. Here's something which may help.'

She handed Nora and Sarah two pieces of slate each, one square in shape and one very small piece for writing with. 'You can practice writing on this and I have a child's reading primer here too.'

Nora was delighted with these gifts and took up the slate immediately. It took a little time for her to hold the small slate comfortably between her fingers and make a recognisable shape with it. But then she started to draw the letters of her name slowly, painstakingly and somewhat ill-formed but Mrs Barnard was impressed by her determination.

Sarah was too overwhelmed by the gift to say anything. It was the best thing anyone could have given her. No more writing in the air or on the floor in soot. Sarah's world had expanded and now she had the means to teach Nora and Joanna to write too.

While Nora was busy with the slate Mrs Barnard drew Sarah aside.

'Sarah, I have rarely seen you smile before today. Teaching Nora must to be good for you.'

'I love it Ma'am, I enjoyed helping the little ones in the foundling home.'

'Do you think you could tell me a little about the home and why you are here, Sarah?'

Since Sarah had opened up to Nora and the others, she found it easier to talk to people. Patsy said a trouble shared is a trouble halved and perhaps that was true for she found telling her story for the second time was less daunting. She went through the main events quickly, but left out John the tapman's part, because she didn't want Mrs Barnard to cause any trouble for him. Finally, she had questions of her own for Mrs Barnard.

'The stories in the Bible are about caring for other people but you are the only person I ever met who seems to care for those less fortunate. Why is that, Ma'am? Why do people spend so much time hurting those that are under them? I don't understand it.'

'I cannot undertake to talk for others Sarah, but each of us in the Society of Friends believes we find God through our daily actions and that all people are worthy of respect, no matter their role or standing.'

'How I wish I could be a part of such a society. No one ever cared for me before Newgate and I do not know how to care for others. Do you think it possible to learn?'

'Yes, I truly believe it is possible, Sarah. Do not give up hope. As yet, there are no Friends in Van Diemen's Land, but I pray that some will go there soon. You must join them when they do and they would surely welcome thee. But until then I will leave thee this book about our beliefs and you do not need others to practise them. Thee are already a child of God and will come to know him through thine own self, thy thoughts, thy deeds and thy prayers.'

Could she really join such a group? Sarah took the book greedily, and with sincere thanks let Mrs Barnard move on to talk to other women.

Mrs Barnard found the difference in Sarah since her last visit to the ship quite remarkable. She wondered how it had come about. It must lie in teaching others to read she decided.

After several hours spent on board, both Mrs Prior and Mrs Barnard found the surgeon to tell him their recommendations. Mrs Prior gave him three names of suitable women and Mrs Barnard just one.

'You may think that the person I recommend is not suitable because of her age and her crime, but I believe that she is more sinned against than sinning. I urge you to give her a chance as she is one of the most intelligent girls I have met and very close to God. She is quiet, but will follow your instructions to the letter, and needs an opportunity to learn how to love herself and other people. She has had no care in her upbringing, and yet humanity shines out of her. She is just unaware of it.'

The surgeon listened attentively and promised that to consider the girl. Reminding the women of his instructions regarding the dangers of spreading smallpox they left the ship for the final time.

Part 2 - Chapter 15

The days followed the pattern which had been set the week before. When the weather was fine the women stayed on deck throughout the day, if it rained they went below to the prison deck.

On Sunday Nora was about to climb up the steps for divine service, when a young, stout woman, fell backwards through the hatchway onto the deck below. Her head and neck were bent forwards towards her chest and she appeared senseless. Nora feared she was dead as she looked so awkward lying there. Luckily the surgeon, passing by at that instant, knelt down, placed his hands around her head and pulled sharply so the neck bones were forced back with a crack. A moment later, regaining her senses, the woman moved her arms and legs but complained of a dreadful pain in her neck. Nora's admiration for the surgeon grew. How wonderful that he knew exactly what to do.

Reverend William Garrard, the new Assistant Chaplain to Van Diemen's Land, had embarked the day before. A young, earnest-looking man, around thirty years of age, he had found favour with Colonel Arthur in Honduras and happily accepted Colonel Arthur's offer of patronage when he was appointed as Governor Arthur of Van Diemen's Land. Now he was on his way to an island where there was a different slavery, white rather than black. Not that he would ever judge it so. It was the natural order of things to try and make useful men and woman from those who did not abide by God's commandments.

The Reverend conducted the service tolerably well and he was largely unabashed by the strangest congregation he had had in his career so far. He told the women about the school starting next week. Children over the age of six were to be taught their letters and about 'our dear lord, Jesus, who died for our sins,' this last phrase made pointedly towards the women before him. One or two looked mortified but he also noted those who were unrepentant looked mortified, but he also noted those who appeared unrepentant and shrugged off his words. He relished the opportunity to work with those loose and fallen women. God would help him mend their ways.

Sarah had a strange encounter with the surgeon later that day. He asked her to read a passage from the Bible and then plied her with questions about her time in the foundling home and illnesses she had experienced there. She didn't know what to make of it but answered him respectfully and with honesty. Only a few short weeks ago, she could not have answered him and would have been shaking with fear, while he became exasperated. This pleased her. She was also quietly thrilled with the progress that Nora was making with reading and writing. It gave her a strange feeling of contentment, which she wondered if she could trust.

The following Sunday, October 2nd saw, the Henry still berthed at Woolwich, and the women restless with boredom. When would they sail, they asked each other daily? Unbeknownst to them, a free passenger, fifteen-year-old Sally Richie was taken ill the evening before and the surgeon's worst fears were realised. It was smallpox and despite Sally having been vaccinated some years ago, she had still caught the disease. The following day Mary Horn from Edinburgh reported that her four-month-old baby was unwell and the surgeon put his plan into action.

Part 2 - Chapter 16

He called Sarah and Jenny, the other woman chosen, to the hospital and told them he wished them to nurse the sick children. They would work four hours and then rest for four hours in turn. They should keep the children's temperatures down by bathing them in cool water and, in the case of little Margaret Horn, not let the mother pick her up, unless breastfeeding, Sally, should be helped to drink barley water and the surgeon called if they were at all worried. They were to note on a slate each time Sally had drunk and how much liquid she had taken.

As the day went on two more babies were carried to the hospital. All had been vaccinated but were showing signs of the dreaded disease. Then Sally Richie's five-year-old sister, Mary, came down with it. Within twenty-four hours three babies and two children joined William Lugg in the hospital. The surgeon's assistants were kept fully busy mopping down fevered bodies, helping the older patients to drink and calming the distraught mothers as they came to breastfeed the babies. The surgeon came by frequently, but he still needed to keep an eye on all the other women and look for signs of disease in other children without unduly alarming all the ship's passengers. This was a losing battle as word passed around and groups of women huddled together anxiously talking and crying. In the midst of all of this, news came that the ship would set sail that evening.

The two assistants were obliged to stay in the hospital away from all the other prisoners. As Sarah rested she wondered why the Surgeon had chosen her for the task. She couldn't understand it. There were many older women, like Jenny, who were mothers and who knew about nursing. She had no fear of the disease, seeing it so many times before, but she knew nothing about nursing. She found herself praying that she could help them and that she wouldn't let the surgeon down. Sarah slept awhile, then ate some food and began her next four-hour duty.

Part 2 - Chapter 17

Sarah

The surgeon was bleeding Sally when I arrived for my duty. I watched as the cup slowly filled up with her bright red blood and I wondered how blood-letting worked. Would it bring down her dreadful fever? I did not dare ask. Her cheeks were flaming and I could feel the heat rising from her skin as I bathed her face with cool water. A rash was forming on her face and body which I knew would develop into open sores. Most likely her looks would be forever disfigured if she survived this. Her eyes flickered open as I tried to get a little barley water down her throat.

'Please I don't want to die, I am frightened,' she whispered from her cracked and broken lips. I, who had so often thought longingly of death as being an end to cold and hunger, stroked her cheek gently with a cool rag, not knowing how to answer. She quietened and then drifted again into a restless sleep. I turned to her little sister, Mary, who was less feverish than Sally and bathed her body and she smiled wanly at me and grasped my hand. I could detect a slight twitching as her body spasmed, but I held her hand a long time until sleep took her. I continued to stroke the damp, blonde curls framing her face, remembering those little bedmates of mine who sank inevitably into fever and death. Why was I spared? I never understood that.

Sally Ritchie shivered and groaned with pain. Her face was visibly swelling but, seeming satisfied that her fever was less, the surgeon ordered me to keep her covered and warm. The other children appeared comfortable, though poor little William's sores had scabbed and were falling off leaving him terribly marked. As my four hours ended I began to feel the ship moving and there was noise above as sailors shouted to each other. The surgeon told me that we had begun the journey and tomorrow I may have a walk on deck to see the ship underway, as long as I don't get in the way of the sailors as they do their work. The other prisoners will not be allowed on deck while the ship moves down the river as it would be too dangerous. I found myself excited by the prospect of the journey.

I am glad my life in London is over and perhaps there is a chance for me in a different place. Though I knew so little of London I will remember the dirt and poverty and hurt. How I wish I could be born anew on this ship and never remember the life I had before. I would like to wipe my life clean as I do the marks on a slate.

Jenny came for her shift and I was pleased to sleep. But my dreams were full of burning or drowning children. I was that relieved when I woke at dawn, to the smell of food and a gentle rocking motion as the ship sailed down the Thames. After a quick meal, I made my way to the hatchway and climbed to the deck. There was a fair wind and the banks of the Thames appeared further away and the river much wider now. The two masts had square sails billowing in the breeze and we seemed to skim across the water. It was a wonderful feeling, and as the gulls wheeled and flew around the ship I imagined myself up there with them, free and flying wherever I wanted. I could have stayed there all day but worried about leaving Jenny any longer so made my way back down to the hospital.

'That poor lass has had such a bad night, see her face so swelled and purple. I don't like the look of her at all Sarah,' she whispered as she left to get to her bed.

And for sure Sally looked very much worse. I sat beside her and though her fever had abated, her eyes were running and red looking. She tried to speak but her throat seemed closed up and she couldn't get any words out. So, I held her hand and talked to her about the ship sailing and what I had seen on deck. I told her that I would like to be a bird, having all that freedom to roam around the sky. I talked to her quite easily, though by now she was insensible to what was around her and did not try to respond. I spent much time with Sally that morning, the other children being less fevered and responding to the surgeon's treatment.

He came by regularly, though he was quite taken up with the other prisoners, who needed him. He looked at Sally with great concern, there was blood in her motions and her urine and he tried to give her medicine but she had great difficulty in swallowing. Taking me aside he told me to just try and keep her comfortable and see if she would drink the barley water. I think he has seen that she will not survive this, which makes me sad.

I left her in Jenny's care for the afternoon, but as I now worried for her all my waking hours I found it difficult to sleep. When I returned to the hospital that evening I saw that much of her body had now a purple hue. Her mother was by her bed and was crying and wailing in despair. The surgeon made her leave saying she should get some rest and there was nothing to do but pray. He made a sleeping draught for Sally but as the evening turned to night what little he could get her to drink had no effect. She tossed and turned and made noises as though she was trying to speak, but she was not aware of her surroundings at all. She messed herself several times and I cleaned her up as best I could, but dark oozing blood kept on coming from her mouth and nether regions. The Surgeon shook his head when he visited her last before he departed for his bed. Remembering the psalm, Mrs Barnard recited before we left Newgate, and I got down on my knees, still holding Sally's hand. I repeated it and then prayed to God to take Sally quickly and bring her into his light. That is how Jenny found me that night. I was exhausted and tearful and so I went to bed immediately, not knowing what I should find the next morning.

Yet the next morning God had still not seen fit to take Sally, though she sank ever further. There was nothing we could do to help her but continue to sit and pray for her and keep her clean. She died in the early hours of the next morning, not long after I left to sleep again. By the time, I awoke she had been consigned to the sea along with the rags we bathed her with and any other items we used to nurse her. Even her mother had not been there at the end, just Jenny who laid her out and wrapped the body ready for burial.

William returned today to his mother, recovered but dreadfully scarred. How the sins of his mother have been visited upon him. I cannot make sense of that. The other children are progressing and will soon be out of danger. The surgeon told me I can go back to the prison deck within two days as the children would be well enough to be cared for by their mothers and him. He hurried off to see a prisoner who had given birth the day before. Jenny told me that the child was born dead and probably dead for some time, given the state of it. How sad for a woman go through all those months of waiting, and then the pains of labour, but no child to hold and to care for.

Over the next two days, I helped nurse Mary, Sally's sister. Her disease followed the same early pattern as it had in her poor sister, but much less severely. The swelling came as did the pustules but there was no more fever and she was able to swallow and even eat a little. She cried a lot but mostly for the loss of Sally than for herself. Her mother, of course, was prostrate with grief and blaming herself for undertaking the journey. She worried about what to tell her husband when she arrived in Van Diemen's Land with only one daughter but laid no blame on him for sending for his family. Why should she feel guilt? She has just followed her husband's wishes.

I escaped to the deck whenever I had a break. In the evenings, I saw the moon rise, sometimes so big and silvery that it shone on the sea and lit a magical, shining pathway through the water. I wanted to step out on it, sure it would take me to a wondrous place where pain and grief did not exist. During the day, the fresh air soothed me and I watched the changing coastline, wondering, always wondering about the land that passed. So many ships sailed by, as we lay off the Downs waiting for a fair wind. An elderly sailor stopped to pass the time of day with me.

'There be East India Men from India and China,' he pointed, 'bringing cotton, silk, tea and spices. You can smell the spices on the wind.'

And it was true, you could smell the most wonderful scents, pungent, rich and sharp and I wondered what they would taste like. There's so much about the world I do not know and want to find out.

Today the surgeon told me to return to the prison after I had washed myself and changed my clothes. My present clothes are to be destroyed to stop infection spreading. I dared to ask him why he had chosen me to help and he said that it was Mrs Barnard who recommended me. He decided to give me a chance and was pleased that he had and intended to write a good report of me when we landed.

I am sure I blushed when he said that and I hope I mumbled my thanks before he dismissed me. I am confused by what he told me but I hugged the thought to myself that Mrs Barnard spoke good things about me, when I didn't even have the courage to speak to her for months. These last few days I forgot my own fears when Sally had so much more to fear than me. I wish she had lived but I hope I helped her a little; it felt useful, it felt good.

The surgeon is keeping Jenny on as a nurse as there are still patients in the hospital including the poor women who lost her babe. Jenny said she isn't at all well and will take a deal of nursing back to health. But I look forward to going back to my friends now. It feels strange to say that word, but it's true. I do have friends who care about me.

Part 2 - Chapter 18

The Journey

The ship left the safety of the Downs and sailed down the English Channel until by October 13th they lay off Portland. Many of the women experienced sea sickness and the prison decks reeked with the smell of vomit when the hatchway was opened in the morning. With the weather being rough, the openings on the deck above the prison remained tightly closed, leaving the smell nowhere to escape. Nora was not afflicted but gained the awful job of emptying bowls of sick into the privy and rinsing them out. Not all women managed to find a bowl quickly enough and cleaning the deck became a filthy job which made her want to puke herself. But at least, when the job was done, Nora and others, who felt well enough, could climb up to the main deck for fresh air while the rest lay groaning below in misery.

Nora was overjoyed to see Sarah return as she missed their lessons and wanted to show her how she had been practising writing.

'Look, Sarah, I can write 'the cat sat on the mat' and my numbers up to ten.'

Sarah smiled her approval of her pupil's progress. Nora asked her about what she had been doing for the surgeon but Sarah told her little and Nora, used to Sarah's silence, did not take offence.

Helen was prostrate with sickness. Every movement of the ship sent her into paroxysms of retching and now she had nothing left to bring up. Patsy was not so ill and she stayed with Helen to look after Davy and coax her into trying a sip of water every now and again.

'What if I can't eat through this journey and my milk dries up?' said Helen terrified.

'Yo will get over it and as long as yo keep drinking it'll be alright.' Patsy was not confident but she willed it to be so. She really liked Helen and saw her as a younger version of herself, hard-working, resilient and down to earth. As for Davy, he was just a sweetheart and his smile lit up her days. She prayed for them both and watched Helen as her fingers moved over her wooden beads and her mouth silently prayed for deliverance.

By Sunday, October 17th they had said a final farewell to the English coast and those who could make it through the hatchway attended divine service on a shifting, pitching deck. Helen was much better and thankfully Davy appeared none the worse for his mother's sickness. She was more than happy to thank God for working his miracle on her, not only that but the outbreak of smallpox was over. Helen felt doubly blessed.

After divine service, the surgeon gave each woman, who was fit enough, half a pint of wine to drink. Sarah and Nora were not used to strong drink and after gingerly sipping it, offered their beakers around.

As the afternoon progressed, behaviour on deck worsened, becoming boisterous and rowdy, encouraged by the sailors, who responded as men do. Several of the women started to sing bawdy songs and danced as the sailors cheered and stamped their feet, but elsewhere it attracted disapproving stares. At the point where Jane and Lizzie, in particular, beckoned to two of the sailors in a lascivious manner the surgeon decided that the women should go back to the prison deck. Most were accommodating, but Jane and Lizzie resisted and began to taunt the surgeon. He decided to set an example otherwise his control would be lost.

'Lock them in the coal-hole for twenty-four hours,' he told George.

Turning to address the women he said, 'When you come out your hair will be shorn, which should teach you some manners.' He gestured to George and another sailor who were holding the women to take them away. He also made a mental note to cut the wine ration next Sunday.

The days passed slowly; some fine with a fair wind and others squally. The women began to get used to the motion of the ship and the children coped better than their mothers. Two women had barely been able to keep any food down since they left the Thames. They grew prostrate with hunger and were referred to the surgeon. He applied cantharidin to the chest, causing a blister to rise to draw out the poisons from the body. Somehow it worked for the women started to eat again after a day or two.

But much of the problem was the nature of the food. While it was plentiful, it was not fresh and Nora despaired of it. She was used to better fare. Rancid salt meat; peas boiled up for hours though still seeming like bullets; ships biscuit, either so hard it could not be chewed or soft and crumbly and full of weevils, she could hardly force herself to get it down.

Even the water was green and scummy and often infested with insects but it had to be used for tea and for cooking the food. So was it any surprise that the surgeon had to deal with diarrhoea or constipation in equal measure?

Helen was so grateful that little Davy was still feeding well. The food was more regular than she was used to but was often no better than those rotten vegetables she had scrounged from the fields or midden heaps. Perhaps being used to such a poor diet she stood in better stead than Patsy or Nora, who could hardly bear to force down each unpleasant mouthful.

It was such a relief to go on deck when the weather was fair and by the end of October the weather became warmer and they started to pass mountainous islands of lush vegetation.

'I wonder where we are? It looks so different from England but quite beautiful.' said Nora to herself.

'It's called Madeira, where the wine comes from. I have called there on other ships,' said a passing sailor.

'Oh yes, my mistress used to have a little Madeira wine of an evening. She said it helped her to sleep. I never thought to see it. I wish we could go ashore, it looks so green. '

'Where you are going has, even more, trees,' replied the sailor grinning, as he walked away to his work.

'Don't you find it strange that we know nothing about where we are going? We have been told nothing other than we will work and probably not come home again,' said Nora turning to Sarah and Helen.

'We should try to find something out about it. Who would tell us, do you think?' asked Helen.

'Perhaps the Reverend?' suggested Sarah, half in jest, knowing what the others thought of him.

'Humph! Perhaps not!' Both Nora and Helen said in unison. Neither had taken to him and he did not appear to care for Catholics. He had not said as much, but there was just a hint of disdain in his eyes when he came upon them using their rosaries. Strangely there was no disdain when he preached directly to the most hard-bitten of prostitutes. Most of whom either laughed at him or pretended to repent, only to call him names once back in their dormitories.

'I could ask the surgeon.' Sarah volunteered still shy and tentative.

'Is he not terribly busy?'

'Well, we could try tomorrow, after service, when he's handing out the wine.'

Nora found it difficult to reconcile this Sarah with the Sarah she knew before in Newgate. Was it telling her story which helped or was it the week she spent helping in the hospital? Sarah certainly talked more, smiled more and her eyes seemed different, more alive somehow.

The following day Sarah asked the surgeon how to find information about where they were going and he regarded her quizzically.

'For such a young woman, you are remarkable. Most of the women here display no interest whatsoever in what happens to them. I find that surprising. There is a book which Mrs Pryor left on board about lands in the southern seas. George will bring it to you.'

He turned away to give out a lime sherbet saying, 'This will guard against scurvy,' following it up with wine, just a quarter pint this time and none for those who had displayed such disreputable behaviour the previous Sunday.

Part 2 - Chapter 19

When George handed Sarah the book, she received it with the reverence one might receive a precious jewel. It was a slim, shabby book, the cardboard cover faded and stained and the inside pages were spotted brown. This did not stop the excitement as the three friends pored over the pages which included several wood-cuts, images of strange creatures and people. Sarah was attempting to read some of the pages, but the others kept trying to turn to the next drawing and then exclaiming.

'Would you ever believe that!' pointing to a kangaroo or a dark-skinned figure wearing nothing but a cloth to disguise his manhood.

Other women curious at what was going on began to take a peek and soon there was a crowd around them. They clamoured for the book to be passed around. All now wanted to see these peculiar drawings. For many women, it confirmed their worst fears that they were going to a place of nightmares and devils. They wished for more wine to forget the images they had seen and cursed Jane and Lizzie for causing their ration to be cut.

But there were a few who asked Sarah to read the book to them so they could find out more about such wondrous lands. After each morning's cleaning and washing, Sarah sat down and the group sat rapt as her halting voice described the places and creatures in the book.

Within a week much of the book had been read and the women drifted away to other pastimes but there was a map at the beginning of the book and Sarah puzzled over it for hours. She had never seen a map of anywhere and was unsure how to read it but it seemed to open up such a wealth of possibilities. She knew such a minute area of London and at one time she thought that everywhere was the same. But this book and the glimpses of passing islands made her aware of how much more there was to learn about the world.

One morning, in early November, land appeared on the horizon and several islands passed by as the day went on. Sarah stood watching as the navy sea gave way to turquoise bays surrounding uninhabited beaches of bone white sand and treeless mountains covered by wispy clouds, shimmering in the heat of the afternoon. It was warm enough to stay there all night and she would have stayed but George came to tell her to go below as the prison was about to be locked.

Sarah returned to the deck the next morning, as soon as the prison opened, to find the ship moored in a large horseshoe shaped bay overlooking a small town. The houses looked different from those in London. Small whitewashed houses with terracotta roofs and untidily thatched stone houses, were dwarfed by a large fortress. A tender was lowered from the ship and rowed to the shore of dark orange sand, the same colour as the hills beyond. Sarah could see people on the shore, two in uniform, most likely soldiers. Others helping to pull up the tender were black and bare-chested. Three sailing ships were moored in the bay and a tiny, shelf-like island, completely flat and treeless lay to the left. She drank it all in.

The tender set off back from the shore laden with fresh produce to the cheers of the women as they sensed a welcome change in diet.

That evening, the women feasted on fresh beef and vegetable stew followed by a strange looking yellow fruit, tubular in shape, which had a soft waxy skin. At first, no one knew what to do with it but a sailor showed them how to tear the skin off and they saw a cream fruit underneath, etched with vertical lines. Tentatively, one or two bit into the fruit and found it, unlike anything they had ever tasted. Some liked the taste but others spat it out in disgust. Jane and Lizzie joked uproariously about the shape of the fruit and other uses they could put it to. They peeled the skin and took it into their mouths and sucked loudly, their tongues snaking in and out of between their lips, watched in horror by Reverend Garrard. With their heads shorn of hair, they looked grotesque, but it had not shamed them in any way. Jane and Lizzie were beyond shame. They did not know how to act any other way.

The atmosphere on board became quite carefree. The warm, still evening scented by exotic flowers on shore, drifting now and again over the ship, relaxed all on board. The women had no sea sickness, their bellies were full and for once they felt happy. Someone started to sing and others joined in. It was way past the time that the prison was normally locked. But the surgeon decided it would do no harm to let them stay on deck for a while longer. Even the free passengers were enjoying the songs and, as some of the prisoners began to dance, a sailor brought out a fiddle and everyone felt the joy that good food and music can muster. Nora sat watching wistfully and reminisced about her father on his fiddle and her mother dancing a jig. It brought them so close that tears pricked her eyes. When the jolly dance ended, she broke quite naturally into Barbara Allen. Quiet soon overcame the audience as they listened to her sweet, melodic voice as they had done once before, adding sadness to the mix.

George felt the hairs stand on the back of his neck. He had found the owner of that voice which haunted him and his heart seemed to beat at twice the normal speed. Nora made some impression, with her obvious good looks, when she came on board at Woolwich. She seemed a timid, shy sort of girl, unlike the raucous loud mouthed majority of female convicts. After he witnessed the love and sadness between her and her family taking their leave, he sympathised, wanted to cheer her up. Later as he went about his work it was hard not to notice her reading lessons with that mousy scrap of a girl who'd helped the surgeon during the smallpox outbreak. He never understood why the surgeon chose Sarah to help. But to give her due, she had really cared for those sick children, despite the foul, noxious smell of the one who'd died.

Now, listening to that angelic voice, he wanted to hear Nora singing just for him, only for him, and he knew he would never cease to want it. Not the kind of sailor to seduce and abandon a maid, he found himself longing to protect this gentle, sweet girl and care for her, with his life if necessary. A sudden despair gripped him. Once they had landed she would be lost to him. There must be a way to change that. First, he must think how to get to know her without incurring the surgeon's displeasure, but it would take some days before he had a solution to that problem.

After three days moored off the little town of Saint Jago and replenished with food, the Henry set sail again. The days and nights grew ever warmer. Many of the hospital patients were fit enough to rejoin their companions and the surgeon had time to spend on deck overseeing his charges. Sarah dared to approach him and tell him she had finished the book he lent her.

'Yes, you had quite an audience around you. It was good to see all that interest. Is there anything you didn't understand?'

'Sir, I have been puzzling over this map.' She showed him the map at the front of the book. 'I don't know how to read it. England is not on it. There are lots of islands, but not Cape Verde where we stopped a while ago. I can see Van Diemen's Land just underneath that big one called New Holland.'

'Ah yes. That big one, called New Holland on your map, has been renamed this very year as Australia. It will take a while to catch on, I should think. This ship will call there after we have dropped you off in Van Diemen's Land. The reason that England isn't there is because this map only covers the southern seas and not the whole of the world.'

'I would like to see a map of the whole world, would that be possible, sir? Do you have such a thing?'

'I should think if we are sailing half way around the world we ought to have a chart that shows it, otherwise, we might not know which way to sail,' he said laughing. 'Yes, I do have a map in another book of my own. I haven't time to give you a geography lesson, but I will ask George to explain it to you.'

George was delighted with this request. It gave him the opportunity he longed for. He would make sure that Nora was with the girl, Sarah, before he gave her the new book and hoped he could spin out the explanation.

'If she asks me any more questions about where we are and where we are sailing to next, do I have your permission to answer her sir?'

'Yes, but mind I do not want any familiarity, George. Be on your guard as many of those women are quite depraved and will take advantage of a fine young sailor, such as yourself. Only speak to Sarah and I don't mind if she is with that young friend she is teaching to read. She seems to be of good character.'

George scarcely concealed his pleasure. He assured the surgeon he would be careful, picked up the book of maps and decided to walk around the deck to see if Nora and Sarah were together. But when he came upon Sarah she was helping the woman called Joanna with her writing. No matter, he could bide his time for a day or two, without arousing any suspicion. With the weather turning hotter by the day several of the women seemed to be suffering other afflictions, which would keep the surgeon too busy for enquiries about Sarah and the map.

Part 2 - Chapter 20

It was so hot! How can people live in this heat, asked Nora to herself? It felt like an added punishment and she prayed to God that it would not be as hot in Van Diemen's Land. The sky was a deep, cloudless blue and the sun a fiery disc, which bore down on her shawl-covered head. Perspiration dripped from her forehead and into her eyes. She wiped it away with a rag for the umpteenth time that day. From her neck, sweat trickled down her spine making her petticoat stick to her skin. She longed to strip off her thick dress and wallow in a cool bath. At night, it was worse, she tossed and turned in her bunk, unable to settle. Sometimes melted pitch from the caulking, between the planks of the ship, dropped onto her body, scorching her skin.

A sail had been erected over the hatchway to capture any breeze, funnelling it to the decks below, which helped a little. Nora would never have imagined that heat could be so tiring, so draining. She longed for rain and a pleasant English breeze. She frowned as she remembered her complaints in Newgate, about the poor summer. Now she dreamt of a cooling glass of fresh water, or even better, a glass of mild ale. Once in her mind, the desire grew and grew until it was all she thought of.

On deck, although there was no shade to be found, it was still better than being in the airless prison below. She and Sarah tried to make hats out of the straw that Mrs Barnard had left. They were having trouble getting started when George found them together and he saw his opportunity. All sailors had their pastimes for long voyages and making straw hats came as second nature to him.

'Let me help you. I can show you the best way to get started.' He broke into their futile attempts, startling them as they struggled with the straw.

'The Surgeon asked me to explain maps and charts to you, Miss Sarah. I was hoping I might catch you, but I reckon you need some help with this first.'

Both girls nodded shyly but were relieved at the offer of help. They watched as George nimbly started to plait the straw, showing them how to create a circle for the crown of the hat. He was a patient teacher and the girls began to understand what they had to do.

As he worked the straw he plucked up the courage to say to Nora. 'I enjoyed the singing the other night. You surely have a beautiful voice, Miss Nora. I reckon I could listen all day and night to you singing those songs.'

Nora blushed but ventured a smile in his direction. 'My whole family loves singing and my father plays the fiddle too.'

'Yes, I remember your father and sisters when they came to Woolwich. They looked fine people.'

'I have three little brothers too. I miss them all dreadfully.'

'I hate to see you looking so sad. I wish it were in my power to make you happy miss.' As he said this he finished weaving and bid them farewell, promising to return with the book of maps the following day. Both girls stared at his retreating figure. Helen came over to them. She had seen and heard most of the conversation.

'It looks like you have an admirer, Nora. George surely is love-struck.'

Nora's cheeks flared. 'Really Helen, he is just being kind and helpful.'

'No. I recognise that look he gave you. He is much taken with you. Just watch your step with him and don't let him take advantage. You're too much of an innocent.'

'George is very polite and proper. I am sure he wouldn't take advantage.' Nora dismissed the friendly warning. Since that first day on board, he had been courteous and correct, unlike some of the other sailors whose rude gestures frightened her. She felt sure George was the same way with all the women and it couldn't be possible that he meant anything by those words. She asked Sarah what she thought.

'What do I know of the ways of men? I can only judge on actions. If they don't scorn you or hurt you they may have some goodness, I suppose, but I cannot really say anything about George beyond what you know already.'

Nora pondered on Helen's words all that day, tossing and turning most of the humid night. She awoke damp and irritable, but after a wash in clammy water and the usual burgoo porridge, only edible with a good-sized dollop of sugar stirred in it, she settled down with Sarah to finish off the straw hat.

They chose the simplest design, just a round disc of straw with string on either side to tie under the chin. It would do its job of keeping the sun from the face and neck. Anything more complicated would take too much time and they were impatient for relief from the sun. That day the sun was stronger than ever and a few of the women who had no covering for their heads began to complain of headaches, nausea and fever. The Surgeon was busy and he required assistance from George for most of the day.

It was not until the late afternoon that George appeared on deck. Nora watched his progress towards her. She was sitting with Joanna practising their spelling. George gave a brief nod and passed by. He did not stop to show Sarah the book he was carrying, which Nora thought strange. The same thing happened the next day. He passed by twice with the book and did not stop to speak to Sarah and Helen, who sat together. However, on the third day after helping with the hats, George stopped to show Sarah the book and this time Nora was sitting beside her. He greeted them both, but Nora noticed that the smile he gave her just lingered a fraction more than it did for Sarah. She felt her cheeks flush so dipped her head to look at the picture he was showing them from the book.

'This is a map of the world. You can see the southern seas you were looking at in the other book are just a small corner of the world.' His finger circled New Holland and the surrounding islands.

He spent several minutes explaining the world map to Sarah, who was evidently very interested. Nora nodded and smiled in appropriate places. She felt tongue-tied in his presence and suddenly very shy. Perhaps Helen was right to be suspicious. Nora did not know what to think about it.

George's hand accidentally touched Nora's hand as he turned the page to show another map. The shock sent a tingling sensation all the way up her arm. She opened her mouth in surprise, and her eyes fleetingly glanced to his face and then she knew. His expression could only be described as wistful. She found she didn't remember anything he said to Sarah after that. He stayed for another minute or so before bidding them farewell.

The same pattern occurred on the two following days. If Nora was not sitting with Sarah, he did not stop. If they were together he stopped and asked if Sarah had any questions about the various maps in the book. Nora, aware that his eyes rested on her face as he talked with Sarah, tried not to look at him. But when her eyes did find his she did not always glance away, for the warmth in his brown eyes drew her in further.

Their fingers fleetingly met again as a page turned. This time it was more than a disturbing tingling. She felt her insides melting and saw that it was the same for him. She knew she should not encourage him, but her body responded of its own volition and he was aware of it. He smiled at Nora even more as he greeted Sarah, but Sarah was oblivious to both of them. She was too wrapped up in the book to notice.

Nora, on the other hand, began to find her heart racing as she watched for him. She was by now careful to sit close to Sarah, whenever he might be on deck. He was easy to spot being taller than most of the other sailors. His wide-brimmed straw hat covered most, but not all of his brown, curly hair and despite the hat, his face was bronzed from the sun. You couldn't call him handsome, she thought, but he has a face with character. His jaw line is too square perhaps, a beard may suit him. His eyes are set well apart and his nose is straight and not overly big. I could do a lot worse, she grinned to herself.

Nora encouraged Sarah to talk about the maps and the journey when they were on their own. While she could never concentrate when George was talking, she thought that she should try to understand what they talked about. She did not want to appear stupid or not interested, so she listened carefully when Sarah read bits out of the book or showed her a map. Nora even asked questions, in the hope that if Sarah didn't know the answer, she would ask George, giving him an excuse to stay a little longer. She did not talk about her feelings to either Sarah or Helen. She wanted to keep it close because it seemed so private and pleasurable and she understood that if the word spread and the Surgeon come to hear of it, then, there could be trouble for George and herself.

Part 2 - Chapter 21

As the month changed to December and the sun was hotter than any summer day in the northern climes of Europe, the surgeon gave out a more generous portion of wine on Sunday; a reward for good behaviour. A pig had been slaughtered which meant fresh meat for dinner. Helen didn't think she had ever smelt anything go enticing. She gave a tiny bit to Davy and watched him chew with his tiny two bottom teeth.

'Remember the taste of this Davy,' she whispered. 'One day we will eat like this every day.' He gurgled at her and laughed.

Everyone was cheerful and in good spirits and they started to sing as they washed their dinner plates and pans. The Surgeon suggested they rest for an hour or two while the sun was at its hottest and then return to the deck in the late afternoon.

Once back on deck the passengers, the sailors and the convicts settled down for a relaxed, communal song and dance. As dusk began to fall the party was still in full swing and Nora felt the lightest touch on her arm. George drew her away from the dancing and they stood side by side, not touching, scarcely breathing, but together alone for the first time. As a song and dance ended and cheers and claps resounded around the ship George whispered.

'Miss Nora, you must know that I have feelings for you and I have hopes that you feel the same.'

Nora gave a barely perceptible nod and breathed, 'Yes, but we hardly know each other,'

'No matter, it's enough. We have another two months before we land, with time to know each other little more. But for now, can I ask you to sing a song for me. Let me hear your beautiful voice.'

George turned away and strode across the deck and Nora, her heart beating fast, moved back to the centre of the deck to join in the dancing. Why did she feel this way? It made no sense. She had known this man for just three months and had spoken less than a dozen words to him. She knew nothing of his past and his character, but his touch burned her skin and she couldn't stop thinking about him.

When there was a break in the dancing Nora stood up to sing 'My love is like a red, red rose.' Nora's father loved the Scottish ballad, often singing it to his wife before she died. The words and tune poured from Nora's mouth with a passion that made George's heart contract. He would never tire of hearing that voice. The audience was entranced and a fiddle began to accompany her, but no one else joined in for her voice was a joy to listen to. She sang with passion, perhaps she had left a sweetheart back home, poor thing. After the second rendition, she sat down to silence, followed by rapturous applause.

That night Nora stayed awake for a long time. It wasn't so much the heat and the noise of seventy odd women and children sometimes snoring, sometimes crying out or getting up to use the privy, which stopped her sleeping. No, her mind was racing in wonder at how quickly all these emotions surrounding George had built up in her mind. Was she just responding to his feelings for her? It was a forbidden attraction. Did that make it more desirable? She wished she knew more about love and could talk to her sisters. They would talk sense to her.

Nora mused over it for a long time. She needed to know more about George and if she could trust him. Suddenly an idea came to her, which would depend on Sarah still being wrapped up in her search for ever more answers about the world. She must make it appear natural and innocent so that Sarah would not guess anything was untoward. Relieved she drifted into a sleep, full of pleasant of dreams for a change.

The surgeon asked George for a report on how the book on maps had gone down with Sarah the next morning.

'Sir, she's like a well that was dry and is now filling up but can't get enough water. You explain something and the next day she has another question and then another. It's as though she knew nothing but thirsts after knowing everything.'

'Yes, I think you are right. She is unlike any other girl I have come across, especially in one so young and timid. I have seen you talking to her and that other girl. What is she like? I hope she's well behaved.'

'Oh, to be sure sir, she never speaks, surprising really for she has a glorious singing voice.'

'She does indeed. Continue to answer Sarah's questions and if you need any more books I let me know. But don't let it interfere with your work.'

'Thank you, sir, I will make sure of that.' George turned away relieved that he had the surgeon's permission to continue to speak to Sarah. He longed to be close to Nora to catch a brief smile, touch her and watch her green eyes flicker on his face, then look away in confusion. The surgeon might put a stop to it at any point if he thought anything was untoward. They needed to be careful.

After breakfast and cleaning the prison deck, Nora sat down with Sarah for her reading lesson. Nora was beginning to attempt short passages from the New Testament and Sarah was quietly thrilled with her progress. Sure, there were plenty of stumbles as Nora sounded out new words letter by letter. Sarah always dreamt of teaching children to read but this was better, teaching friends. The pleasure it gave her went beyond words.

In Newgate, she had dreaded the long voyage, believing they would be at the mercy of the sailors, despite assurances from the Governor. Even she knew that with money in their pockets, sailors liked nothing more than to spend it on booze and doxies. She had seen it often enough as she collected the empty plates in the bar. She thanked God for Surgeon Carlyle keeping order and for Mrs Barnard for recommending her to him, giving her the courage to ask him questions.

Up until the time they boarded the ship Sarah's life was nothing more than a nightmare. Now she was waking up. Being confined to the ship was as natural to Sarah as it was unnatural to someone such as Helen. Sarah's world had been a series of prisons, the foundling home, the inn, Newgate and now the ship. But being on the ship was like moving from a darkened room out into a beautiful landscape, full of life and colour. It was not just the ever-changing sea, nor the birds, nor the fish she sometimes saw when looking over the side, but the possibilities.

She remembered the phrase in the Bible. 'Whereas I was blind, now I see.'

She could not put into words the feelings of quiet delight in the broadening of her horizons, the friendships she was making and the growing feeling that her life might have a purpose.

When Nora's lesson finished and they were sewing she started to talk to Sarah about the map book and asked a question she had planned the night before.

'George knows a great deal about the world. How long do you think he has been a sailor?'

'Probably since he was a boy. I wonder why he chose the sea?'

Nora smiled to herself; this was going to be easy. 'Do you think he always intends to be a sailor?'

Sarah didn't answer because she was imagining the freedom of sailing the seas and visiting so many strange countries. Why would anyone want to give it up? Not for the first time she wished she were a man and could choose such a life.

When George passed by later that afternoon he pointed out land on the horizon. 'That's South America.'

'Will we be stopping there?' asked Sarah.

'Not unless we need more provisions.'

Both girls were disappointed. They longed for fresh meat and vegetables. It was near enough five weeks since they had stopped at Cape Verde and the memory of that meal still lingered.

'Have you been there?' asked Sarah as she looked in the book for the right map. When she had found it, he pointed out roughly where they were, south of the Caribbean Islands.

'Not South America but several islands of the Caribbean. I am always troubled by the plight of the poor slaves.' George saw the bemusement on their faces.

'Over the last two hundred years, they have taken thousands, maybe millions of blacks from Africa to work the land and they live in appalling conditions. Men, women and children, were stolen from their homes and then sold to rich plantation owners who exercise absolute control over them. It distresses me to see them being treated worse than dogs. They sell them like cattle, auction them off to the highest bidder. They stand there naked and in chains, a slave market, they call it. It's sickening.

On my first ship, there was a man, Cyrus, a slave and a runaway. He made it to Canada and thought by joining a ship he could make it back home to Africa. He told me tales such that I cannot repeat. He had the marks of his mistreatment on his back and hands, where he had lost both little fingers as punishment for some wrongdoing. Only the little fingers mind, nothing that would stop him from working. Yes, Cyrus made a big impression on me.

The wicked trade is declining now, thanks to the Royal Navy. But those poor souls, I sometimes despair of the cruelty of man.'

George also had trouble with the idea of sending his fellow citizens half way around the world, sometimes for trivial offences. But he didn't voice that, after all, he was complicit.

'How long have you been at sea?' Sarah broke into his thoughts.

'I ran away to sea at twelve. My pa had died and my mother married a man who took pleasure in beating me for anything and everything. My mother just stood by, saying not a word in my defense, or lifting a finger to stop him. I cannot forgive her for that and I've never seen her since. That must be why I hate seeing others needlessly beaten.'

'So, will you always be a sailor?' asked Sarah again, probing further.

'It's all I know, miss, but when I have enough money I want to buy a small fishing boat. There are many opportunities for a young man or a family in Van Diemen's Land.' George let his eyes rest on Nora's face as he said this. She had the answer she was looking and it made her heart sing. 'Now I must go and do my work but the surgeon has offered other books for you, Miss Sarah, when you are ready.'

Sarah's face glowed with pleasure at the thought of more books but Nora hid her own smile. This time she had listened carefully to George's replies and would mull them over for the next few hours, if not throughout the night.

Part 2 - Chapter 22

Just a few days later the women came on deck after breakfast to find a scene, so ludicrous, it was hard to fathom. A sail lay propped on the deck, its hollow filled with sea water. Next to it stood a strange painted creature dressed in a long grey wig carrying a trident, professing himself to be King Neptune. By his side, lounged a sailor dressed in odd pieces of women's clothing. He wielded a brush like a gentleman might wield a sword. Some of the women cried out as they recognised their own clothes which had gone missing during the voyage.
King Neptune called for a slimy to come forth. One of a line of young sailors was pushed forward. He was made to sit in a chair facing away from the water-filled sail. The oddly dressed sailor asked his name and age, but as soon as he opened his mouth, a brush of tar, coated with the detritus from the animal pens, was painted across his face, amidst laughter from the assembled crew.

'What' going on?' demanded several of the women, ready to rebel if anyone dared to do the same to them.

'Why we are crossing the line today and King Neptune demands his due,' declared the sailor with the brush. 'I, Davy Jones, must shave these slimy pollywogs who have never crossed the line before.' And he proceeded to drag a large razor shaped wooden stick across the sailor's tar strewn face. As the sailor squirmed and tried to avoid the razor, Davy Jones shoved him backwards from the chair into the water, amongst gales of laughter from older sailors. They had been through this on their own first crossing of the equator, now they enjoyed seeing it happen to others.

'They don't mean to do it to us, do they?' asked Sarah grabbing Nora's hand.

'If they try it they will get a right kicking.' shouted a stout, tough-looking woman with arms folded tight across her chest.

Captain Ferrier assured the women that they would not be subject to the ministrations of Davy Jones. Sigh with relief, they sat on the deck, giggling at the spectacle. The next man tried to give his names and age without opening his mouth but was forced to in the end as his fellow crew and the women too cried 'louder, we can't hear you.'

Once the sailors had been through the initiation the water started to get splashed everywhere and several of the women got a soaking after all. But they did not mind. The general levity of the occasion came on a bright sunny day when the sea was flat calm and everyone was disposed to be relaxed and content. The ceremony had done its job of raising morale midway through a long voyage and it had not got out of hand, which was sometimes the case. But with the Surgeon and Captain in watchful mode, the rest of the morning passed merrily and, in honour of the occasion, another pig was slaughtered.

Amidst the gaiety, George once again took an opportunity to speak with Nora. 'There will be music and singing again this afternoon. Will you sing a song for me, just for me, sweet Nora?'

Colouring slightly, Nora dipped her head in agreement and murmured softly 'If I sing 'The Last Rose of Summer' you will know it's for you.' before she moved away to join Helen.

'I look forward to it sweetheart.' his fingers brushed the air where she had been. He felt completely bewitched by this young woman and longed each day for the chance to stroke her soft, curling hair, the colour of brazen sunsets, or to kiss her lips. Never before, had he experienced this tumult and the pain of love, but he recognised it now. His stomach was in knots, his heart hammered in his chest whenever he caught a glimpse of her and his eyes threatened tears when he thought of losing her.

Later that afternoon, as Nora sang the second verse of the song she promised, he vowed somehow to love and protect her always. With difficulty, he turned his face from hers so she should not see the tears in his eyes.

I'll not leave thee, thou lone one, to pine on the stem
Since the lovely are sleeping, go sleep thou with them
Thus kindly I scatter thy leaves o'er the bed
Where thy mates of the garden lie scentless and dead

Nora looked for him as she sang and caught his face briefly before he turned away seeing an expression which was familiar to her. She wasn't sure why and she puzzled over it for hours later that night. She wished she was more experienced in the ways of men. Oh, how she wished she could curl up in bed with her sisters and talk about the way they had imagined their future husbands. How it would be to love a man. Then it struck her where she had seen that expression before. It was the same way her father looked at her mother when she was singing a song for him. That recognition ended all doubts she had about George. He loved her and that was enough for her. A peace she had not experienced since childhood lulled her to a dreamless sleep.

She had to tell someone she was in love and there was only one person she wanted to confide in. It was Helen and Patsy's turn to clean out their dormitory but Nora asked Patsy if she would swap. Patsy only needed a little persuasion as her knees were troubling her and she welcomed not having to get down on them to scrub the floor.

When Nora knew they could not be overheard, she told Helen about her feelings for George and how he felt the same way and asked what she thought.

'You reckon I didn't notice? It's as plain as anything for all that cares to see. You think you have hidden your feelings, but I've watched you since the first day he came up to you and Sarah. Think back, Nora. I told you then how it was.'

Nora nodded in anguish. 'You think others have noticed?'

'Maybe not, it depends on where they are looking, but if I know, then plenty others could too.'

'Oh, my Lord! If the surgeon gets to know George will be in great trouble.'

'Where do you think this is going? Has he promised you anything?'

'No not really. We have so little time on our own, but I feel sure he's honourable. He's talked about buying a fishing boat in Van Diemen's Land.

'Be careful. Don't allow him any liberties and don't talk to him on your own is my advice. The next time I see you together I will look around to see if anyone else is taking an interest. Dear Nora, you are such an innocent and I would hate you getting into trouble. I suppose I am one to talk, but here is some not so bitter experience on which to call.' She picked up Davy and thrust him at Nora to make the point. Then folding him back in her arms she made him giggle by covering his face with little kisses and tickling his bare toes.

Nora thanked her friend but was now worried. The equanimity with which she gained her sleep last night was undone. In many ways, she wished she had kept silent, then at least she would have held on to that blissful feeling she had woken to.

Helen was as good as her word. When George came to deliver a new book for Sarah later that day he lingered longer than he ought. She looked carefully for those who might be taking too much of an interest in the threesome. Most of the women were engaged in their sewing, reading or chatting. The younger children were playing, watched closely by their mothers who did not allow them to stray too far or go anywhere near the open hatchways. The reverend was holding his school for older children in the stern of the ship and the surgeon was busy with his patients. That just left the crew of the ship. Those on duty seemed to be busy apart from two who were talking closely to each other. She recognised them as ones who liked to leer at the younger and prettier women. Alarmingly, she caught them glancing across to George and then they nudged each other in the ribs and laughed. She couldn't read their lips, or overhear what they said, but she was sure they had noticed George and Nora and most likely not for the first time. She decided to keep a watchful eye on them over the following days.

Part 2 - Chapter 23

Christmas approached and some of the women tried to make an effort by sewing little items for the children on board or a new apron or a decorative addition to their straw bonnet. Others were laid low by dysentery, keeping the surgeon busy.

Davy was six months old and had spent most of his life on board ship. Helen no longer swaddled him but had made him a dress out of her apron. He sat on the deck playing with scraps of cloth and a stuffed cat which Patsy made for him. Helen loved to watch him discover what his arms and legs could do and each day seemed to bring a new discovery. He was thriving from spending so much time in the fresh air and by now he was eating a little of the oatmeal burgoo as well as suckling her milk. He now had two front teeth in his top gum and had managed this without too much discomfort. She had been worried about the tales Patsy told her about teething and how her children had each suffered. But this time Davy just had two fitful nights and then two perfect white teeth appeared in his top gums to match those below.

When he was born in a dark, gloomy cell set aside for the sick at Nottingham prison, Helen fretted that he wouldn't survive the privations of the prison let alone the awful journey down to London. She had swaddled him tightly in a thin, torn blanket as she perched on top of the coach in an unseasonably wet July. But here he was laughing and cooing at her as she played peekaboo or pat-a-cake-pat-a-cake-bakers man with him. Her heart filled with love for this babe as she looked for his father's features in his chubby face. She dared not think about the future so she relished the present where each had the other's, undivided love.

Helen told her friend about the attention the sailors were paying her and George. In turn, Nora had let George know that he needed to be careful. They spent less time together and Nora was careful not to sit always with Sarah when she was on deck, so George could still answer any questions Sarah had. Nora and George watched for each other and passed occasional smiles and they began to think any danger had passed.

A muted Christmas and New Year came and went. Although the surgeon did his best to bring cheer, none of the women felt in much mood for celebration. Divine Service on Christmas Day brought back thoughts of families, and if you were very lucky a goose and a dark, rich fruit pudding. On the ship, it was the usual rations. Land had not been seen for some time and the women were sick of the endless sea. They were approaching the Southern-Ocean and they were grateful that the unrelenting heat had diminished. One day a sailor perched above in the rigging called out 'whale' and all the women and children craned their necks for a look at the beast. There was not one, but several huge bodies moving through the water and sometimes blowing out jets of water high into the air.

Sarah was entranced and stayed watching long after most of the women had gone back to their pastimes. On another day, she leant over the side of the boat to see what George pointed out as 'flying fish' and she watched as silver fish, with fins more akin to wings, leapt out of the water, gliding over the waves, until falling back into the sea and then leapt out again. They stayed with the ship for hours, as though escorting them on their journey, but then Sarah noticed larger bodies joining them. She asked a passing sailor what this new creature was. He leant over the side and told her they were porpoises and Sarah wondered if the surgeon had a book about everything that lived in the sea.

Davy had begun to find a way of moving around by a mixture of rolling and shuffling on his bottom. Helen laughed to see his antics and often chased him on her knees, making him squeal with delight. One particular day in early January, he enjoyed himself so much that Helen was late in returning to the prison deck for dinner. She and Davy were alone on deck save for a few sailors. It was a fine, breezy day and the ropes were covered with the women's laundry. Davy managed to work his way around a horizontal timber and Helen crawled close behind him when she heard voices coming from behind one of the masts. At first, it was just snatches of conversation, but then her ear picked up more understandable phrases of the conversation.

'..... letting us get near these women'

'Yes, they're all prostitutes anyway. .... why .... a little comfort? It's ... too long since we left London.'

'Anyways, we got a little arrangement with ..... women and we wondered whether ... .You could have that one you're always ...... Not that plain chit; the one who sings.'

'What are you talking about?' Helen heard George's voice grow louder and she gathered Davy up in her arms and put him to her breast so he wouldn't make a noise. She crouched lower down, hidden from view by the laundry and the sails.

'Come on, we've seen you looking ..... Well, we reckon we can break .... prison. The locks are quite flimsy and we .... the women back to our hammocks easily enough. We're planning for tomorrow night.'

Helen didn't hear George's reply as his voice became muffled.

'Well .... thought you'd be raring to have a go at her, her being so young and juicy an' all.'

'Don't even speak like that of her. You ....' Helen heard scuffles and then some final menacing words, louder than the before.

'Don't you dare tell George. We're going to have some fun and if we're stopped we will know who told, and that body will be food for fishes before we reach land and maybe that body's friend an' all.'

The men moved away. Helen sat shocked and scarcely breathing. She didn't recognise the other men, but George was named and she knew his voice. From what he said he didn't agree to join in, but what if he changed his mind? Or what if the men decided to take Nora anyway? Helen knew she must do something but what the men said scared her. If she was named as the snitch, then she or even worse, Davy, could also be food for fish. It wouldn't be difficult to conjure an accident. She only had until tomorrow night to think of something. One thing was certain, she'd not tell Nora any of this because she would get into a right panic about George being harmed. She might do something stupid that placed everyone in more danger.

She waited until the sailors left to go about their business. With her heart in her mouth, she wrapped Davy in her shawl, with just enough material remaining to go over her head. She crept towards the hatchway, praying none of the men could see her or recognise her. As she descended into gloom and safety, she breathed a sigh of relief, thankful that she had given up on wearing clogs months before.

Helen worried throughout the afternoon, chewing her nails whilst Davy slept. Eventually, she decided that the best course of action must be to let the surgeon know via a trusted third party, the reverend. He had to be of use for something she thought. The more religious of the women sought his advice on religious matters from time to time. No one would think it suspicious, only a little strange, that Helen should talk with him.

Next morning, she waited until his class with the children had finished. She would tell anyone who asked that she wanted Davy to be baptised. It was true that she worried about there not being a Catholic priest in Hobart and it was not right that he remained unbaptised. She felt that deeply. But Reverent Garrard was not the man to do it. Davy must wait for a Catholic priest.

Plucking up the courage to speak to the reverend was a big enough ordeal in itself, but she had to save Nora or even any of the other women who might be at risk. She walked to the stern as the reverend dismissed the children for dinner. She felt nervous, tongue-tied and he did not help her by looking as though he too was impatient for his dinner.

One she started to speak she found the words sped out of her mouth. He asked her to start again and this time to talk slowly. She repeated what she had heard, how frightened she was for herself, her friends and possibly George. She told him she thought George appeared reluctant.

'They say they will come tonight, sir. I think there were two or three, maybe, even more, in on it. Can you have a word with the surgeon, sir, to see if he can stop them? But please, I don't want my name given. I am frightened for my son.'

Reverend Garrard looked shocked at her tale. He realised how serious it was and how brave of this woman to tell him about it. Perhaps not all of these Irish Catholics were irredeemable. He patted her hand, absent-mindedly. He needed to tell Surgeon Carlyle at once.

Thank you for coming to me and I will not tell him your name or describe you. Do not worry about that. We will pray to God for his help in this matter.'

Helen thought a few Anglican prayers were a small price to pay for keeping her name a secret. It also looked less suspicious if she were seen praying with the Reverend. She knelt down with him for a moment and prayed for deliverance from evil. Amen to that.

That night Helen waited nervously for the prison to be locked. She could not see the gate from her cell and she did not want to arouse suspicion by standing where she could see it. But she did hear chatter move through the prison towards her. Something strange was happening. The noise came at her like a wave. 'The surgeon and the reverend are standing outside the prison and the surgeon had a pistol in his waistband,' the noise said.

'What's going on?' the women asked each other. Several stood around the gate ready to report back. The surgeon told them to go away to their beds. He sounded fierce enough for them to obey.

As nothing more seemed to be happening the women settled down to sleep. It was past midnight before voices were heard, followed by shouting and then cries. A loud shot woke the few women who still slept and a few cried or screamed in shock. For a while, it was bedlam until the reverend entered the prison to calm the women. It took several minutes for him to get to Helen's dormitory.

'Do not be afraid, ladies. The surgeon had word that some of the sailors would try to break into the prison tonight for evil purposes, which I think you can imagine. We have apprehended the culprits and the captain has been called to deal with them. Nothing else will happen tonight so get back to sleep please.' He left to pacify other women.

Helen was relieved but then saw Sarah who was shaking and moaning in terror. Her face was always pale but even in this dim light, she could see her eyes staring at the gloom but somehow not focusing on anything but what was in her imagination.

'Nora, can you fetch Sarah some water please,' said Helen. She tried to soothe Sarah by stroking her hair gently and shushing her. They both tried to get her to sip a little water, but it was no good. Patsy tried talking gently to her as you would a young child after a nightmare, but that didn't work either. Sarah lay there with her eyes wide open, unblinking, no longer shaking, but rigid, unable to move.

'One of us should sleep next to her in case she needs us. If she is no better in the morning, we must tell the surgeon. She doesn't appear to know we are here. I am really worried about her,' said Nora frowning.

Patsy, Helen and Joanna agreed, not knowing what else to do. Ann was no longer sleeping in their dormitory, as she had found space with some of the other women, who suited her better. Nora crept into Sarah's berth as Helen had Davy with her. It was a tight fit, but she held Sarah and as light began to seep into the prison deck, she managed a fitful couple of hours' sleep.

Sarah

'Oh Lord, please not again. I can't go through this again. You helped me escape it and now it's back. I can't do it. I can't. Please let me die.'

Part 2 - Chapter 24

Breakfast time arrived and the women were agog at what had happened during the night. Rumours were circulating that a man had been killed and several injured. With only one shot fired that didn't seem likely, thought Helen. She kept her own counsel and refused to join in with tittle-tattle. Helen was more concerned with Sarah who still did not speak, though her eyes were now closed. She lay prone in her berth, immobile and unaware of what was happening around her.

'I don't know whether she slept at all. I've never seen anyone like this before. It is as though her mind has gone.' Nora stroked Sarah's back but got no response.

'Nora, we must call the surgeon as soon as he opens the prison. Er ain't right.' Patsy tried to pinch Sarah's cheek quite hard but there was no cry of pain or even any fluttering of eyelids. 'Er's in some kind of trance and I ain't never seen the like of it.'

Joanna agreed to wait by the gate and as soon as the surgeon and George arrived, she begged them to come and see Sarah. Once in the dormitory the surgeon examined Sarah briefly and told George to carry her to the hospital. Nora begged that she might go with her friend and the surgeon gave his consent. George lifted Sarah in his arms then hoisted her over his shoulder, with no response from Sarah. Nora trotted along behind, too concerned about Sarah, even to take the opportunity of talking with George, beyond asking what had happened the previous night.

George turned a worried face to Nora. 'There was an attempted break-in to the prison, but the surgeon got to hear of it and caught them in the act. That's all I know.'

Nora was surprised at his tone and demeanour; he seemed to be very ill at ease and remained silent until they reached the hospital where Sarah was put to bed by Jenny. George left to return to the prison and Nora watched him go with even greater concern.

'Ah, poor thing! Whatever's happened to her?'

Nora gathered her thoughts together and told Jenny about the night's events and Sarah losing her senses.

'I'm sure the Surgeon will help her. I do hope he can because she's a good girl, very quiet to be sure but her heart's in the right place. I remember how she cared for Sally, the girl who died of the smallpox. Sarah talked to her and prayed for her all night. I couldn't sleep and heard her talking. She were that gentle with her. Such a good nurse she'd be, given half a chance.'

Nora looked blankly at Jenny. Sarah never told her much about what she was doing with the surgeon in the week before they left England, beyond saying that she just washed and fed the patients. The way she said it had sounded trivial and almost tiresome and Nora was glad she hadn't been chosen for the task. But yet again Sarah continually surprised her. There was so much she didn't talk about and Nora wondered what else she had kept to herself. She grasped her friend's hand, pleading with her to wake up. That was how the surgeon found them an hour later.

'Miss, can you stand to one side so I can examine her properly and while I'm doing that tell me what happened to her last night.'

Nora recounted how Sarah reacted to the shouts and the gunfire and then proceeded to give Sarah's history as far as she knew it. She told him how frightened Sarah had been when she entered the prison, and how she scarcely spoke a word for the first three months.

'Sarah seemed so much better, lately, less afraid. In Newgate, she would jump at her own shadow. Please make her better,' Nora pleaded.

The surgeon listened patiently. Then, turning to Sarah, he examined her thoroughly, prodding and pinching to try and get any response, without success.

'I believe she is in a kind of hysterical stupor. I have read about such cases, of course, but never seen it. I must warn you it may make take time for her to recover.' Turning to Jenny he said, 'We will try cold baths and if that doesn't work I will apply a blister, which I believe can be beneficial' He turned back to Nora saying, 'You can stay here a while for now. Come and visit her each day. Talk to her; your voice may help to rouse her.'

Nora thanked the surgeon, although his words did nothing to relieve her anxiety. He did not sound confident that Sarah would recover quickly. She drew up a chair took Sarah's hand and began to talk. Nora prattled on about anything that came into her mind; the voyage; what life would be like in Van Diemen's Land. She asked Sarah questions praying she would answer then glancing sadly at her face when she didn't. Nora must have been doing this for twenty minutes when she heard the Surgeon's angry voice through an open door.

'I am very disappointed in you. You have misplaced my trust, George. Could you not have come to me and told me rather than let me hear about it from Reverend Garrard? He at least did the right thing.'

Nora was horrorstruck. George was in trouble and she stopped talking to Sarah so she could listen. George spoke softly but she could just manage to hear him say.

'I am truly sorry sir, but they threatened me. I know I should have told you but I was concerned not only about myself.'

'Who else did they threaten?'

'I'd rather not say, sir.'

'I can't make you. But you are hiding something and I won't tolerate it. We caught the culprits red-handed but even now the captain won't punish them properly, so I don't know if they will try it again. Will you tell me if you hear of it?'

George remained silent for a few seconds but then said, 'I doubt they will try to involve me again sir. Do they know who gave them away? Will you tell them it wasn't me? I am afraid of what they will do if they think it was me that gave them away.'

'Pah! I will not waste more time on you, you lily-livered scoundrel. You are dismissed, I will ask Captain Ferrier for another sailor to take your place as my assistant.'

As George left, the door slammed behind him, kicked shut by the furious surgeon. Meanwhile, Nora sat in shock, her cheeks flaming and her heart hammering in her chest. George was told about the plan and did nothing. Was he a coward as the surgeon suggested? She didn't know what to think. She tried to bring her thoughts back to Sarah but sat there with tears rolling down her face, almost in a stupor herself. When the surgeon came in and said he was going to try a cold bath for Sarah, Nora was relieved to leave.

'Don't worry too much, miss, we will do everything to help your friend,' he said, mistaking the cause of her tears.

Nora wiped her eyes on her sleeve and stumbled back up to the deck. She found Helen and collapsed distraught into her lap, narrowly missing Davy who was sitting chewing on an old piece of thick rope at Helen's feet.

'Oh, my Lord! She's not died, has she?' cried Helen, in consternation.

'No, she's just the same. The surgeon says she could stay like that for days and he's going to try a cold bath and a blister to rouse her. But it's George I am worried for as well. He's in trouble for not warning the surgeon. Surgeon Carlyle called him a coward, Helen, and I can't but think that he is. If he knew about the plan why wouldn't he tell on them?'

'Shush, shush. This isn't something we should talk of here. There's too many folk around. I need to tell you something where we can't be overheard.'

Nora accepted that reluctantly and sat staring at nothing in particular. Thoughts about Sarah and George tumbled around her brain making her head ache until she felt Helen's hand on her and realised that it was time for the midday meal.

The rancid meal was quickly over. It could not be savoured, just chewed and swallowed. Chew, swallow, grimace, the food tasted awful, but they got it down. In these last few weeks of the journey, the women longed for any fresh food. Had they been offered a crust of warm soft bread and cool water from a well, Helen thought she would have fought over it.

Patsy and Joanna wanted to hear how Sarah was, although there was not much to tell beyond what they already knew. Nora told them that she intended to visit her that afternoon and report to them if there was any change. Helen said she would clear away the crumbs and clean the table. Patsy and Joanna drifted off back to the deck and Nora begged Helen to tell what she knew.

Helen sat down with Davy, looking around in case there was anyone within listening range and told Nora about the conversation overheard two days ago. She explained that she caught snatches and had to piece it together.

'But you did hear him being threatened?'

'Yes, and I think so were you, because they knew he liked you. I feel sure he was trying to protect you, by not speaking. So, don't be too hard on him.'

'So, who do you think told the reverend? Did other people overhear?'

Helen was dreading this question. Should she own up and put her life, or even worse, Davy's life in danger? Would Nora believe her if she denied it was her? She looked at Nora's face to see if she could detect any suspicious look, but there was only puzzlement.

'They must have tried to involve another sailor, or perhaps they talked about it too openly and someone else got to hear.' Helen decided to bluff her way out of the situation. She would not risk her son. Nora's face cleared.

'Yes, you are probably right. We have to be careful, don't we? It is not something to discuss openly, or others might get the idea one of us told. Don't worry I'll not speak of it again.'

Helen didn't dare breathe a sigh of relief, until Nora left, saying she would go and visit Sarah. Davy sat on her lap playing with a strand of her hair which had worked loose. Helen laughed happily as he tugged at it and tried lamely to tuck it away out of reach when she heard a scream and then a cry of pain.

She leapt to her feet, placing Davy on the floor of the cell and closing the gate behind her she ran to the main gate of the prison, scrambling up the ladder, almost tripping on her skirts.

Nora was on the floor and two other women were kicking her. As she got closer she recognised the two by their short, cropped hair. It was

Jane and Lizzie. Helen launched herself at Jane and bowled her over onto the floor, hitting her as hard as she could in the stomach to wind her. Then before Lizzie had a chance to react she sprang up from the floor and jumped on Lizzie's back, grabbing at her nose and scratching her face. With a howl of pain, Lizzie tried to shake her off, forgetting Nora, who managed to get to her feet and grab one of Lizzie's arms, twisting her wrist as hard as she could.

The noise of the fighting women drew a few of the other women down from the deck above to watch and shout encouragement to whoever they fancied. No one came to separate them until the surgeon arrived in time to see Jane on all fours groaning but still trying to hit Nora. Lizzie, having shaken off Helen, at last, was kicking out at both of the younger girls who in their turn landed occasional punches on the older women. Blood was pouring from Lizzie's face from the many scratches that Helen had inflicted and also from her nose which was bent, most likely broken.

Bellowing in anger, the surgeon waded in and calling for help he separated the fighting women, receiving several blows himself before he got them to stand red-faced, scowling and panting. The reverend and a couple of sailors arrived with handcuffs and all four were quickly cuffed and led away to the hospital to have their cuts and scratches tended and also to face a furious, weary surgeon.

Hearing Helen scream that Davy had been left alone in the prison the reverend sent for Patsy to rescue and tend to him.

Part 2 - Chapter 25

The surgeon attended first to Lizzie, the most obviously injured. Her bent nose grew puffier by the minute and her face was scratched and bleeding badly. She had several minor bruises on her arms, but those would fade quickly. As the surgeon tended to her nose and face he asked her what the fight was about and who started it. Lizzie stayed mute. He was fast losing patience with these women and demanded to know what had happened, but still, Lizzie stayed silent. She was no snitch; others might be but she would never talk. Despairing of any answer from Lizzie he called for a sailor to take her away and to lock her in an adjacent cabin.

Nora came in next. She had been kicked once or twice in the ribs before curling up in a ball to protect herself and now she struggled to breathe. The surgeon examined her and found her ribs to be bruised but not broken. He ordered bed rest in the hospital next to Sarah which delighted Nora. She was easily able to tell the surgeon that she had no idea why Lizzie and Jane jumped on her. They had lain in wait for her obviously, and one shouted 'It's your fault, you mealy-mouthed, tell-tale piece of Irish shite.' But she couldn't say those words to the Surgeon; it would have been just too embarrassing to repeat them.

Jane, like Lizzie, would not talk and was also led away to be locked up in the cabin. Helen had just a few minor bruises and scratches. When asked about the fight she told the Surgeon that she did not see how it started but heard screaming and ran to find Nora on the floor being kicked and did what any friend would do.

'I had to look after her you see, it was two to one and Nora's no fighter.'

'And you are?'

'Only when it can't be avoided, and to protect myself and my family. On this ship, Nora is my family.'

'Well, you seem to have fought with some result, judging by Lizzie's injuries.'

'She deserved it,' Helen said defiantly, though inside she was remembering his threat about reduced rations on that first day when she stood up to Anne.

Surgeon Carlyle sighed and told her she was to go back to her son. Helen couldn't leave fast enough and once out of the door, she grinned and almost ran to find Davy.

A few minutes later the surgeon sought out the reverend and asked him if he had any knowledge of why the women had been fighting.

'I can only suppose that the older women were those hoping to have relations with the sailors last night. But the sailors were caught, and the women looked to blame someone.'

'But Nora wasn't the one who told you, was she? If that had been the case I might have dealt with George a little more leniently. He could have told her to save himself a beating, though I would still think him a coward.'

'No, it wasn't Nora. But from what I have heard George may have been trying to protect her. Reading between the lines I think he is smitten with her, and she was threatened somehow, although she did not know it.'

'The stupid fool! I should never have let him talk with Sarah and Nora. I suppose I let that happen. She is a pretty young thing and her singing voice is quite divine.'

'A gift from God indeed. It is a shame she is not of our religion.'

Later the surgeon considered the events of the last twenty-four hours. The voyage was in its final weeks but was now dragging on and the women had little to look forward to when they arrived. They would be sent out to work almost immediately, some never to see the friends they had made on the ship again. The population of Van Diemen's Land was around only twelve thousand, but spread throughout an island the size of Ireland and still largely unexplored. With burgeoning communities, both in the north and south there was widespread demand for female servants.

He hoped that the majority of the women had learnt the benefits of cleanliness and sober living on the ship. Some may even have been receptive to the religious sermons and now be prepared to live a decent life. There were, of course, others, like Jane and Lizzie who were, in his opinion, the very worst kind of women, wanton and worthless. It was unlikely that they would last five minutes in a respectable household and were destined to spend most of their time in the female factory, causing mayhem. The only option would be to split them up.

'Ah what if we could take one of them on to Port Jackson, then they really would be parted' he thought. He resolved to ask the governor for permission to do that on arrival in Hobart Town. Meanwhile, he decided to keep the two locked up and out of mischief for the remainder of the voyage.

Leaving all that aside, for now, it was time to visit his patients in the hospital. Nora was sleeping in her bed but looked comfortable. Sarah had been given a cold bath without effect. Her eyes remained closed and her limbs stiff and unresponsive. Jenny told the surgeon that she had not uttered a word or even a sound since being brought there that morning, even when being immersed in cool sea water.

' In that case, we ought to try cupping. Make her ready, please.'

The surgeon went to find the box of metal cups as Jenny loosened Sarah's petticoat. On his return, he took out a cup, then taking some cotton he immersed it in alcohol before setting it alight and grabbing hold of it with forceps placed it in the cup, drawing out the oxygen. He deftly removed it and then placed the cup on Sarah's chest. Her skin was drawn up into the vacuum almost immediately. Sarah moaned, but did not open her eyes. He repeated it again several times, but there was no further reaction.

'It is a good sign that she moaned. I wonder what her life has been to bring her to this?' he spoke quietly to himself.

'I hope you can make her better, sir. She's a real, good lass.'

'She's a very unusual girl, that's for sure. I will come by this evening and see them both. Pray for some improvement, if not I will try some Spanish fly on her skin. Maybe a blister will get a reaction.

'I pray so, Sir.'

He still had to talk to the captain about the behaviour of his sailors and try to persuade him to punish them, which Captain Ferrier seemed reluctant to do. What a day this was turning out to be. Reaching Hobart Town would be most welcome indeed.

Part 2 - Chapter 26

Sarah

I'm burning, My skin's burning. Oh, God, it hurts. I can hear voices above me. Am I in hell now? Forgive me Lord, please not the pit! I tried to be good, truly I did. I was led into evil. You must know I never wanted it. I wanted to escape but didn't know how. Where was I to go? Who could have helped? There was no one then. Mrs Barnard, please pray for me. Nora, please pray for me.

Part 2 - Chapter 27

As Jenny bathed Sarah's face in cool water, she thought she detected a slight change. It might have been an eye movement behind a closed lid; maybe the slight twitch of an eyelash or a whispered sound. She wasn't sure. It could have been all three but they were so slight as to be almost unnoticeable.

When Nora woke from her sleep she was given some tea and plum duff, though her ribs and stomach were now very sore and she did not really feel like eating.

'Come on dear, you must try to eat. The surgeon is a great believer in food helping people get better. Why, that poor lass who lost her baby, right back at the start of the journey, he's fed her Donkin's preserved meat every day and she's on the mend at last. I didn't think she would survive, she were that poorly.'

'How is Sarah?' Nora couldn't see Sarah's face from her prone position.

'I think the cupping might do the trick. The surgeon came back this evening to apply it. I'm sure she moved a tiny bit not long after it was applied and she moaned too. When I first watched him doing that to women, I couldn't believe it would do any good. Why would it help, I wondered? But what do I know about medicine? I never had a doctor when my wee mites were sickly. There wasn't the money. It was God's will if they lived or died.'

'How many children did you leave behind, Jenny?'

'Two living, but they are near grown up now. My sister-in-law says she will look out for them, my husband being in his grave these five years past. They are both in service, so I have no need to worry about them.'

Nora said nothing. Being in service had been her own downfall but perhaps Jenny's children would not be as stupid as she had been. She lay back and Jenny left her to doze some more. She was vaguely aware that the surgeon came back to check on her and Sarah. But it was dark now and a sound awakened her. She listened for a moment and then found she was in urgent need of the privy. Gingerly she got up from the bed and, wincing in pain, she peered in the gloom for a night bucket. After relieving herself she made her way back to the bed, but stopped short when she heard a sound from Sarah's bed. Sarah's hands were pulling ineffectively at the dressing on her chest and her mouth was moving but Nora could hear no words. She bent lower but cried out herself as her bruised ribs objected. But the cry made Sarah's eyes shoot open and though barely audible, Nora heard.

'No, no, please don't. Nora, pray for me.'

Nora stood in shock at hearing her name. Then despite her own pain she dropped to her knees beside Sarah and grasped her hand. She could only think of the 'Lord's prayer' to begin with and repeated it several times before she remembered Mrs Barnard reciting the twenty-third psalm. She recollected how it had calmed them all in Newgate and began to recite it, finding she remembered the words as well as the scene. Sarah and she had read it together several times and somehow it was etched into her brain.

Jenny found Nora, asleep, the next morning, sitting up beside Sarah's bed, still holding her hand. Sarah looked less rigid and more peaceful than she had been when brought into the hospital.

Nora woke to hear Jenny instructing her to get back to bed. Every movement was agonising. Her body was both stiff and sore and later when the surgeon examined her, she saw how the bruises were turning indigo and violet all over her chest, stomach and the backs of her legs.

'You really are lucky not to have any broken bones. I am concerned that there might be some internal injuries. Have you managed to eat and drink or pass a motion?'

Nora told him she had little appetite and had only passed water. He ordered up a dish of preserved meat to tempt her and told her that she should stay in the hospital until he was satisfied her internal organs were working as they should, and she could breathe without difficulty.

Helen came to visit that afternoon, having been given permission by the surgeon. Finding Sarah still not woken from her stupor, she gave her a kiss and tried to rouse her, but soon gave up and turned to Nora.

'You should hear the gossip in the prison. He hasn't let Lizzie or Jane back, so there are all sorts of rumours about what he has done with them and why we were fighting. I just told them to mind their own business. How long is he going to keep you in here?'

'I don't know but as soon as I get my appetite back and can use the privy. He said something about breathing too. To tell you the truth, I wouldn't mind staying here. You should taste the meat I got for dinner, it wasn't anything like that salted meat they give us and not really like fresh meat either, but it was that tasty. Jenny says it comes out of a tin, not a barrel.'

'You are making me so jealous.' Helen smiled and then gestured towards Sarah. 'It doesn't look like there's much change with Sarah.'

'I am praying she will come out of it.' Nora proceeded to tell her what happened the night before. She also thanked Helen for saving her from an even worse beating.

'Jane and Lizzie seemed to think it was me that told on the sailors, but I suppose they think that George told me. I wish they would let me talk to him to find out what happened and his part in it.'

'You will be kept apart. The surgeon must know who was mixed up in it. I saw George today and he asked how you were. He looked that upset and before I answered he was told to move away. Most likely they are keeping a close watch on him.'

Nora frowned and she felt tearful. She was already missing his attentions.

'What if we can't talk before we leave the ship? What if this is the last time I will see him. Oh, I do love him, Helen, despite what's happened.'

Helen shushed her friend and carefully gave her the gentlest of hugs before leaving with a promise to visit on the next day.

Nora and Sarah had been in the hospital for three days. Nora was getting stronger and her bruises were beginning to turn yellow, a good sign the surgeon told her. It still hurt to breathe and she found it more comfortable to sit propped up, rather than lying flat. Her appetite was getting back to normal and in another few days, he thought she could leave if she continued to improve. She found she was getting very bored without the companionship she had got used to on the ship. Helen visited every day and brought her sewing so that she had something to do, besides worrying and praying for Sarah.

With no sign of real improvement, the surgeon had resorted to applying Spanish fly onto Sarah's chest to raise a blister. Her skin was sore and angry looking. Nora watched as the surgeon drained off the liquid in the hope it would dispel the evil from her body, likewise, the emetic he gave her to purge the poisons inflicting her soul. Sarah's body went rigid whenever the surgeon was treating her or when Jenny struggled with a tube to get liquid into her mouth and then into her stomach.

'She's going to waste away if she doesn't wake soon. I can only get a little soup down her and I'm not sure the soup I can make from dried vegetables is good enough. I just wish we could get some fresh meat and vegetables to make a nourishing broth.' Jenny asked Nora to come and try to calm her, but it rarely helped as Sarah resisted all efforts to make her take sustenance.

She became peaceful only when being bathed or left alone during the day but as the darkness grew she became more and more restive and anxious. Nora got out of her bed several times to hold her hand and talk to her and pray for her but without much effect. Sarah still did not speak or show any awareness of where she was.

The weather was deteriorating as they crossed the southern Indian Ocean from the Cape of Good Hope towards Van Diemen's Land. The small ship jerked wildly in huge waves bringing many of the passengers to their knees with nausea. Those who had not suffered before, found they were no match for these waves. The prison was awash with sickening women and children. There was little point and no room to bring them into the hospital, the surgeon decided they must ride it out.

But one night, a storm, more violent than any before, began to blow. The howl of the wind sounded like the very devil and it froze Nora's blood. The wooden spars, creaking loudly, juddered until Nora, felt sure they were going to snap. The hatches fastened tight against the sea, did not keep out all the water. Instead, it seeped through the timbers of the ship, dampening everything in its path. Nora trembled in the dark, praying for the ship to survive. Despite the wind, she could hear women from the prison, as frightened as she, screeching and screaming, as though tormented banshees. It went on for hours. The ship rose up on enormous waves, give a huge shudder and then fall back into the void left by the wave. When it fell, the sound was shocking. Everything moved and groaned, as though being torn apart, timber by timber. Each time it did this the women shrieked in terror fearing the ship was about to turn over and all of them cast into the angry sea.

Nora knew she would be thrown from her bed if the storm worsened and there was no chance of sleep. She got out of bed, still wincing from the sharp pain in her ribs, and made her way over to Sarah. As she did so, there was an almighty crash and she hung on to Sarah's bed in panic, just in time to stop Sarah from being thrown out to the floor.

'Oh dear lord, are we all to drown?' cried Nora terrified.

'Nora, you shouldn't be here. The devil shouldn't have taken you.'

'Sarah you're awake! Thank the Lord! I worried you would never wake again.'

The ship rose up again and then settled so deeply in the trough that Nora's stomach fell quickly and she retched.

'Why would he take you? You're so good and innocent.'

Nora retched again and when her stomach settled asked Sarah what on earth she was talking about.

'Hell, we're in hell, aren't we? The darkness, the screaming, the burning and the choking, where else could we be?'

'Oh Sarah, we aren't in hell, we're still on the blasted ship and there's a violent storm. Can't you hear the wind tossing the ship around like a toy boat? I am so scared.'

Sarah was silent. Was it true? She didn't remember much, only terror, and what she took to have been the devil and his female helper, delighting in tormenting her with their instruments of pain.

'If you are right, Nora, tell me what happened. I recognise this place.'

'It's the hospital on the ship and we are both patients here, Sarah. You have been so ill we despaired of you.'

Nora clutched Sarah's bed as the ship veered first one way then violently another. Anything loose rolled back and forth across the floor.

'Sarah, we must get on the floor. Let's pull our pillows and blankets off the beds and try to wedge ourselves under that heavy desk over there. Otherwise, we are going to get hurt.'

Nora helped her friend get out of bed, but Sarah was so weak that Nora struggled to help her get under the desk. Once accomplished, she tottered off to fetch blankets. She managed to make a nest of sorts for them both and wrapped Sarah up tight. Putting her arm around Sarah's thin body, she began to tell her what had been happening from the moment the shot was fired. The story took her mind off the ship's battle with the elements. At least if we are going to drown, then we'll be together she thought.

'And they were only trying to feed me?' Sarah asked as Nora finished the story.

'Yes, and I tried too but you struggled and resisted so much. Can you think, Sarah, why all this happened? Why did you collapse and appear dead to the world?'

'I'm so tired Nora. Let me sleep now.' Sarah settled back in the blankets and closed her eyes.

'You can sleep in this storm?' Nora was outraged. Here was Sarah back from the dead and she just wanted to sleep and how could anyone sleep when the ship might go down at any minute. But Sarah refused to open her eyes again and after a while, Nora heard her breathing change and an occasional gentle snuffle as sleep overcame her.

The wind was abating slightly and Nora, resigned to getting no more out of Sarah, gave in and tried to sleep. Perhaps they would be saved for another day and God did not yet want to claim their souls.

Part 2 - Chapter 28

She was astonished when she woke the following morning to find that not only was the ship still sailing, but Sarah was sitting up in bed and drinking tea, supplied by an overjoyed Jenny. Nora climbed out from under the desk, pulling her blankets with her. Jenny helped her make up her own bed and then gave her some tea and gruel, whispering that their prayers had worked.

The surgeon was inundated with cases of seasickness and bruised female bodies. The sailors, in their hammocks, rode out the storm in relative comfort, but women had tumbled from beds or fallen as they made their way to the privy.

'I think you are fit enough to go back to the prison.' The surgeon told Nora after the rush had subsided.

'Please sir, just one more night.' Nora begged and coughed piteously. She wanted to talk to Sarah privately, wondering when she would have another opportunity.

'Very well, one more night.' he glanced at Sarah and understood her motives. Did they think he wouldn't know what they were up to? He smiled to himself.

'And as for you, Miss Sarah, you gave us a fright. You are very weak and need some building up. I think you will be with us until we land in a fortnight or so.

'Are we so near?' they both chorused. He nodded and left them.

After supper, when Sarah had managed to eat a little of the tinned meat and some pea soup, Nora asked her to talk about what had happened to make her go into that stupor.

'I don't want to talk about it.'

'Oh, but you must. It is always better to get these things out in the open then we can help you.' replied Nora firmly. 'Fear can tie your stomach and brain up in knots. I know that. But, Sarah, it almost killed you. Think about that. What if it happens again?'

'You don't think the shame of it will kill me? I might prefer death.'

'Whatever do you mean?' cried Nora shocked. 'I know you, Sarah. You're a good person, and nothing you say will make me believe otherwise.'

'It's not me but the deeds of others which shames me, defiles me and makes me hate myself. I can't live with it, Nora, I have tried. I began to think I might have a chance when we set sail because the sea is so cleansing and the air, this clean, pure air we breathe now, gave me hope. But it's all gone. I am back in the prison I have made for myself.'

Sarah looked in such despair that Nora got out of her bed and climbed in with Sarah, holding her and stroking her hair. They lay there together, Sarah sobbed and Nora held her, kissing her tear-streaked face.

'I lied. You remember when I told you my story? I didn't tell you the whole truth.'

'Don't worry about that, just try and tell me now.'

'There was another girl at the tavern, Rose, a bit older than me, maybe fifteen. She had been the skivvy before me, even came from a foundling home. Not mine because I didn't recognise her. She wore a red dress which barely covered her bosom and her face, so painted, it looked like a mask.

At first, she was quite kind to me but she changed. As soon as the bar opened she'd be in there chatting to the drinkers and encouraging them to buy more and more. They pawed at her and it sickened me to see it. Sometimes she went upstairs with a man and did not return for fifteen minutes. I only took the food in and she served it to them, just pie and mash, that's all we did. But she got harder and colder towards me. I think she was unhappy. She had a smile painted on her face, bright red lips fixed into a smile, but her eyes were dead.

One day I heard her crying and then heard a slap. I poked my head round the door to the bar and she was there with the innkeeper's wife. The wife was real angry and tears streaked Rose's face, the red paint running over her chin making her look like a sad clown.

'You should have told me before this,' the mistress said. 'It might be too late now. You'd better come with me.' And she dragged her up the stairs, struggling and crying at the same time.

I went back to the kitchen and started on another load of potatoes, but not long after I heard such screams as you wouldn't believe. I was frozen to the floor. The innkeeper came in and caught my face with the flat of his hand.

'Get a move on, you idle wretch. Take no notice of that screaming. Rose has a stomach ache and you'd think she was dying, but she ain't. She'll be as right as rain tomorrow.'

But she wasn't and nor the next day. I asked the old cook and she told me that she'd been with child and they'd tried to get rid of it but Rose died instead. I felt sad for her, but I didn't know what was coming.'

Nora gasped and said, 'Oh no Sarah, they didn't,' but couldn't finish the sentence.

'About two days later, the wife gave me some soap and told me to wash everything, including my hair. She came out to the pump and watched me wash. Then she sat me down in the bar, it was early, before the drinkers arrived, and she gave me a drink, gin she called it. I spat it out and she grabbed me by the hair and forced it down my throat, then another and another until I was senseless.' Sarah breathed hard and willed herself to continue. 'When I woke up I was on a bed dressed in Rose's dress, but it was rucked up to my waist and this old man was on top of me. It hurt and I struggled. He may have been old but he was strong. He pinned my arms down, said that he liked a bit of spirit and rode me like a horse. I was screaming and crying but he just carried on, biting my breast and I was sure he was tearing my insides until at last he cried out and shuddered. Then he got off me, there was blood on the sheet, and before I had chance to cover myself he nodded at the blood, opened the door, where the wife was waiting, dropped two gold sovereigns into her hand and said, 'very satisfactory' and left.'

Nora didn't say a word. She was too shocked but held Sarah tighter. They were both crying. A minute or two went by when Sarah gathered her courage to finish off the story,

'She told me that my life as a skivvy was at an end and I should be pleased. Life as a whore would be easier, especially in a good tavern such as theirs. It would help if I had more meat on my bones, but she would feed me up. No more scraps for me, I might even get a pie to myself,' Sarah grimaced in bitterness.

'Then she talked about painting me to make me prettier. I wanted to choke, to retch. I just kept thinking of Rose's eyes. She ignored my horror, for it must have shown on my face, but she didn't care, She banged on about learning to be nice to the customers. If I was good at my job, then I could earn enough money to put by for my old age. They wouldn't get two guineas again for me, that was only a virgin price, but maybe half a crown, and they would let me keep sixpence. Rose never got to be old and probably not the one before her neither, I should think. Had she no idea that I would rather drown than become a whore!

The wife went off to celebrate the golden guineas by getting so drunk she didn't get up the next day. I put on my old rags and went back to the kitchen vowing never to wear Rose's dress, but I didn't know how else to rebel. I was still trying to puzzle out how to escape when the innkeeper caught me. He said now I'd been plucked he could have me whenever he wanted for free. The rest you know. It was John who killed him but I was glad, so glad, may God forgive me.

With her out of the way and the innkeeper dead, it left John to run the tavern. He told me he planned to marry the widow and then he would own it. I think he had been looking for the opportunity to get rid of the innkeeper and took it when he could. But I don't blame him. He saved me from that life.'

'You really are safe now, Sarah.'

'Do you think so, Nora? I don't. What if we are assigned to someone like that innkeeper? Will we be protected? I fear not and I can't go back to that. I will not,' she paused and then said, 'Nora I'm tired, will you stay with me until I'm asleep.'

'Of course, I will and please don't be afraid, Sarah. I am sure it will be alright.' Nora was horrified by Sarah's story but could not think the same thing would happen in Van Diemen's Land. They wanted maids and wives, not whores, didn't they? By all accounts, they would soon find out, only fourteen more days until landfall. Despite the summer heat of a January night in the southern hemisphere, Nora shivered.

Part Three

Part 3- Chapter 1

February 1825 Van Diemen's Land

'Land Ahoy'

Word flew around the prison and the women, eager and relieved to see their new home, scrambled up to the top deck and rushed to the port side to view inhospitable mountains and a rugged coastline. Nora felt Sarah's bony hand grasp hers as they gazed at the land to the north. Sarah had been let out of the hospital the day before thinner, paler and even quieter than before, but alive and for that Nora was grateful.

By the next morning, tiny islands with sheer cliffs came into view and then disappeared. Nowhere was there any sign of human habitation, no distant town lined the shore, not so much as the smoke from a cooking fire, let alone a cottage. Nora thought it forbidding and began to get as frightened as Sarah evidently was.

In the afternoon, the ship sailed into a wide channel and they saw trees, thousands of them, so many trees but strange, not recognisable by colour or shape. Through the dense bush, tall, straight, pale-barked trees appeared ghostly and forbidding. Long fingers of dead white branches intermingled with parasol-shaped canopies of a yellow-greenish hue. No English oak or Scots pine here, no ash, no beech but giant eucalypts, strange pines and tree ferns overhung by steamy clouds.

To Nora's relief, smaller boats were glimpsed at last. As they drew nearer fishermen and whalers gawped at the display of women lining the deck and then there was pandemonium.

It is debatable who cheered the loudest or gave the rudest gestures. Certainly, those women, who had been on the town, in common parlance, did not fit the surgeon's view of demure womanhood. He began to force the women away from the edge of the ship and back to the prison with the help of several sailors, grinning with anticipation at the pleasures of Hobart Town.

Sometime during the night, the journey ended and the movement of the ship ceased. Towards dawn, Nora and Patsy woke up and wondered what was wrong, used as they were to the motion of the ship. It seemed unnaturally still with only the slightest creaking from the masts, now bare of sails, and the familiar cry of gulls.

At seven in the morning, the Surgeon entered the prison to find it subdued. Women sat around in small groups, holding hands, worried that friendships cemented during the voyage were now under threat. Many were in tears dreading the thought of being split apart, not to see each other again. Even staying in touch would be difficult for few could write.

Nora sat with Sarah who was mute with misery. She was physically better but terrified at the thought of losing Nora, her lifeline, and without her, she doubted she would keep her sanity.

Those with children, like Helen, felt sick with anxiety and, as soon as the Surgeon appeared, bombarded him with questions about keeping their children with them. He couldn't or wouldn't answer them and they clutched their little ones to their chests, weeping. As children do, they picked up on their mother's distress and started bawling noisily.

The Surgeon stood there. This was even worse than he had feared. On male convict ships, there was none of this raw emotion when they arrived, sullenness, bravado yes, but not such fear and sorrow. The men had done with that on leaving the mother country. He put his hands up and asked for calm. Slowly the women and then the children quietened, turning tear-stained faces toward him.

Some were still whimpering but the surgeon was able to speak and be heard at last. He told them that they would not leave the ship that day. First the sick must be taken to the hospital in Hobart Town. He would accompany them and then report to the Governor.

'Officials will come onboard to ask you questions. Answer them truthfully. Keep your tags safe for when you want to reclaim your boxes. But for now, I wish you all well and may God be with you.'

His job with them was done. He had written a brief report on their behaviour and maintained his journal of the voyage. Now he could look forward to visiting his estate in New South Wales and introducing it to the merino sheep he had on board.

The women, given a further day's reprieve, gratefully thanked him. And so the day progressed. The port officer boarded, followed by the Colonial Secretary and the women were mustered for his examination. Satisfied they had no complaints about their treatment and that their general health was good he left and for the last evening on board the women had time to say their own farewells.

Sarah sat glued to Nora's side, silent but with fears tumbling through her head. How could she live without her friend? She doubted it was possible. Helen feasted her eyes on David. Please, God, they would let her keep him. She spent the night in silent prayer.

The following day, the Muster Master and the Principal Superintendent of Convicts arrived. Provided with the surgeon's indent of prisoners and his conduct report, they examined each woman as to their previous history, their trade and their crime. The authorities appeared to have enough information about them already to make sure the women knew it was not worth their while to lie.

Written down in black and white, their crimes and their conduct laid bare for the judgment of those in charge. To this would be added the least infringement of colonial standards of behaviour. Drink too much, it would be noted and punished; likewise, an insolent comment; a refusal to do a duty, or engage in a sexual relationship; none of which was a crime but would be treated as such. This they had yet to discover.

Once their details had been written down they were sent to the deck to wait for a boat to take them ashore. Helen was the first of the three friends to leave the prison. She hugged her weeping friends tightly, wished them luck and grasping Davy made her way up to the deck, blinking in the warm, summer sunlight. What she saw in front of her was a small town, scarcely more than a village, rising up a gentle hill. Beyond were patches of cultivated land and yet further still a tree-clad rocky mountain, she would come to know as Mount Wellington. Solid handsome looking buildings surrounded the harbour in front of her. She turned slowly around, noticing other sailing ships in the bay and smaller vessels plying back and forth amidst the sparkling water. But one thing was certain she had never seen such a beautiful place. Yes, there was smoke and all the smells of a fishing port but it was the light, the colours, the shining water and the untouched landscape beyond which grabbed a sudden hold of her heart and gave her hope.

They should have called this place New Ireland, she thought. How it reminded her of Cork and her untroubled early childhood. 'Whatever happens next, remember this feeling,' she said to herself and then to Davy.

'This could be a good place to bring up a family. We just need to find the right man, a husband for me and a father for you, someone strong who will fight for us both.' And she kissed Davy's head softly before being hurried along to climb into a tender that would take them both ashore to a new life.

It was Nora and Sarah's turn to leave. They stood on the deck still holding hands, amazed at the sight before them. Used to London they could not believe how small Hobart Town was. If they both stayed in Hobart there would be no need to write letters, it was so small they would surely bump into each other often. Sarah looked at the forbidding mountain and the surrounding bush and faced with the reality, rather than woodcuts from a book, suddenly became terrified and grasped Nora's hand tighter.

Nora glimpsed George in the rowing boat coming towards the ship. He had delivered a cargo of women to the quayside and was now returning for the next boatful. She had not seen more than a fleeting sight of him over the last few days. Once she thought she had caught him smiling at her but he hurried off at someone's command. Faced with never seeing him again, she despaired, her whole body heavy with sorrow.

Guided to the side of the ship, Nora climbed down the rope ladder into the waiting boat below. A hand grasped hers to help her into the boat. As she removed her hand, a tiny slip of paper stuck in her palm and she knew that it was a note from George, who was now helping Sarah. Fearful of being seen, her fist closed around the scrap of paper. She would read it later but her spirits rose and she dared to smile at him as he lifted Sarah into the gently rocking boat. Nora smiled all the way to the shore, wishing the journey was longer than the few minutes it took, because from where she was sitting she could look at his face as he did hers. The last she saw of him was rowing back for the next group. But he had held her once more while lifting her out of the boat and then steadied her as she stumbled, unused to dry land. That same tingling feeling gripped them both as their hands touched for the last time. She heard his whispered 'wait for me' as he turned to help Sarah and she nodded, dumbly, her eyes awash with tears, the slip of paper still grasped tightly; the only thing left of him now.

Heaving a large sigh, she turned away and joined the rest of the women on the quayside, happy at least to see Helen and Davy again, however briefly. As soon as Nora dared, she looked at the scrap of paper. It had been torn from a book, probably one of the ones that Sarah had borrowed. Alongside the text in the margin were written a few misspelt words.

I luv you, Nora. Wait to years and I will cum bak to marry you.

Nora kissed the paper and turned towards the ship, hoping to catch a glimpse of him but all she could see was sunlight and black shapes, as tears misted her eyes and then dropped in fat blobs onto the paper. She spent the next hour trying to catch sight of him but other rowers now brought women to the shore and she was too far away from the ship to make out any faces.

Reaching land, the women stumbled and swayed, their legs unable to support them; so used to the movement of the ship, that solid land now felt unnatural. But they had an hour to get used to it as they waited under a burning sun for all the women to be landed. The older children, happy at first to play a game of tag, soon became hungry, bored and fretful. They wanted food, they needed water but nothing was provided for them. The women were used to that; so it had been at Woolwich, but it made them resentful.

Once all the prisoners and their children had landed they waited to be addressed by the newly appointed Governor. Nora watched him approach. His air of authority could not be denied. He was a slim man, around forty years old with a soldier's bearing. His face, dominated by a long, slender nose did not at first appear unkind but she had the impression that he would not stand for disobedience. When he started to speak, she heard the tone of a man who was used to getting his own way. There was none of the softness that she had sometimes detected in the surgeon's voice.

As he began to lay out the facts of their life in Van Diemen's Land he raised hope at first.

'Work hard, follow the orders of your masters, avoid drink and other bad influences and within a year or two of good behaviour, you may find a husband.'

The women smiled and nodded to each other. His tone changed.

'Fall into bad ways and it is back to prison with hard labour, maybe bread and water rations. Continue to behave badly then your head will be shaved or an iron collar fitted, maybe even the stocks. We expect your masters to report any misdemeanour. Obey their instructions, at all times. That is all.' It sounded simple, brutal and their spirits sank.

Helen marched along with the other women towards the prison, known in Hobart as the female factory. She thought what a sad and bedraggled bunch they were, conscious of her stained and salt-stiffened dress. Fashionable ladies under parasols, watched silently, speculatively. Would one of these ladies be her mistress? Would she let Davy live with Helen? She was hot and parched with thirst and Davy must have been too for he cried and struggled as she carried him. She would have liked to rest but could not. They were being chivvied along.

Sarah found the stares of the men unnerving. The better-dressed ones passed by unaware or uncaring. It was the other men, labourers, convicts even constables, who looked them up and down, nudging each other, pointing and leering. She had seen the looks Rose was given in the tavern; she recognised it here and shivered.

Once at the female factory, separated only from the men's prison by a high brick wall they were divided. Those unfit by nature or demeanour to be assigned were led to the second story where they would be set to work washing and spinning. Each woman was given new clothes, two petticoats, two dresses of brown serge, boots, a straw bonnet and an apron. The women were both grateful for their clothes but immediately ashamed of the drab uniform and began to scheme how they might brighten it up.

Part 3- Chapter 2

Helen

February 1825 Hobart

'Can you cook?' asked Mrs Mason.

'I can bake a potato and boil up a rabbit.'

Mrs Mason sighed. This was worse than she thought. She studied the young, angular woman standing before her, uncomfortable in her ill-fitting convict garb.

'You must address me as Ma'am and I doubt you will find a rabbit on the whole of this island.' She reproved the sullen girl before her. 'Can you wash sheets and iron and make a bed?'

'We slept on straw if we were lucky, but on the ship, we had sheets and I washed 'em,' then remembering, added 'Ma'am.'

'Oh, dear Lord! Well, what can you do?'

'I can sew and clean and help with the harvest, Ma'am.'

'I cannot have my domestic servant helping with the harvest, especially here in Hobart Town.' Mrs Mason was becoming exasperated. 'Well, let's hope you can learn your duties quickly. As you can see I am with child. It is due within the month so I need someone to do the heavy work.' She did not tell Helen about her last servant, or the one before that. These women were they all useless?

She recounted the conversation with her husband as Helen was in the kitchen washing pots after a simple dinner of boiled potatoes and cold chicken. 'I really don't know if it's going to work,' she said. 'She has so little ability.'

'Yes, but she has the child and is still nursing him,' he said trying to mollify her. 'If you have trouble nursing yourself, she can do it. There are hardly many wet nurses in Hobart to choose from.'

'Hm, I suppose you are right dear, but if I can nurse myself and she isn't working out can I get rid of her?'

'Again? She has only been here a few hours. You know you may not easily be assigned other one after the last two you sent back. These women are in short supply,' he warned, somewhat wearily.

'Oh, I am sure I can engineer an excuse.' she said.

Unaware, Helen had finished washing the china dishes wondering why anyone wanted such flimsy dishes, so easy to break, as she examined a chip in one of the plates. Davy gurgled in the corner where he was trying to eat a clothes peg.

'Come here my darling.' She gathered him up and undid her bodice. Crooning she sat on a chair and fed him, so pleased that she had been sent to a mistress who agreed to Helen bringing her son. She could learn all these things the missus wanted eventually, although Helen thought some of the work was pointless. Why have all those ornaments if they needed dusting every day? Still, she was grateful to have a small box room and a truckle bed where they could sleep and be fed and clothed. The Governor, in his brief speech, promised if she stayed out of trouble she might find a husband in only a year. A year would go quickly enough with Davy to keep her company.

At eight months, old he was learning new things every day and she no longer envisaged a life without him. Helen kissed his head as he finished feeding and held his soft body to her until he struggled and gave a loud burp. Later while lying in bed she looked back over her day. It had all been so strange and new.

A constable walked her to the house. He seemed a brutish kind of man, heavily scarred and pockmarked with meat cleaver hands, so she was pleased that the journey was short and silent. He did not enter the house but left her as soon as he had introduced her to Mrs Mason, her new mistress.

Mrs Mason showed her straight to the kitchen, housed in a small separate room at the back, with Helen's box room next to it. In the kitchen, a log fire smouldered in an iron grate above which stood a metal trivet. For the moment, a kettle hung over the fire gently steaming. Pans of all sizes hung on the wall beside the fire, some of iron and others of copper. On another wall, there were wooden shelves containing earthenware pots and pewter dishes. Above them were china dishes coloured blue and white and with patterns of trees and strangely shaped houses. Mrs Mason told her it was Willow Pattern and to be used only when they had no company. Under the small, single, window stood an enamel bowl for washing pots. Elsewhere lay various buckets tubs, brushes a mangle and a washing board. In the centre of the room stood a small, table and a rough kitchen chair.

It was a smaller version of English farmhouse kitchens. Helen remembered tramping round as a child and sometimes a friendly farmer's wife would give them a stale loaf or a few vegetables if they knocked at the door; may even have let them stand inside waiting, while the good wife gathered a few treats, a rosy apple, some nuts even a tart. Mostly, when they knocked, the wife shouted them away with fearsome gestures. This Mrs Mason had a face like those women with small blue eyes which bore into you. A constant frown was already creating tiny lines around her mouth, and her only five and twenty, thereabouts; a woman to be wary of, Helen sensed.

This was a much smaller kitchen, not meant for the whole family to enjoy sitting around the table to share a wholesome meal. It was hot but lacked warmth that a large noisy family brought to a kitchen.

Mrs Mason instructed Helen to keep the fire banked up with logs from the store in the garden and to draw water from the well outside.

Inside the brick house had polished wooden floorboards which would have gleamed in the strong sunlight, but for the drapery that appeared to cover most of the windows. The parlour was so awash with colour and pattern that it dazzled Helen. Four chairs in a deeply upholstered red material surrounded a handsome fireplace and the same red cloth hung at the windows, driving out the light. Two small polished tables of dark wood sat between the chairs. The walls were covered in a heavily patterned paper depicting strange coloured birds and delicate flowers of red and purple. On the floor was a rug, not made of bits of old cloth but thick and shimmering with pattern and colour. Helen thought it the most beautiful thing she had ever seen and knelt to touch its softness. Mrs Mason told her it was a Turkey rug and seemed rightly proud of it. Helen wondered where she had bought the furnishings. Hobart did not appear big enough to have shops where such things could be bought.

The dining room was similar, richly papered and curtained, this time in blue and cream stripes. A large table, of the same dark rich wood, shone in the centre and six chairs with dark blue velvet seats were tucked in underneath. In the centre of the table was a large, silver candlestick. A cupboard stood against the wall opposite the window. Nestling inside were plates and cups, not of wood or pewter but of thin translucent china covered with pattern again, this time of purple fruits and swags of green leaves. Helen had never seen anything like this house. Sometimes she had wondered what was in the big houses she passed and now she knew. She was confused. All that colour and pattern has addled my brains, she thought as she drifted into sleep.

After a breakfast of fried eggs, bread and tea Helen sat sewing in the kitchen the following morning, her spectacles perched on her nose. Mrs Mason walked in and Helen scrambled to her feet bobbing a curtsey.

'I have written down a list of your duties, Helen.'

'Oh, I can't read Ma'am.'

'What! Well, why have spectacles if to not to help you read?'

'Mrs Fry gave them to me to help with sewing Ma'am. My friend Sarah tried to teach me reading but I couldn't get on with it.'

'Mrs Fry! You have met Mrs Fry,' Mrs Mason exclaimed in disbelief. Everyone knew of the women who went into prisons to help the women. Why she would stoop so low as to do that was a mystery to Mrs Mason. It was bad enough having a convict in her own house.

'Oh yes, a real lady that Mrs Fry.' Which Mrs Mason took to mean that in Helen's eyes she herself was not! Really the impudence of the girl was too much.

Mrs Mason reeled off a list of duties starting at half past five in the morning and finishing at ten in the evening, which had Helen's head spinning, knowing she would not remember half of it. She wished Nora was there to help her. If only she had thought to ask Nora what the duties of a house servant were so she could be better prepared.

Mrs Mason's saw Helen's eyes glaze over and lost her temper. 'Pay attention, Helen.'

'Yes Ma'am,' she mumbled miserably. 'Can you tell me it all again.'

A week later as Helen was removing the tea things from the parlour one of the visiting ladies asked Mrs Mason how she was finding her new servant.

Waiting barely for the door to close she replied. 'It is a real struggle to teach her anything. I swear she has lived in the fields, not a house for all the use she is. My china is chipped and smashed. She manages to burn milk for heaven's sake and you will never guess what she did when I told her to beat the rug.'

'What?' they exclaimed.

'She got down on her hands and knees and hit the rug where it lay on the floor. Can you believe it?'

The ladies tittered with mirth and then a whole stream of complaints about their own convict servants began to emerge.

Helen had listened behind the door, her face burning with shame. It was a lie. She had bent to stroke the rug because it was so beautiful. She had tried so hard to understand her duties, but Mrs Mason just assumed she would understand things that were unfamiliar to her. Nora would be a much better servant for this fancy woman and her fancy ways and Helen wondered longingly about her friends. She ached to talk to them because she felt so lonely in this unwelcoming house; her only solace being Davy. Would things improve when the baby arrived? Surely Mrs Mason will be more concerned with her own child than Helen's shortcomings.

Helen got part of her wish on the following Sunday. Mrs Mason felt unwell and Helen was instructed to attend Anglican divine service and return promptly to prepare the midday meal. As she walked into Saint David's church Helen glimpsed Nora's coppery hair under a grey bonnet and made her way over to sit beside her. Nora wasn't dressed in the ubiquitous brown serge convict dress, surprisingly, but in a smart black dress and jacket and her face was wreathed in smiles as she caught sight of her and Davy.

'Ooh Nora, you look so lovely in that outfit. Wherever, did you get it?'

'My mistress feels herself a cut above the rest of society in Hobart and wishes not to be reminded we are convicts. She's real la di da. When she found out that I had been a housemaid in Westminster she almost swooned with delight. Oh Helen, how I have missed you. How are you getting on?'

'Badly. I can do nothing right it seems. My mistress makes fun of me to her friends. What I wouldn't have given for your advice these past days. She confounds me and confuses me with all her instructions. It is not a big house, but she fills my day from morning to night with her constant, silly jobs. I scarce know how I am going to survive there without throwing summat at her.'

'You poor thing! Shall I visit and show you a few things to impress her, like how to get glasses sparkling?'

'Would you, can you? Oh, please do, Nora.'

'I am sure I can get a morning off. Does your mistress go out at all?'

'Not at the moment, while she's waiting for her confinement. It could be anytime now, judging by the size of her, and then she tells me that she will spend two weeks lying in. I could hardly believe that when she told me.' The service was starting and voices hushed so Nora leant over and whispered.

'Good. I will ask Mrs Parry if I can have a couple of hours off a week Wednesday. I have quite a bit to tell you.'

By the time, Helen arrived back at the house in Argyll Street the doctor and midwife had been called and Helen was asked to boil water for an imminent delivery. All through the afternoon, the master paced around his bit of garden while the mistress groaned and cried out in pain. Helen took the master a cup of tea but was told to bring whisky instead, which he proceeded to drink throughout the rest of his wife's labour.

Late in the evening Helen heard the high–pitched squealing of a baby and a while later the doctor appeared to tell of the birth of a daughter, mother and baby both well. Helen was needed to take away the soiled sheets and clean up the room and then take tea to the Mistress. Remembering her own confinement in Nottingham Gaol, she felt a rush of sympathy towards Mrs Mason and chattered softly to her. How delighted she must be with her beautiful daughter. Would Mrs Mason like her to brush her hair and get some warm water for bathing her face?

'Oh, do go away, Helen. You are giving me a headache. Where is Mr Mason? Tell him he may come and see me now.'

'He is asleep in the parlour Ma'am. I can try to rouse him for you.' Helen doubted she would succeed given the full bottle of whisky he had consumed before and after the baby's birth.

The next ten days were fraught. Mrs Mason stayed in bed and Helen was at the beck and call of her mistress and master. Nothing seemed good enough for them. Her duties increased; now Helen had to change and wash the baby's swaddling or take her away to rock her when the little mite started to cry so that her mother could rest undisturbed.

Davy was neglected and cried to be picked up and Helen felt so guilty for refusing him, knowing she was behind with her duties. She fell into bed for six short hours at night before waking bleary eyed to start another endless round of washing, polishing, cleaning, cooking and nursing all over again. Helen had not made it to church the following Sunday and her tiredness made her forget that Nora was coming to visit until she heard a rap on the kitchen door.

'Goodness Helen, you look a wreck.' Nora took in the scene. There was Davy on the floor crying with his arms outstretched, Helen had the new baby tied to her chest with a shawl and the kitchen was cluttered with dirty dishes and piles of laundry. Nora picked up Davy to soothe him and, recognising her smile, he subsided into contented cooing. On the ship, he had been cosseted and played with by all the women in the dormitory and he missed the attention.

Helen sat on the kitchen chair and burst into tears. 'I don't think I can do this much longer I am so exhausted. The missus is still in her bed and deigns to feed the baby but not much else. I suppose I should be grateful that she doesn't want me to feed her too.'

'Right, now you sit there Helen, let me give you a hand. I do not have to be back until 12.00 and we can talk as we work. First, let's drink a cup of tea.'

Helen took a cup to Mrs Mason before settling down to drink hers with Nora.

'I heard voices Helen, who is it? You don't have a man in the kitchen with you? I will not countenance any male visitors you know.'

'Oh no, Ma'am, Mrs Parry's maid has come to teach me how to look after you better.'

'Colonel Parry's maid?'

'Yes, Ma'am I believe so. She was on the ship with me and she was a housemaid in Westminster.' Helen was not above subtle flattery of her own.

'Really, that sounds a good idea, as long as Mrs Parry agrees.'

'Yes Ma'am, she did ask first.'

Mrs Mason sank back into her pillows for more rest. At least the baby was sleeping and put down to lie beside her in a basket. Helen didn't understand this lying-in business. Her mother was up and about with a few hours of giving birth. There was no luxury of lying in bed for days on end or giving birth in a bed. So much easier to give birth on straw, she thought to herself, just throw away the straw and what a waste of good linen. She'd boiled it and rubbed at it but you could still see the rusty marks of blood on it.

By the time, she got back to the kitchen Nora had her hands in hot water and was half way through the dirty dishes. Davy was back on the floor eating pieces of apple placed on a wooden plate beside him.

'We should have two hours of peace now. Please, Nora, show me what I should be doing in this damned house and let me have your gossip.'

Nora showed Helen the tips she had garnered over the years, such as the use of old newspaper for cleaning windows, vinegar for cleaning glassware, stale bread for marks on wallpaper and so forth, while keeping up a steady chatter. She told Helen that Lizzie left the prison the day after Helen had been assigned and was returned to the ship to be sent on to Port Jackson.

'Good riddance, but I bet that Jane was unhappy.'

'She was to be sure and didn't stop cursing you and me for the rest of the day, by all accounts. And do you remember that pretty girl from Kent, the one called Eliza.'

Helen thought for a minute and then nodded.

'Well, she came back from her assigned mistress and got sent back to the ship too. The story is that she was reassigned to a lady travelling on to Sydney but I heard it might be because the surgeon had taken a fancy to her. That loud girl, Ann from Kent, said she noticed him giving her the eye. He was always telling the women off for taking a fancy to the sailors, and all the while he was up to the same thing.'

'Do you think Eliza wanted to go with him?'

'I don't know. She was a good girl. Do you think he will marry her?'

'Men such as him don't marry the likes of us. Poor girl, what will happen when he tires of her?' Neither cared to think about that and Helen changed the subject. What of Sarah, do you have any news?'

'No I don't, she was still waiting for assignment when I left and I worry about her. She isn't strong like you and you're being worked to the bone here She's not been in church either.'

Helen felt so much happier having had Nora to visit but it did not last long. By the end of the week, Mrs Mason was back on her feet and the baby was taking up much of her time, but she still found time to scold and criticise Helen. Six more weeks went by with Helen worked off her feet, getting just two hours off to go to divine service on a Sunday and by mid-April, with the weather turning cooler, Helen was stretched to breaking point.

Sunday started off as normal but Helen managed to burn the master's bacon and Mrs Mason came into the kitchen bearing the plate with two singed rashers in a foul temper.

'This is not how the master likes his bacon, Helen. Have you learnt so little in the past two months? How do they expect me to make a servant of you? You're quite hopeless and not worth your keep. My best china is all chipped, you have scorched the linen, your cooking is just dreadful and I despair of you improving.

'Ma'am, I do my best. If you gave me less to do I could take the time to do it better. I'm always in such a rush to get everything you want done.

'Don't you dare be impertinent! It is not your place to tell me what to do. I am the mistress here and you do what I tell you to do.'

Helen, fearing that she would hit Mrs Mason, threw off her apron, gathered Davy in her arms and told her mistress that she was going to church and stormed out of the house, leaving Mrs Mason speechless with rage.

'That's it,' she told her husband 'She has to go. I cannot bear the sight of her another day.'

When Helen returned an hour late from church, because she had been sobbing in Nora's arms, a constable waited for her in the kitchen.

'You are to come with me girl,' he said. 'Your master has made a complaint against you and you are to go before the magistrate tomorrow. Gather your belongings.' With some relief, Helen did as she was told. Neither the master nor the mistress bid her goodbye and so she left the unfriendly household with Davy in her arms. Five minutes later they were back in the damp, gloomy, female factory.

Helen was just glad of a rest and spent the afternoon playing with Davy, sleeping when he slept and eating the poor rations that were offered to her.

Helen came up before Magistrate Thomas. She had lasted two months in Mrs Mason's house. She was accused of disobeying orders and being late back on Sunday after church. Helen couldn't argue with that, but given the chance, would have replied her mistress was unreasonable and too demanding. Of course, she didn't get that chance and found herself sentenced to three months in the factory, crime class. What crime, she thought? I never stole anything. Is it a crime to be late or to burn the bacon? Apparently so!

Part 3- Chapter 3

The Female Factory Hobart

Back at the prison, the first thing Helen did was to ask for Davy, but to her absolute horror, the superintendent told her he had been taken to the nursery to be weaned, him being older than nine months. Helen screamed his name, again and again, unbelieving and in utter anguish, until the guards dragged her away sobbing, and choking on her tears.

Crime class was just another room in the ramshackle prison designated for those women who had done something the authorities did not approve of and separate from those where women waited to be assigned.

Helen's first night there was horrific. Left alone to weep and grieve for Davy, her breasts oozed milk and ached constantly. She imagined his terror at losing his mother and felt sure she could hear his cries of hunger amongst the other noises of the prison. What had he ever eaten other than her own milk and the odd crust of bread and boiled egg, and only since they landed in Hobart, before that just oatmeal burgoo. Could he survive without her milk? Her mind conjured up nightmares of Davy alone and frightened and starving and her sobs grew louder. She wasn't aware of the shouts to shut up around her, but as dawn broke she became aware of a hand on her shoulder and soothing sounds. At last, she turned around and saw, in the gloomy light from a murky window, an old crone who smiled toothlessly at her.

'There, there my dear, hush, I know what you're feeling,' she said.

'No, you can't. It's my Davy, my joy. They've taken him from me. He's not weaned and they've stolen him.'

'Yes, but you will see him again my dear. Hold on to that. You will see him again.'

'Do you think so? Will they look after him?'

'They take all babies at nine months to wean, so they know what to do. I've seen it happen time and again.'

'And they're alright, after I mean?'

'Yes, for the most part.' The old lady made a slight grimace involuntarily, but in the half-light, Helen didn't notice and she attempted a wan smile of thanks. 'Try and get some sleep, dear, It's still early.'

Helen settled back down, quieter now and eventually drifted off until the aching of her breasts awoke her to grieve all over again.

Later that morning she sat on a bench in the small upstairs room with several other women in crime class. This room was to be her home for the next three months. She would sleep, work and eat here, with just a small yard for exercise. But it wasn't a patch even on Newgate. Too small for the number of women it held, too damp and cold for the coming winter, it was dirty, not even weatherproof and more fit for animals than women. Water oozed on the floor and dampened the mattresses lying directly on top.

Mrs Fry should see this place, thought Helen. Looking around at the state of the room Helen reckoned the authorities could not care about them, but only consider them a nuisance who didn't deserve better. Davy may be better off where he is. In here he could catch a chill, no doubt about that. Surely the conditions in a nursery would be better, wouldn't they? She imagined a warm room with clean bedding and kindly women to help soothe the children when they were upset at missing their mothers. Yes, that's how it will be and it comforted her.

Helen recognised a few of the women. Like her, they had been on the Henry, but she knew them as the roughest and most argumentative of women and Helen had no interest in renewing their acquaintance, however unavoidable. She looked around at the women she didn't know, trying to judge their character by their faces and demeanour. No Nora or Sarah here. But there was a woman sitting quietly on her own, older than the rest, maybe fifty years of age; her hair straggly and grey, hard work and poverty etched on her face. But there was kindness in her watery eyes as she glanced at Helen, and then she realised that this was the woman who comforted her during the night. Helen moved over to sit beside her and received a smile, such as it was, because her few remaining teeth were blackened from a lifetime of pipe smoking.

'I don't suppose you have any baccy on you?' she said.

'No, I'm sorry, I don't.'

'Ah well. I didn't think you would. It's a week or two now since I had some, but it soothes my pain.' She held up her twisted hands for Helen to see.

'I'm too old and crippled to be of much use as a servant, so they keep me here. I'd starve otherwise.'

'How long have you been in Van Diemen's Land?'

'Well now, I came on the female ship five years ago, the Morley it was called. For the first three years, I was a servant in a reverend's household but then my hands got so painful and I dropped everything. Smashed the cups, dropped the dinner plates with good food flying everywhere. I couldn't even peel a potato so he let me go. Next, I was a washerwoman in a laundry and for a while it was alright. The hot water helped ease the pain at first, but then my hands got raw and bled so it was even more painful. There was this overseer, who was always swearing at me to work faster, so one day I just tipped a jug of hot water over her damned head. She yelled and cursed and called murder, so now I'm here and here is where I will stay till I drop; pray God soon. I can't say I'll be sad to go. I'm tired of all this.' She gestured around the room. 'These women are the lowest of the low. It is nice to see a new and friendly face here, though I feel for your loss. Tell me about your little one, Davy, is it? How come they sent you here?'

Helen told her briefly of her ten weeks at Mrs Mason's and about her 'crime'.

'Oh, they don't need much of an excuse to get rid of people, especially such as her. She sounds an uppity woman, maybe not brought up with servants but thinks she can lord it over all and sundry. I wouldn't take it to heart, but the trouble is there's quite a few like her. My name is Mary, by the way. How old is your little boy?'

'I'm Helen. Davy is nigh on eleven months and beginning to stand up, not far off walking. Why do you think they let me keep Davy when I was assigned to that woman?'

'No dear, you think. You said she was confined while you were there.'

Helen thought for a few seconds and then cried 'Oh dear Lord. I understand now.' Helen was stunned and angered by the deviousness of Mrs Mason. She remained silent for a moment until Mary broke in with another question.

'Are you Irish?'

'Born there but we travelled around Nottingham for a few years.'

'I'm from Hampshire, never travelled more than five miles from where I was born till I was took for trial and got sent here. You married?'

'No, but I had a sweetheart. He's married my sister now.'

'I was married and had three boys. Husband died twenty years back and left me penniless. The parish gave me a little help but it was never enough and the boys died one by one. Terrible hard it is to see your children die; you never get over it. When the last one went, I reckon I went mad. I'd raised him to thirteen, that were seven years ago, but soon after he started with the cough, just like his brothers, and I knew he would go. All that year I prayed to God, just leave me one, but he didn't listen.' Mary's eyes were staring out into the room and she stopped talking, her sorrow evidently still raw.

Helen crossed herself then and stroked Mary's twisted hand. This woman had been through far more than Helen. She must try to cling on until that time. In three months, she could visit Davy. It would be tough, but it had to be got through.

The days passed slowly in crime class. There was work picking and spinning wool but not enough to keep them more than half occupied. Some evenings the women managed to catch the attention of men passing by the barred window, persuading them to pass up drink or tobacco on the promise of a future favour. The drink and tobacco got passed around and on those evenings Mary was content to smoke her clay pipe in silence and Helen clicked her wooden rosary beads whilst praying that Davy stayed safe from harm.

She was comforted by the Catholic priest, Father Philip, who visited the Irish women on Sundays and prayed with them. She was pleased to confess her sins for the first time in years and his blessing afterwards gave her great solace. The Father was a good and kindly priest and she told him how she wished Davy were baptised. He told her of the chapel he was building. Without money or paid labour, it would be rough and ready, but he hoped she would attend service there and she promised to try. He vowed to visit Davy in the nursery and bring her news of him as well as baptise him. She kissed his hands in thanks and asked about Godparents. We can deal with that when you leave here he told her.

On tobacco-less evenings Helen sat with Mary and chatted. After that first night, Mary didn't talk about her family but about the women, she had met in Van Diemen's Land.

'As I sees it, there's four ways to get through this, and I've seen enough pass through here.

First way is not to knuckle under. These women fight the system and end up in an out of here, some with their head shaved, or wearing an iron collar, but they keep on fighting or trying to escape. Few manage to escape for long. The bush or the blackies get them first, or worse still they become a moll to the bushrangers and get passed around till they's all wore out and drown theirselves. Leastways, I don't recommend fighting the system.

Second way is to work as a servant but not very hard and do something to get you back in here where you can doss around with your mates.' She pointed at a group of women. 'Those lazy good for nothings while away their time playing cards, having a gossip, but at the end of their time, they've got to work to earn a keep or find any husband who's fool enough to take them on. Those that can't do either end up in the bawdy houses or worse.

Third way is to drink yourself to death. Lots do it. It won't take long. Again, you'll be in and out of here and there'll be no one to care for young Davy. There ain't no orphanage nor workhouse for him in Hobart, so he'll starve quickly enough or get given to someone as an apprentice if he's lucky.

Fourth way is to keep your head down; Do enough work so they keep you on and don't answer back, no matter what they says to you. Don't fight and don't drink and look for a man who's done his time, got a bit of land and wants a woman to bear his children. Never take on a drinker. He'll beat you when he's drunk and he'll drink each day to forget the stripes he's earned on his back. Helen, the life of a poor woman in this world is nought but hard work, sorrow and pain. You have to get by the best you can, feel your way through it.'

'Mary, you are right. I've always known that just from my own mother, but a poor man has it hard too.'

'I'm not saying they don't. But you'll see the gangs of men in their convict slops, they go out to build roads and saw down trees at about eight in the morning, but by five or six they've finished for the day. How long did you work for your missus?'

'From five in the morning until ten at night.'

'There's your answer. Did you ever hear of a poet called Mary Collier?'

'I don't even know what a poet is?'

'Someone as meks up rhymes. She ended her days in Hampshire and my old granny used to recite a poem she wrote about the labouring woman. This Mary, she were real famous in our parts a number of years back. She took exception to a poem written by a man about how hard they have to work at harvest time and how easy it is for a woman just to glean while chatting to her friends. Well, I never forgot how it ends, it's the story of our lives, ain't that the truth!' Mary took Helen's hand in her gnarled fingers and started to recite the verse slowly and with great feeling.

'With heavy hearts we often view the sun,

Fearing he'll set before our work is done;

For, either in the morning or at night,

We piece the summer's day with candlelight.

Though we all day with care our work attend,

Such is our fate, we know not when 'twill end.

When evening's come, you homeward take your way;

We, till our work is done, are forced to stay,

And, after all our toil and labour past,

Sixpence or eightpence pays us off at last;

For all our pains no prospect can we see

Attend us, but old age and poverty.'

Mary spoke with such emotion that both were silent for a while.

At last, she released Helen's hand. 'Tis the only poem I ever learnt. But it speaks true, so I've no need for others.'

Helen could tell that Mary spoke a lot of sense confirming what they had been told when they got off the ship. Somehow, she'd have to curb her temper, deal with the tiredness and just get through the work she was given. In five years, maybe less, she would be free, but it was vital to find a man to marry and the right one at that, listening to Mary's advice.

Slowly the three months passed and Helen took her leave of Mary. 'Don't let me see you in here again, my lovely. I sure as hell don't want to see you outside either. I'll be cut free within the year and I won't find a job, not with these hands. Just let me meet my maker, that's all I ask. Starving to death in a ditch don't attract me at all.'

Helen kissed her poor old face. She could see tears gathering in her rheumy eyes.

'Bless you, Mary. I'll say a prayer for you every Sunday. If you should leave here I'll always find a crust for you. They tell me I am going to Mr Ogilvie's at the British Hotel in Liverpool Street. I promise I'll work hard so they'll be pleased with me.'

Part 3- Chapter 4

The British Hotel was a much larger establishment than the Mason's small home. A two-storey building, it had seven handsome windows facing the street on the first floor, chimneys at either end of the roof and a veranda shading passers-by and customers of the hotel and brandy vaults.

The constable led Helen into a warm kitchen via the servant's entrance and she was pleased to see a jovial woman who introduced herself as Cook, another female servant and a spotty faced youth around the same age as Helen. July coldness had seeped into their bones on the short walk and they were pleased to be offered a cup of tea. Once the constable left, Cook led Helen to the mistress's parlour to be introduced.

Mrs Ogilvie was roughly the same age as Mrs Mason, in her mid-twenties, and there the similarities ended. She welcomed Helen with a warm smile, asked about her experience as a servant and did not appear too fazed when told of her limited abilities.

'Cook will look after you and explain your duties, won't you Cook? I am sure you will soon learn for you seem to be a neat, orderly woman and I hope not prone to drink?'

Helen shook her head at this. 'Oh, indeed not Ma'am, my son depends on me.'

'How old?'

'He's just thirteen months Ma'am. He will be walking now most likely. I haven't seen him for three months. Will it be alright to visit him? He's in the nursery.

'Ah, the same age as my youngest daughter. I have three children, a boy and two girls. You might be asked to take them for a walk in the fresh air, if we don't have many guests for lunch. Can I trust you not to get into any improper conversations with men, or neglect the children in any way?' Seeing Helen nod again she had one more warning. 'This is a hotel, as you realise from the name. There will be male guests and I will not countenance you having any relationships with them. Do you understand?' Helen showed she understood and Mrs Mason gave her the agreement she had longed for. 'Ask cook if she can spare you for an hour a week to visit your son.'

Helen broke into a smile, bobbed a curtsey and left with cook to go and start learning her new duties and to be shown around the building and the rooms she would be cleaning.

And so, Helen's second chance began. Once again, she had to be up by 5.30 in the morning to set up the dining room for breakfast, lay a fire in winter, help serve the breakfasts, clean the bedrooms and change sheets when necessary. Next, it was preparing for dinner, serving and clearing away, then an hour off before preparing for supper time at six o'clock. The other servant girl, called Betsy, a sweet, pretty girl, but not quite the full shilling, did the laundry. Ted, the spotty youth, was porter and boot boy and very enamoured of Betsy, who was entirely unaware of his adoration.

But the work was shared and they had a laugh or two as they busied themselves. None of the women served in the bar, so bed came at the reasonable time of nine in the evening. Food was plentiful and well cooked. The master and mistress expected the work to be done to a high standard but did not criticise if it was completed on time. Helen found that she slotted in and learnt the best way of doing things by copying the others. The only downside was making sure the male guests did not become too familiar with her. One or two tried it on but Helen became adept at slapping away a stray hand or two and delivering a sharp rebuke to suggestive comments. Generally, this was accepted and if any complained, Helen told them to speak to the mistress of the hotel and they soon backed off.

Best of all cook agreed that Helen may visit Davy before church on a Sunday, if she got up earlier to complete her chores. Helen found her excitement mounting as the week went on. She could scarcely contain it when Saturday came and by Sunday morning she was a bag of nerves.

At the appointed hour, she dashed from the hotel and ran the short distance to the nursery. She knocked on the heavy wooden door and after a few seconds, a beefy woman opened it a few inches. Seeing Helen, she stepped outside planting her feet apart blocking the entrance, and her expression showed Helen she was unwelcome. Helen asked to see Davy Fitzgerald but the woman replied brusquely that it was unsettling for the children if mothers turned up. It would be far better for David Fitzgerald if his mother stayed away until she was free to collect him from the nursery.

Helen was not about to be fobbed off by a convict and she was could see the woman was a convict by her clothes. She demanded to see the person in charge and planted her feet on the step and prayed that she looked as determined and fierce as the woman in front of her, although her insides felt as though they were turning to jelly. The door was slammed in her face. Helen did not move hoping that meant the woman had gone to find the matron. A minute or two ticked by with Helen feeling frantic but refusing to let her fear overcome her. She might as well be in the prison if they would not let her see Davy. She heard footsteps behind her as the door began to reopen. Helen was just about to demand to see Davy again when she heard a familiar voice beside her.

'Ah, Miss Fitzgerald, have you come to visit your Davy?' it was Father Phillip. 'I thought you may be here, as you weren't in the factory.'

'Yes, I have, Father Phillip.' Helen turned towards him and he could see the anxiety in her eyes.

'Ah, Matron, I promised Miss Fitzgerald we would visit him together today. Shall we go in?' He walked in through the door and Helen followed, with matron standing back to allow them access, her face showing her displeasure but she dared not refuse the priest.

'Miss Fitzgerald is a pious God-fearing woman, Matron. Her visits will be good for Davy.'

Helen and the priest walked into a largish room. It was the smell that hit her first. In front of her was an array of filthy, straw mattresses where mothers lay nursing their babies. One was weeping as she hugged her baby tight to her chest.

'She's being moved to the Female Factory tomorrow," whispered Father Patrick. "I will come back to pray with her in a minute.'

Helen shivered; there was little enough warmth in the dying embers of the fire. The priest led her on to the next room. She gasped at the fetid air as he opened the door. Children of all ages sat on the dirty floor, ragged and unkempt; their eyes hollow in their pale faces. A couple of female convicts played cards in a corner, ignoring children and visitors alike. Beyond the room was a square of outside space, but it was a cold day and the door was firmly closed.

Helen remembered Sarah's description of the foundling home but surely this was worse. The children weren't even occupied. She scanned the faces for Davy, but not seeing him, began to edge her way around the mattresses, her heart in her mouth. Please let him be here she prayed. Father Phillip put his hand on her arm and then pointed to Davy. Oh, thank the Lord, there he was, poor mite. Although she would recognise him anywhere, he looked so forlorn and far too thin for her liking. She reached out and picked him up but he started screaming.

'Davy, Davy it's me, Mama.' The howling didn't stop.

'He doesn't know you. He's forgotten,' whispered the priest. 'I've seen it so many times. Give him time.'

'My darling boy, please remember me.' Helen smothered him with kisses and pulled out a sweetmeat she had brought from the hotel. He took it and while sucking turned his tearful face to her, appearing to study it. 'Please remember me, my sweet. I know, you like this,' and she began to sing an Irish lullaby. He studied her face and then smiled and her heart almost fell through the floor.

'Thank you, Lord!' She raised her eyes to the ceiling and crossed herself. 'I promise I will come every week to see you, darling boy and I will get you out of here as soon as I can and I will bring you something nice to eat...' and on she went, saying anything to make him smile again. But her hour was soon over and she had to leave him once more. His arms stretched out to her, crying inconsolably. She turned away weeping and left him behind, his screaming followed her through the door.

'See that's what I meant,' said the woman who had opened the door first. 'Visits unsettle them. You would have done better to stay away.' Helen did not trust herself to answer, as she might be tempted to hit her.

As she shut the door of the nursery to walk to church, she leant on the wall for a minute, sobbing. Father Phillip followed her out.

'The nursery's a disgrace, I know, but don't blame the matron too much. She's given little enough money to run it, and the convict helpers well you can see for yourself how much use they are. The matron says you may visit on Sundays for the moment, although permission may be withdrawn if... at any time really.' He looked sorrowfully at her.

'Thank you, Father. You've been a great help. But I must go. I cannot miss church.' She bent down and kissed his hand, then turned and ran, her eyes still brimming with tears. One thing was now certain, she could not go back to prison and leave Davy alone for another three months in that place.

The day before she had been excited at the prospect of seeing Nora again, and it was still true that she yearned to see her friend. But she had left her heart in the nursery. Once in church, she peered around for Nora's smart black dress but didn't see it. Taking another look, she caught sight of Nora, back in female, convict garb and looking weary. Helen made her way over to sit beside her and Nora jumped to her feet and grabbing her in delight. Seeing her friend look quizzically at her dress, she laughed in embarrassment.

'Yes, I know, pride before a fall as they say. I'm not with Mrs Parry anymore, more fool me I suppose. She informed me last month they were being sent on to Sydney and would I like to go with them. I thought about it but worried George wouldn't find me so I turned it down.'

'You goose; I could tell him when he comes looking.'

'But I would miss you and Sarah too, not that I know where Sarah is yet. Jenny told me she is up country, whatever that means. Anyway, just before the Parrys left, I was told a new mistress, had put in a special request for me. You will never guess who.'

'Not that dreadful woman, Mrs Mason!' Helen gasped in horror.

'Yes, her indeed. She was so smug when I arrived. I reckon she feels she's got one up on all her friends. She can't help parading me in front of them. Nora worked as a lady's maid in Westminster, don't you know, and then she preens and purrs so much I want to be sick.'

Helen, at first aghast, was unable to stop herself from laughing and Nora joined in. The congregation in front, waiting for the service to begin, glared at them for their unbecoming behaviour, so they stuffed their hands in their mouths until they calmed themselves once more. The laughter helped to ease Helen's sadness.

'How I have missed you,' said Nora, echoing Helen's feeling. 'It's not that bad at Mrs Mason's because she has got a skivvy now as well. She kept the girl she got after you. She's a bit of a gossip, but harmless, although she's fond of a tipple.

'Oh, I blame myself that you're there. I told Mrs Mason, when you came that morning, how you had been a maid in Westminster and she was really impressed.'

'Helen, don't worry. I might have been sent somewhere far worse or even out of Hobart and then we wouldn't see each other at all. Now where is Davy and how is he?'

Helen broke down and wept, unable to say much. Throughout the service, she made no attempt at singing but was grateful for the times she could kneel on the hard stone floor, the discomfort she felt was her due for leaving Davy. She longed to smuggle him out of that place but knew she could lose him for longer. There would be no mercy if she tried it.

Before they left the church, Helen quickly told her friend what had happened and how heartbroken she was. Nora was distraught for she had learnt to love Davy.

'There was me going on about my troubles and all the while.' she couldn't finish the sentence but hugged her friend tightly.

Later that week, after Mrs Mason's friends had been to call for afternoon tea she came into the kitchen frowning with displeasure.

'I hear that you behaved badly in church with that useless girl, Helen. Your behaviour reflects on me and I think it is unwise that you have anything to do with her in future.'

Sorry Ma'am.' Nora's mind scrambled for something to say that could give her a reason to continue to see Helen. 'I am little Davy's godmother and it is my duty to make sure he is brought up in righteousness. I was just pleased to hear about him after such a long absence. It won't happen again; I will make sure of that.' Nora was amazed at how glibly she lied and totally without shame.

Mrs Mason looked doubtful at first, but unwilling to take her maid further to task, given her ability and normal demeanour, she decided to let it pass with a final warning.

'Very well, but I expect you to have a good influence on her rather than the other way around. If I am told of any further reports of bad behaviour, then you will know what to expect.'

'You're learning gal,' said Sal, the skivvy, as Mrs Mason left the kitchen. 'Yer got to play her at the same game. We mustn't let them win all the time. Crafty is what yer got to be, 'specially with her type,' she said conspiratorially.

While Nora wasn't about to confide in Sal, she agreed with the advice but didn't trust the woman not to blab, especially when Sal had been filching the wine left over after dinner. She just nodded and carried on with her work.

Part 3- Chapter 5

The weather in midwinter was bitingly cold but not icy. There was snow on the top of Mount Wellington but neither of the two friends got much chance to see it. They continued to meet each other at church for a precious of hour on Sundays. Mindful of being observed, they behaved modestly and demurely for all who watched, whispering gossip and news to each other as they knelt for prayers.

Sometimes, when the hotel had few guests, Helen was asked to take out the Ogilvies' children for a walk. She loved to amble around Sullivan's Cove watching the small boats unload catches of fish and whale meat. She longed to show them to Davy and wished he were there to enjoy it, remembering how he loved to be outside. It would be a rare treat for him to splash in the puddles and run around in the fresh air. There were always larger ships in the harbour too and Helen occasionally had to run the gauntlet of drunken sailors making their way back to the ships from the many bars and brothels of Hobart. If it was one of those days she walked the children further south, towards Battery Point, to watch the red-coats drilling. But she ached for Sundays to hold Davy in her arms once again.

Every time she went to visit him, she longed to take off and run away with him. Instead, she brought little treats, showered him with love and tried to make him giggle. The hour went too fast. She asked her Mistress if she would let Davy live at the British Hotel, but while Mrs Ogilvie sympathised, she said it was not a suitable place for a child and he would get in the way of her work. Not a suitable place for a child indeed, she scoffed to herself. Were there not children living in the house already?

But winter passed and the weather was warming up again. Helen waited in church as usual on a fine Sunday morning in late November. She watched as the front pews filled up with gentlemen and their ladies in fine clothes, convict men to one side the church and convict women to the other. The male convicts in grey uniforms eyed the women as they walked past but any comments here were punished, unlike at Newgate Prison. Helen did not pay much attention to the male convicts. She would be looking for a free man with a trade or some land when the time came. Nora arrived and joined Helen in the seat she had saved for her. A number of other convicts from the Henry were present and she noticed quite a lot of whispering between them, even when the service was underway. As soon as the service was over women from the Henry started to gather outside of the church doors.

'Did you hear the news?' Jane Smith had a broad grin on her face. Nora felt herself shrinking. Whatever the news, Jane was going to delight in telling her.

'It's the Henry, it's only gone and got shipwrecked.' She laughed to see Nora's stricken face. 'Yes, that sailor you was sweet on, I bet he's feeding the fishes as we speak.'

'How do you know about the shipwreck?' Helen caught a hold of Nora as she stumbled, her face ashen.

'I heard this fella talking outside the pub. He had money in the cargo and ranted that he'd lost a packet.' She smirked now and Helen longed to hit her again. What a shame so many people were around to observe and judge. She could tell that Nora was distraught.

'Was anyone saved?' asked Nora in a pleading whisper.

'Shouldn't think so. If they were, they probably got eaten up by them cannibals. I hears it was near some of them islands. That James Cook, he was boiled up to be eaten, weren't he? I remember that silly chit Sarah, reading about it.' Jane cackled with glee when Nora screamed 'No.' and beat her hands against Jane's chest. Jane just shoved Nora away where she sank to the ground crying.

Several of the congregation, leaving the church, were wondering what was happening. Whatever it was, it all appeared unseemly and so disrespectful outside the church.

Helen hauled Nora upright and then dragged her away from Jane before she could say anything else. Nora's eyes were awash with tears but she blindly let Helen lead her away. Helen decided the best place to take would be her to the kitchen of the British Hotel and dragged her sobbing friend to the kitchen door.

Helen had just got Nora sat down and was explaining to Cook what had gone on when Mrs Ogilvie entered the kitchen.

'Whatever is the matter with the poor girl?' she asked in concern.

'She's had some bad news, Ma'am. Her young man, it appears, has drowned,' replied Helen, speaking quietly to Mrs Ogilvie, so as not to upset Nora even more.

'Oh, dear me, how awful for her. I will get a drop of brandy for her and Cook, please make her a cup of sweetened tea.'

Mrs Ogilvie was as good as her word and returned a few moments later with a finger of brandy in a glass which she encouraged Nora to sip.

"Ugh, it tastes awful."

"It will do you good, dear." Nora took another sip, which was not as bad as the first.

Between the tea and the brandy, Nora started to calm down. She began to feel light-headed and attempted to smile at Mrs Ogilvie, before sipping some more.

'Helen, walk her back to her mistress, dinner will just have to be a few minutes late today. Hurry up though, will you, as there's quite a lot to do.'

Mrs Ogilvie left the kitchen and Helen got her friend to stand up, somewhat unsteadily. Cook gave her a wet cloth to wipe her face and they set off to the Masons' house. Nora didn't feel like talking and Helen, not knowing what to say to help her, kept her arm linked through Nora's, giving her little words of encouragement every now and again.

As they arrived at the Masons' house, Nora turned and said 'Thank you Helen. I don't know how I would survive without you. But you best get back now. Your Mrs Ogilvie is really nice and I'm glad for you. Don't worry, I will be alright.' Turning towards the kitchen door she entered and didn't look back.

Helen was worried but understood why she did not want Helen in the kitchen. Mrs Mason would make it hard on Nora. She had told her about the attempt to stop them from seeing each other. Helen had laughed and said that she would love to ask Father Philip to re-baptise Davy and have Nora as godmother if ever she could get Davy out of that damned nursery. But for now, she made her way back to the hotel to resume her duties.

As soon as Nora entered the door she was greeted with such malevolence that it undid all of Mrs Ogilvie's and Helen's kindness. Mrs Mason ranted and raved about the frightful exhibition she had made of herself. How Mrs Mason had been shamed in front of her friends and now she could even smell strong drink on her breath. Nora burst into tears once more. Was there any point in trying to defend herself? It was impossible to believe that Mrs Mason would listen to any excuse, had she the strength to open her mouth and give one. Her heart was broken; who cared what happened next. Still feeling unsteady from the brandy, Nora stumbled, then to her utmost shame she retched and deposited the contents of her stomach over Mrs Mason's shoes and then, thankfully passed out on the floor of the kitchen.

Part 3- Chapter 6

The Female Factory Hobart

Inevitably her appearance before the magistrate, charged with disorderly conduct, neglect of duty and drunkenness, was no surprise. Thinking back to her first court appearance, Nora felt resigned to punishment. There seemed little worse they could do to her. Her despatch to the cells for three days on bread and water and three months in crime class created no fear, just great weariness and a desire to sleep off the pain of George's loss. At that moment, Nora did not think she would ever be happy again.

She didn't mind the dark cell. She shared it with a Welshwoman who barely spoke English. Neither did she mind the bread and water. Silence was all she craved. She reminisced over their brief meetings, the songs she sang for him; the way her skin felt when he touched it; the smiles he gave her. She loved George, she knew that, but now he was lost she did not know how to bear it. It was like being torn apart again from her family, only worse, for he had been her future.

These last six months, she daydreamed for hours whilst doing her chores. She pictured a pretty cottage with a bit of land by the sea and a family, little James and George and maybe another Nora, or perhaps she would call her Helen. Those dreams kept her cheerful, despite Mrs Mason petty demands. She had counted the months off until last Saturday; a year and four months until he came for her she reckoned. She loved to imagine where he was and pictured the ship as it sailed the seas, calling at strange ports. Now all she hoped for was that he hadn't suffered, trying to push the image that Jane left her with from her mind; it was too unbearable.

She also thought a great deal about her family, wondering if they had received the letter that Mrs Parry said she would post for her. What a kind mistress she was, so different from Mrs Mason. She had given Nora a sheet of precious paper and then seeing Nora's difficulty with a quill and ink, wrote the letter for her. Nora was relieved to tell her family of the good position she had, how she was settling in well to the life in Hobart town. It was all gone now. Back where she started and it sickened her. She had made the worst mistake possible in not going to Port Jackson with the Parrys.

The three days passed and Nora was led out of her refuge into the room set aside for crime class. It had not improved since Helen was there and it fitted her description, damp, dirty and crowded. She half-heartedly looked around for the woman called Mary that Helen had told her about. No one fitted her description so perhaps she had achieved her wish to die.

However, there was a familiar face or two and Nora's spirits sank further when she saw Anne Farrow mockingly walk toward her.

'Well, If it ain't Miss Goody Two-shoes!'

Nora nodded hello, but said nothing. Anne looked utterly dishevelled and her convict dress was in tatters.

Anne, caught her looking at her dress and said, 'I didn't care for working from dawn to the middle of the night so I walked. Spent time in the bush, didn't I, trying to find a friendly face and a place to hide. All I found were trees, more trees and shrubs so dense, it made it impossible to get through. I reckoned I would die out there. I couldn't find so much as a berry to eat and scarcely any water.

After a day or two, I came across a chain gang and begged the overseer to get me out of the bush. I was that glad the overseer was there an' all. Those men on the chain gang looked a desperate lot, I can tell yo. I were afraid for my life. Oh, but yo should have seen them, some must have been whipped till their skin was off their backs. I've never seen such scars. I never wants to see another tree in my life either, let alone the snakes and the devilish creatures that chills your heart when you hears 'em screech and squeal at night.'

In spite of herself, Nora asked Anne if she saw any wild black men in the bush. Nora had seen a few black children in Hobart, but they were dressed in ragged dresses or trousers and apart from their skin and wiry hair had not thought them too strange.

'No, thank the Lord. I was hoping for a bushranger. I hear there's groups of convicts who have escaped and roam around thieving and such and I had a fancy to join one of their gangs. But the countryside ain't like England and that's for sure. It's wild and untamed, fit only for the black men, if yo ask me. But they'll never make a servant of me. I'd rather spend my time in here than skivvy. I spit on their bleeding work,' and with that, she gathered up a great globule of phlegm and spat it out at Nora's feet.'

'That's like what I did to my mistress, only it was brandy and my breakfast,' laughed Nora, ruefully.

'Bostin!, Did yo really? Well, I'll go to the foot of our stairs! Oh, and there was I believing yo had no spunk at all.' Anne clapped an arm around Nora's shoulder and squeezed her. 'I want to hear all about it. Now I know yo think I was a bitch on the ship and probably I was. A year of Patsy most likely drove me to it. The number of times I wanted to give 'er a right lampin. Imagine being stuck with the same woman for days and months and 'er going on so about 'er saintly husband. I saw him once when he visited and he was nout special, a lot older and more withered than 'er. I shouldn't think he was long for this world. But, enough about Patsy; we women should stick together and thumb our noses at the rest. So stop your mythering and come.'

'But it's women who have ruined me, every time. Why should I trust you, Anne?'

'Yo're right. Don't trust me. I'm no good, but we might as well rub along. Here come along and meet some of the other 'no goods'. I have a drop of wine and by the looks of it, you could do with a drink.'

Nora didn't care anymore, so she allowed herself to be led across the room to meet the other women. If this was to be her home for three months then she had better, as Anne said, rub along with the occupants, or her life could be even more miserable. She wasn't going to tell them any more than they needed to know, just that she had had another fight with Jane Smith, got drunk and now she was here. She pushed her heartbreak to the back of her mind. It was weakness and weakness would always be exploited by someone.

As she later discovered most of the others were here for absconding, fighting and drinking in any case. The authorities seemed to expect it of them. They were the dregs of society and fighting, drinking, whoring was all they were good for. But the women's behaviour fed off society's disapproval of them, and as Nora lived and worked beside these women she reluctantly began to admire their refusal to knuckle under.

They delighted in making up lewd and bawdy songs; their masters and mistresses being the butt of their venom. Knowing that Nora had an exceptional singing voice they tried hard to get her to join in. At first, she declined, being too embarrassed and not really understanding what it was they were singing. Anne took undue pleasure in educating Nora about the suggestive words and meanings, which Nora greeted initially with the utmost mortification. But drip by drip her innocence was stripped away. Nora felt she should have fought somehow against it. That is what her father and sisters would expect. However, eighteen months of imprisonment amidst the outcasts of society led her irredeemably down this new, path. She could never regain her naivety and slowly she accepted that her life was now to be spent amongst women who had nothing further to lose. Wasn't it best to go down fighting?

So, she started to sing with them and, like the time in Newgate, when they screamed and banged their dishes in protest, she felt a release in singing and in the drink which was readily available from the men outside. Soldiers and constables were happy to oblige them, often assisting those who wanted to escape this very insecure prison for an evening of debauchery. The Superintendent admonished them for their bawdy songs and threatened the women but they took no notice. What, more bread and water, an hour in the stocks, a shorn head, who cares, do your worst mister. We sing because it is all that is left to us.

As the months wore on Nora's grief and distress grew less as her heart slowly withered. Her singing became louder and more colourful and her pain was shoved away into a place her mind refused to go.

Part 3- Chapter 7

Sarah

When I came up from the prison deck and saw Hobart for the first time I was terrified by the space and the strangeness of it all. Where were the people, the noise and bustle of a city? There was such an expanse of sky and water and a land, I felt suddenly alone.

A single spire stood out against the sky and from the ship I could see many large buildings and several smaller ones being built. The whole of the little town seemed to be still under construction. Beyond the harbour and rising up the hill were poor mean houses, which looked as though they had been thrown together in a hurry. Very few were more than a single storey and some of those scarcely more than a wall and lean-to giving shelter against the elements. The heat of the day when we landed made me wonder if it were always warm, and so shelter against the cold and wind was not so important. But later I found out that houses needed to be built according to your funds, and a house would grow piecemeal, maybe over years. I found it difficult to take in that this little town was barely older than me and me not yet full grown.

The next few days were difficult to bear and once I even wished for that dark oblivion to return. First Helen and little Davy left and then Nora; I sobbed to see her go. In the night, I was in such a state of fear, dreading being sent to work in a tavern or bawdy house, that I am sure I started rambling. A doctor was fetched and he had me taken to the hospital where they put me in a bed next to a Scottish girl I knew from the ship's hospital. While she sank further into that world from which I had emerged, I was calmed by the sight and care of Jenny who had been assigned directly to the hospital. I think she gave me a draught of something to help me sleep, for I slept the best part of the next day, and when I woke the bed next to me was empty. I pointed to the bed and Jenny just shook her head.

I stayed in the hospital for ten days and Jenny talked to me whenever she could and I spoke to her of my worries and fears. I can only think she must have told the doctor because he recommended I be assigned to a family out of the town. Peace and quiet and hard work will cure you he told me before I left. I cannot but agree and I thank him and Jenny for that kindness, though my heart aches for my friends, who I have not seen or heard of in over a year and a half.

There is no paper here. The family, father, mother and three boys do not read or write. The youngest is about the same age as Helen's Davy, but there will be another child soon, as I can see her belly is swelling.

The master and missus tell me they are free children born of convicts in New South Wales but raised in Van Diemen's Land. They were amongst the first settlers and they count their blessings for that. When they married, they were allotted some fine land and help, namely Isaac and later me. We all work from sunup to sundown, even the older children and then we sit down together to eat the fruits of our labour. There is not much talking beyond discussing the next chores to be done, but kindness is always present; such kindness that I feel my soul healing. Why even when a family of blacks comes to the door the missus always finds a few scraps of food for them, though there is little enough to spare sometimes. In return for the food, they bring her leaves of plants and mime how to use them, pointing to their throats or stomachs. They go away peaceably, the women covered only by kangaroo skins and the men with strange scars and naked as they day they were born, save for a tiny strip of cloth covering their privates. We have learnt not to be scared of them and for the most part feel sorry for the land and the life they lost.

Isaac has been with the family for four years. He is a sad, lonely man because he misses his family back in England so much. He is a lifer, like me though neither of us talks about what brought us here and the family don't ask. It is better not to know, they say, for we take people as they are and not what they were.

So, we go on through the days and there is a calmness and peacefulness in the steady work and an easy companionship, I never felt before. As I try to read my Bible in the poorly lit cabin after supper, I search for that inner light that Mrs Barnard told me about and sometimes I think I can see it glimmer.

On a Sunday, if we don't walk the three miles into Sorell for a service, the family ask me to read the Bible and I am happy to oblige. If it is warm, we sit outside under an old gum tree for an hour and they listen to me read. After we sing a song they were taught by their parents or that Isaac used to sing with his family. But then you see tears coursing down his lined and weatherbeaten face till they drip into his greying beard and disappear in the thicket somewhere. I think of Nora and tell them of my dear friend with the beautiful voice and they profess a wish to hear her sing. I can't imagine how that will happen.

If it is too cold to be outside, we gather in the room where we sit and eat and the children sleep. The master, Henry he's called, has made bits of furniture from trees he had to clear before his land could be tilled, but mostly the children sit on a rag rug. I sleep in the scullery out back and it's cosy in winter but too hot in summer because a fire is always banked up for the cooking. There's is one bedroom for the master and missus. And old Isaac, well, he sleeps in the wood shed or out under the stars if it's a warm night. I asked him once if he were not afraid of snake bites sleeping outside, but he said that they wouldn't bite if he was quiet and still. He likes to look at the stars, even though they look different from the ones at home. He told his wife before he left England that when he saw the stars he would be thinking of her and she should do the same and think of him.

'Trouble is,' he said, 'it will never be at the same time for here it is night when in England it is day and vice versa.' I found that hard to believe. How could it be a different time in two places? I wish I could ask the surgeon. He would tell me if that were true.

It is spring now and I am growing to love this land. I don't miss the city and its smells. I love the smell of new cut hay and the sight of a white cockatoo with its bright yellow crest, rather than the plain old English sparrow. I love the sounds of the animals, the gentle lowing of the cattle, the cluck of the black native hens and the strange calls of other birds, unlike the screech of noisy London gulls. At dawn or dusk, we are visited by those jumping animals they call kangaroos. At first, I was frightened of them, so big and wild. But whilst they hop about slowly in the paddock when they move off, they jump so graceful and strong that I believe that God made them so for a purpose, known only to him. I imagine this land as paradise and when I read the creation story the master always says that this is our Eden and the missus nods her head.

But today is different. A stranger carrying a bulky sack came to the door looking real travel-worn, his clothes dirty and dusty from the road. The man announced himself as a pedlar, just taken up the work after his ticket of leave, in case we were suspicious. He tried to interest the missus in ribbons and pots and all sorts of trinkets. She told him there was no money for such like, but she did have need of some cloth to make work overalls. Replying that he was on his way back to Hobart he promised to bring some cloth in about a month, then turned around and started back up the track. I asked the missus if I could give him a message for my friends and she agreed, so I ran to catch him.

He was reluctant, I could tell. But how am I to know where your friends are assigned he asked me. If you would go to the hospital and ask for Jenny she might know, was all I could think. I just need them to understand I am well and perhaps Nora will write or you could bring a message back I pleaded. Shaking his head, he set off back for the road and I felt it was but a slim chance that he would do what I asked. But it raised hope in me and I went about my tasks in the dairy and in the kitchen garden with even more of a spring in my step.

Part 3- Chapter 8

November 1826 Hobart

There was such excitement to have received a message from Sarah. Jenny bumped into Nora on the way into church and told her the news. All this time Sarah was working on a farm near Sorell, not too far distant from Hobart. Jenny told Nora that she apparently looked well and longed to hear from them. If they could find a way to write a few lines before next Sunday, Jenny would give a message back to the pedlar before he set off on his travels again. She couldn't wait to tell Helen.

Nora was assigned to a shopkeeper. She had been there three months and was coping with the work by switching off her mind. Her previous assignment, on leaving the female factory, did not work out because of Nora's insolence. Remembering cheeky songs about this same Mrs Lunt, her new mistress, Nora had burst out laughing on being reprimanded for something or other. There followed another week on bread and water in the cells.

But now Nora felt better. She was sneaking a drink every now and again, but everyone did that. It was quite remarkable how she had developed a taste for it when once she thought it horrible. She felt the loss of George keenly. Weekly it grew more difficult to picture his face, and days went by without her thinking, if he had survived, I would only have three months to wait before he came back for me. It was no good dwelling on it because it just made her want a drink, and then another, to take away her sorrow.

Helen tried to cheer her up, but she was also unhappy about Davy being in the nursery and not getting the care she could give him. Every Sunday at church Helen regaled her with 'he looks too thin and is not getting enough to eat' or 'he is too wan from being indoors too much' and worse still 'he's so very unhappy and wants me to take him away.' Nora went to visit him once with Helen, but she found it so upsetting, she could not bring herself to go again. Guilt and anguish, is that my lot in life, she thought There surely isn't any laughter.

The only thing that cheered Nora was receiving a letter from her family. One had been waiting for her after her second time in the factory. She read it and read until the paper became soft and torn from handling, and she could barely read the faded words. Her brother wrote that Mary was expecting her first child and if a girl would be Nora. The whole family lived together, but the young couple hoped to rent a room nearby when they had enough savings. The boys were all learning their letters now and so Nora should expect more correspondence as they wanted the practice. They missed her of course but were glad she was settled with a good mistress. How Nora smiled wryly at that. Her good mistress hadn't lasted long enough by half. Still, this one wasn't too bad and would help her write a note to Sarah.

Helen worried. She had so many things to worry about sometimes it made her feel sick to her stomach. Davy was now used to her only coming on a Sunday. They both lived for that, but leaving him became harder and harder. Every spare minute she made clothes for him so he would be warm, but oftentimes she saw his clothes on another child. How did that happen, she wondered? Did the other children take them off him or did the helpers not care what they were dressed in. She tried asking Davy but, even at two and a half, he did not speak much and cried when she tried to ask him. Rather than upset him, she stopped asking. She made sure he ate on those Sunday visits. Cook was very good and let her have titbits to take. But she worried how much he ate during the week. She'd seen older children snatch food from the younger ones. Thank goodness it was spring and the cold weather at an end. Perhaps she could stop worrying about him catching a chill, but then there were so many other illnesses he could catch in that awful place.

She found out that when children got to three years old they would be taken to church on a Sunday and her visits to the nursery must stop. Helen used to watch the line of children entering and leaving church, their convict mothers peering over the pews for a sight of them. After the service, they ran alongside the children as they made their way back to the nursery, calling out their names or pressing sweetmeats into their hands, tears flowing down their faces. Helen dreaded the day when she might be one of those mothers. How would Davy cope without her Sunday visits?

She worried about being reassigned or getting into trouble again. Helen needed to stay in Hobart and this assignment was the best she could hope for, so she steered clear of drink and she stayed away from the male guests. That didn't mean she wasn't looking for a husband, but so far, she had no luck. Unlike Joanna from the ship, who married within twelve months of arriving, and even Patsy at forty-seven had found a man, forgetting all about her dear Charles at home.

By now, Helen knew she was not handsome enough to attract a free man. Settlers went for women with an unmarked, attractive face and a curvy, well-endowed figure, not a scrawny, plain-faced woman, with a child to boot. No, it would have to be a ticket of leave man. The trouble with those was either they weren't seriously looking for a wife or had no means to support one, and yet were always up for a fumble or a quickie. Helen knew enough not to fall for that again. Davy, bless him, was more than enough worry for her and should she become pregnant again, she would lose her assignment and her freedom for a year.

She worried about Nora too; shocked at the change in Nora once she left the prison. She was much thinner to be sure, but Helen expected the weight loss, given the paucity of food they gave you. No there had to be something else. Nora's talk was more brazen for one thing, and there was a kind of brittleness about her now. Helen heard how Nora mixed with Anne Farrow and her type in the prison, so that would explain much but it was more than that. It was the emptiness which upset Helen so much. Nora rarely smiled, never laughed now, unless told a bawdy joke. A light had gone from her eyes. It was as though she no longer saw pleasure in the world. Worse still Helen smelt drink on her breath, even on a Sunday morning. Now carry on like that and further trouble could not be far away.

But this Sunday morning Nora was wreathed in smiles as she told Helen about the message from Sarah.

'Isn't that such good news? Oh, I am so happy and relieved. We can write to her. What shall we say?'

Part 3- Chapter 9

Sarah

December 1826 Sorell

The pedlar returned yesterday and he gave me a letter but not only that, he brought me some paper, a little stained but I can use it, and something called a pencil to write with. Fred, for that's his name, showed me how to sharpen the lead with a knife so I can write with it. I was so grateful to him until he spoiled it by asking for a kiss. No, I told him, sorry but I couldn't do that. I gave him a penny instead. The missus thought me silly, what's in a kiss, she said. No harm was ever done by a kiss unless it doesn't stop at one and she laughed.

Nora's letter says that her new mistress has a shop and she would have thrown out the paper because of the dampness. The pencil is just a fraction of what it once was, so the lady let her keep the stub. To me, it is precious because I don't know how long it will last. I have six weeks to write my reply before he comes back again and I intend to write all about my life on this farm and how happy I am to be here. I hope the pencil lasts that long.

It will be Christmas in two weeks and we are fattening up a pig; it will be a right good feast the missus has promised. There will be fruit from the orchard and plum pudding and we are to go to Sorell in the new cart to attend service on Christmas morning. The new church is almost built, they say, and so we won't be using that barn as a church anymore. The missus will stay behind to see to the dinner and because she's now quite big with child, says she doesn't want to bounce around in the cart. I asked her if she was hoping for a girl this time and she says no, boys are needed to work the land. Like me, she rarely gets to leave the farm, other than on the odd Sunday when we can be spared. There's just too much to do and if anything's needed, the master has to fetch it on his horse. But he doesn't like to leave the land either unless it is to sell extra produce, so we make do. Sometimes a farmer from a nearby farm will come by when the bull is needed or he has a runt that he wants to swap for honey.

I'm good at milking and churning so we have plenty of salted butter and cheese. I look after the chickens and collect their eggs, but I can't bring myself to kill any when they get too old for laying. Old Isaac's done some butchering, so when it's needed he'll sharpen his knife, and he tries not to worry the calf or the pig. He'll hide the knife until he's ready, and then slit its throat cleanly and holds it, talking softly until it sinks to the ground and the bright red blood pools around it in the straw. Sometimes the other animals watch and I often wonder if they're frightened or angry. The missus told me not to be so daft but Isaac, he says we're all living things and a pig will scream its fear in a slaughterhouse so he tries to make their passing easier. He'll fondle an old hen and scratch its neck before he twists it real fast and it's done in a flash. He reckons it makes the meat taste sweeter if the animals are not afeared before they go.

Three years ago, I'd never seen or known any of this.

Part 3- Chapter 10

Late January 1827 Hobart

Two years, two years, two years... Nora kept mumbling this to herself. He promised to come for her in two years, so only another week or two to wait. Oh, the bitter shame of it. Why did the shipwreck have to happen? She felt so tired and depressed; her head ached in the blistering heat of the summer's noon. She took no pleasure from the blueness of the sky or the sparkling water of Sullivan's Cove that day, as she walked through the town to pick up a letter for her mistress. A ship had docked the day before from England and her eye caught the glimpse of a rowing boat between a new convict ship and the shore. She stayed to watch, hoping for a miracle and that George would be in that boat He wasn't, so she turned a corner towards the postal office, her head down and her eyes smarting with unshed tears.

The letter was there but also one for Nora herself, which she did not expect. It was only two months since her last letter from home. She recognised her brother's writing and her heart leapt a little, perhaps it was news of her sister's baby. She would leave it until her work was ended for the day and it would be there to look forward to. God knows she needed cheering up.

The banging on the kitchen door of the British Hotel the next morning attracted Cook's attention and she was none too pleased. Lunch was behind schedule and there was a full complement of guests. As she opened the door a sobbing creature fell in. It was that friend of Helen's and she was in a right state, caused by drink, why the girl reeked of it! Cook called for help and Betsy came running.

'Betsy, go and find Helen now and don't let anyone know about her,' Cook said pointing with distaste to the figure crumpled on the floor.

Helen abandoned the table she was setting and rushed to the kitchen.

'Oh, my word! Whatever's the matter, Nora?'

'I shouldn't think she's capable of telling you,' said Cook. 'But one thing is clear you have to get her out of here and get yourself back to work as soon as possible. I will cover for you for twenty minutes, no longer.'

Helen had no idea where to take her but she hauled Nora up and manhandled her out of the door, shocked again at how light and thin she was. She hadn't realised, too bound up with her own worries, most likely. She felt guilty. Now where to take her without being seen by a constable? Helen grasped her friend and stumbled up the street with her until she found a small wooden fenced garden. Over the fence, she saw sheets flapping on a washing line. Remembering how laundry helped to hide her from the sailors on the ship, she opened the latch on the gate and dragged Nora into the garden, shutting the gate silently behind her. The back of the house had a separate, brick kitchen, masking the gate from the house. Helen noticed mimosa in full flower further down the garden and calculated that she could hide Nora behind the foliage. She managed to drag Nora into the heady scented bushes and breathed a small sigh of relief. She felt the washing and found it to be quite wet, certainly a long way from the iron. With any luck, it would not be taken in for two or three hours.

'Now tell me what's happened?' she whispered, in terror of being discovered. But then she realised that Nora had passed out and she did not look likely to come around soon.

What to do, what to do? Helen's mind was in turmoil. Could she leave Nora here and come back after serving the dinner? Would she still be here? What if she came 'round and staggered through the streets of Hobart until she was arrested? But what will happen to Davy if I am arrested? She shook her friend and begged her to wake up, aware of the minutes ticking away. She tried pinching Nora's face but it was no good.

Helen forced herself to think it through. Is Nora going to get into trouble for this? Helen decided on balance that she was. In fact, she didn't see how to avoid it. Nora must be in neglect of her duty already, and she was so drunk that it couldn't be disguised. So, after trying to waken Nora once more and failing, Helen decided to go back to work and beg Cook for an hour off after lunch. Unless someone came out to take the sheets from the line, Helen didn't think Nora would be seen. She crept back down the path, past the washing, looked over the gate to see if anyone was passing then rushed back to work.

For the next two hours, she was beset with anxiety and guilt. How could she have left her friend? Cook told her she had done a wise thing, but it didn't help. What if, even now, Nora was under arrest and realised she had been abandoned. She might never speak to her again. As soon as the meal finished and the dishes cleared away Cook let her go for 'only for an hour, mind.'

Helen rushed back to the garden and, seeing the sheets still on the line, opened the gate once more and crept towards the bushes. Nora was still there and awake. Helen crossed herself, thanking God for his mercy.

'I didn't know where I was. The last thing I remember was banging on your door, so I thought I had better stay here.' Nora's words came out slurred.

'What's happened?'

Nora's mind struggled to remember, then it came of a sudden and she gasped and would have screamed, but for Helen clamping a hand over her mouth.

'Shush, shush. Careful we mustn't be found here.' Helen glanced around wildly to see if they'd been heard but seeing nothing she nodded to Nora to continue.

'It's my Da. He's died. Something in his belly burst. Helen, I cannot take anymore, truly I can't.'

Nora was falling apart and incapable of acting to help herself. Helen despaired. There was nothing to say. For the first time, she wondered if her gentle, mild-mannered friend would survive this latest shock. To get through everything that God was throwing at Nora, you had to be tough, and toughness was not something that Nora owned in any quantity. Helen sighed and realised that the only way she could help was to get her back to her mistress and plead with her to not report the matter to the constable.

Helen struggled to make Nora stand. Her legs wanted to go any way other than in a straight line. It may have been funny in different circumstances; right now, it put the fear of God into Helen. Instructing Nora to be quiet, Helen half dragged and half carried her to the gate. Once there, she put her arm around Nora's waist, holding her as tight as possible, and gave her a rag to put against her face, telling her to pretend she was crying. Nora had no need to pretend.

She got Nora through the gate and started to walk her steadily towards her mistress's shop. Passers-by stared and Helen muttered her friend had received bad news and was not feeling herself. Eventually, she got her into the shop but was horrified to see the wife of a magistrate being served by Nora's mistress. There could be no escape for either of them. Helen wanted to scream Davy's name. She had let him down; he was lost to her, but for how long this time?

Nora was first up before the magistrate next morning. He took note of her bad news, having read Nora's letter for himself. But her mistress said that it wasn't the first time she was drunk. The magistrate read her previous conviction. He felt there was no option but to commit her to the cells for a week on bread and water, followed by three months in gaol and then to be assigned to country service, away from the temptations of Hobart Town.

As for Helen, her mistress spoke well of her. Yes, she neglected her duty and left her master's service without leave. Cook didn't dare say she had given her permission. A week in the cells on bread and water and she may return to her master.

Helen could not believe her luck and left the dock saying, 'Thank you, Sir, thank you, Ma'am.' A week was not a problem. Davy would miss her but he wouldn't forget her again.

Part 3- Chapter 11

Sarah

February 1827 Sorell

The missus and her baby girl are dead! Everything was so good, we were happy and now this. It's all at sixes and sevens. The children cry sorrowfully for their mother. The master works from sunup 'til sundown and scarcely comes near the house, other than to sleep. It's as if he can't bear the place without her. I've not seen a smile or a laugh on anyone's face these last two weeks. I miss her too. She was a good missus and fair to me. I knew none better. I remember when I arrived and was so scared; not knowing what to expect. She didn't try to soothe me. She wasn't that kind of a woman. Plain speaking and plain to look at, but she showed me what to I had to do and let me get on with it. By and by I came to like her and respect her. I'm worried about how things are going to be now.

Neighbours brought food and offered help, and I was pleased to accept it, because I know little of cooking, beyond peeling potatoes. The Missus always cooked. One of the neighbours, Mrs Daniels, has offered to teach me how to cook a few simple meals, but I have so little time now with everything else to do. I must ask the master if we can get another girl, but I'm scared he might bite my head off, him being in a bad mood and sorrowing so much. Mrs Daniels says she will ask him for me.

He's told Mrs Daniels he will think about it, but not until after the harvest is in so I must struggle on for another month. The two eldest boys have been roped in to help with the chickens, but the little one just follows me around all the time asking for cuddles. Whenever I pick him up to soothe him, he screams if I try to put him down. So, we make a game of it and he thinks he's helping me when I milk the cows and churn the butter. I never knew kneading dough could take so long, especially with a two-year-old wanting to help. The flour seems to get everywhere.

There's to be a harvest feast at the Daniels's farm three weeks on Saturday and we are bidden to be there. The master is reluctant, but Mrs Daniels insists and gave him a piece of her mind about getting back to normality, saying the children needed to learn how to be happy again.

Mrs Daniels has a good soul, but is what Nora would call, a gossip. She told me that folk need to look out for each other. There are dangers she said. I know of snakebites and bushfires, but she told me terrifying stories about Matthew Brady and his gang of bushrangers holding up the garrison in Sorell, setting all the prisoners free and then shooting the garrison commander. They had to take the poor man's arm off. Thank goodness, he was caught and hanged just a few months ago. The missus never told me stories of him roaming around. She must have known how frightened I'd have been.

Then there's the blacks. But they're harmless, I said to her. Around here they may be, she told me. But there have been attacks and murders elsewhere. You need to take precautions. It saddened me for I thought them gentle creatures and suppose they must have been driven to it.

Late March

I am so confused. I don't know what to think as It is only two months since the missus died, but the master has told me we should marry. It started with a dance at the harvest feast. There being Scottish folk around, someone played the bagpipes and someone else suggested a dance. The boys and I were so happy watching the fun, and then he came up and asked me to dance. I tried to refuse, but he took my hand, wouldn't take no for an answer. I was too busy concentrating on not stepping on his feet, for it was a fast Highland Reel. After all, I had never danced before. Content as I was to sit and watch on the ship. Anyways I laughed so much, as we tripped and stumbled around, but thought nothing more of it. A week later, I caught him looking at me as I served him the boiled chicken and potatoes that I was so proud of. I must have been grinning with pleasure, for not having burnt the food, and he smiled back. It was good to see him cheerful, and the boys, seeing him smile, perked up no end and started to chatter. For once, there was happy talk at the table.

This morning as I was milking the cows, he came in and sat on the ground beside me. I was worried that I'd done something wrong. He asked me my age and I told him seventeen or thereabouts, and he said old enough to marry then. Oh no, I told him, I don't think I shall ever marry.

He asked why ever not and told me I was a good girl; that I worked hard and cared for the children. He said many a man would want me.

I told him that I was too plain and that marriage scared me.

'Well,' he said, and taking my face in his hands and turning it towards him, said 'I would marry you. You are a fine girl, the children like you and I want you to be my wife. I need a wife and the children need a mother, most of all little Billy, he's taken quite a shine to you.'

I was dumbstruck. I tried to get up, but he held me fast and I started to cry.

He said, 'Has someone hurt you because you look so fearful?'

I nodded to him and cried even more so that I could hardly see for the tears. He let go of me and I wiped my face on my sleeve.

Waiting a while for me to calm myself, he said, 'I'd never hurt you, Sarah. Mull it over, won't you? You need help with the children and your other jobs. I believe you will make a good missus, so we'll leave off getting help for a week or two and hopefully you will change your mind.'

Mrs Daniels told me later I would be a fool to say no. 'You love it here, don't you?' she said, and I nodded. 'What if he marries someone else and she then gets rid of you. How would that make you feel?'
She saw the terror in my face. Even the thought of having to start somewhere afresh didn't bear thinking about. 'He's a good man, isn't he? Once again, I nodded. I could not fault her argument.
'Is it what happens between a man and a woman that troubles you?

She must have seen the tears well up in my eyes again for she put her arms around me as a mother would and patted my back gently.

'Being forced and being married and taking pleasure in each other is as chalk is to cheese,' she told me. 'He will be gentle and if you grow to love him, as I am sure you will, it can be the most wonderful thing to lie together.'

I told her she was the kindest neighbour that I could ever have and I would pray for the wisdom to see the right path. It was her turn to nod. As she left, she told me that she expected to call again in a week and bring me some of her raspberry jam, hoping that I'd come to the right decision by then.

Oh, how I prayed over the next two or three days. The master was around the house more now the harvest was finished. He did his best to help out. He told me he loved listening to me read from the Bible, and I started to grow a little more comfortable in his presence, but still, I sought a sign.

Early April 1827

Today I received a sign. This morning the pedlar arrived bearing a letter from Jenny. Helen had been to see her and was really upset. It turns out the Nora is in a bad way. She received news that her father is dead and that, on top of George being drowned, has sent her to drink and she's back in prison. Jenny writes that Nora is due to be released from prison shortly and sent to the country. Helen asks if there is any way my master and mistress could take her as she knows being with me would help her, but to make sure I keep her away from drink.

Well, there's little enough drink here that I have ever seen, other than the mild ale which the missus brewed. There is nothing that would please me more than to have Nora here. I thought and prayed about it for the rest of the day, and at last, my mind is made up. This evening I sat down with the master once the children were abed.

'Have you come to a decision?' he asked.

'Yes, I said, I have prayed for a sign and it has come and if you will agree I shall marry you, Henry.' And I told him about Nora and how she saved my life on the ship and now she needed our help to recover.

'The doctor told me before I came here how country air and hard work would cure me and it has. Maybe it can do the same for Nora, so please say yes and I will marry you tomorrow.'

He sat for a long moment looking at me and then said, 'You don't need to marry me to save your friend. I would try to do that anyway. I want you to marry me because you want to be my wife and a mother to our family. We could be happy together, Sarah.'

I think I looked at him properly then, for the very first time, and I saw such goodness and kindness in him that I fell in love with him, right at that moment. At least I think it's love. Something shifted within me, as though an unseen hand grasped a hold of my heart and squeezed hard, and suddenly it seemed to beat to a different rhythm, faster, slower, even skipping a beat altogether. Never did I believe I might love, but my heart is now singing with the joy of it.

How selfish of me to ask that of him and not offer my love in return. I knelt before him and promised to love him and the children. I told him to look into my heart, as it now belonged to him. He reached down and picked me up and told me I had should never kneel before him. We would marry and live as equals, not master and servant. Then he kissed me tenderly on the lips and I did not shrink but let myself be enveloped in his strong, brown arms. I felt safe.

'I am home?' I whispered looking at his face.

'Yes, Sarah, this is our home.'

Later he led me to his bed and he was so gentle and loving that it was as wonderful as Mrs Daniels said it could be.

Part 3- Chapter 12

Mid-April 1827 Sorell

The last two weeks had been a whirlwind of activity for Henry and Sarah. Permission to Marry needed to be applied for, though unlikely to be refused. Since Sarah had landed in the colony no black marks were noted against her name, and she was marrying a free settler. She would continue to be assigned to him until set free by the system. Henry told Sarah that they could apply for a pardon for her in a few years.

Banns needed to be read in the new church of St George in Sorell. Mrs Daniels delighting in her matchmaking, offered to do the wedding breakfast, while her husband promised to give Sarah away. She assured Sarah that marrying within three or four months of a wife dying was not seen as unseemly, but practical in a colony where survival, especially of women of childbearing age, was often against the odds.

The children accepted the idea and were not unhappy. Billy treated Sarah as his mother already and the two older boys, Harry and Edward, liked and trusted her, although they continued to mourn for their mother. But now Harry shyly asked Sarah if she would teach him to read and Sarah, glancing at Henry, saw his nod of approval and loved him all over again. She was to get her childhood dream of helping children with their reading, but Harry would also learn to write, she intended to make sure of that.

Sarah was in emotional turmoil. Love was so unexpected. She had not the words to describe her joy. She found herself singing at her work and viewing the world in a different way. As the autumn days shortened she watched for the changes, not dreading the onset of winter, but marvelling at the subtle alterations in light, the earlier sunsets, the touch of gentle rain and then it struck her. This land was her land; she would live here until she died. Gone the desire to sail the seas and discover more about the world. This tiny corner of Van Diemen's Land was hers to know and care for. God had blessed her and she vowed to thank him every day.

There was so much to do before the wedding. So many fruit and vegetables needed bottling for the winter, thank goodness Henry's wife had taught her how to do it. Sarah allowed herself to start thinking of her as Janet, rather than the missus. She had no recipes for Janet's cider or pickles, so once again she asked the redoubtable Mrs Daniels for help. Now Sarah had paper and the nub of a pencil she wrote them down, determined to ask Henry for more supplies, as she could hardly hold the pencil, it was so small.

She thought of Nora and how she longed to take care of her. Henry said he would do his best to have her assigned to him, but it was not usual to ask for someone in particular and so there was no guarantee.

'Tell them your new wife knew her family back in England and we are concerned for her.' advised Sarah.

'You don't think they will put two and two together and realise you came out on the same ship and were friends?'

'Maybe, but it has to be worth a try, Henry.' Her pleading look made him smile. She was a clever little thing, this new wife to be, but unused to the ways of the world. He would like to bet the government agent might be more swayed by the promise of a leg of ham.

'Please, can you also send for my box that came with me on the ship? In it, there's a dress I want to wear for our wedding. I can't get married in this convict uniform.' She handed him her tag and he promised to take it with him into Sorell, where he was to meet the reverend and the government agent.

They picked a day in May for the wedding once permission came through. Meanwhile, work on the small farm continued as normal. But at night, after the children were asleep, Sarah and Henry explored each other's bodies with increasing delight. And in the mornings Sarah sang as she prepared breakfast, her voice not as melodic as Nora's, but she could hold a tune. Her happiness was contagious and Henry, while he still thought fondly of Janet, who helped him build this farm over ten difficult years, now found himself yearning for the evenings with his family and nights with Sarah.

When did he first think of Sarah in that way, he wondered? Certainly, when she arrived on the farm his wife told him that the new servant reminded her of a wounded animal and he couldn't but agree. A thin and scrawny girl, scared of her own reflection, he remembered being disappointed with how weak she looked. But with good food, she filled out and even grew an inch or two. She was willing to learn and soon became a great help to his wife, beyond that he took little notice. When she started to read from the Bible on a Sunday, he liked her voice and the feeling she put into the words, noting how reading calmed her. The first time he saw her smile was when she played with the boys as an older sister might.

But when his wife and new daughter were dying, it was Sarah, who ran herself ragged nursing them with gentleness and devotion. She cooled their fevered skin with water fresh from the well and tried to coax the baby to drink milk dripped from a cloth into her tiny puckered mouth. He regretted not spending more time with his wife in her last hours, but he dared not let the wheat rot in the fields, or how could he feed the boys next year? His only comfort was that Sarah was with them, caring for them. After they died he threw himself into the harvest to numb the pain and the guilt he felt.

No, it was after the harvest that the emptiness and loneliness hit him. He realised that marriage was not only a necessity for the children, but also for him. He missed the easy companionship and honest love of a woman. But how might he go about the search for a new wife? He dreaded what might be involved. Henry had grown up with Janet, her parents were neighbours and marriage seemed sensible, the next step, and it worked. They each knew what the other thought without the need for words. It may have lacked passion but it was comfortable, uncomplicated. Henry had no idea how to meet another woman or how to court her. He disliked the idea of marrying someone he did not know. But when would he have the time to find out whether she would suit being a farmer's wife and a mother to his boys?

It was Mrs Daniels who suggested he dance with Sarah. She came up to him while he was drinking cider with Isaac.

'Go on,' she said. 'You've a face like a dog without a bone. You need some fun, and so does that girl. I'll look after Billy.'

Then he caught sight of Sarah in her shabby, patched convict garb. Her face shone with laughter as she watched the dancing, and the boys laughed with her. Billy lay peacefully on her lap, half asleep, his thumb firmly in his mouth. His heart leapt with love, as he watched his family and, with butterflies in his stomach, he found that the answer was living in his own house.

Part 3- Chapter 13

Nora stepped out of the prison section of the female factory and on to an open cart; one of seven women assigned to the country. An unsympathetic, convict constable chivvied and chided the women until they and their scanty belongings were loaded. A box lay on the floor of the cart. With a pang, Nora recognised it as similar to the one she had been given on the ship, which was still somewhere here in Hobart. She fingered the tag at her neck. Would her dress have survived all this time? Maybe it was moth-eaten or even adorning another convict woman? Had George survived she would be looking forward to wearing it now, an April bride.

The cart began to roll slowly northwards, pulled by two overworked, tired horses. The women sat silent and grim-faced, fearing life in the country. Most had been town dwellers and never set foot on a farm and wondered if running away back to town was an option. But they had been given a stern warning to work hard for their new masters or face a worse punishment next time.

The last few months had almost destroyed Nora. For the first week, her craving for a drink nearly sent her mad. She couldn't keep any food down, let alone the dry bread of her punishment. Her shrieking nightmares bounced off the thick, stone walls of her solitary cell.

When she entered the crime class of the Female Factory, she made no effort to talk to any of the other women and they left her alone. There was something about her eyes which disturbed them. They looked empty. She was set to picking oakum apart; the tarry, blackened rope tore at her nails and then her fingers. She lost hope, lost all sense of self. Believing she had been the cause of her father's death, the guilt ate into her, like a worm burrowing into her skin. It was a wonder she had tears left to cry but they scarcely ceased. When she wiped her eyes, the tar and blood streaked her cheeks until she looked like some ancient Celt, mourning the loss of her warrior husband.

Sent on to the laundry, her fingers recovered, until burnt by the lye soap, but her mind did not. Without Helen or Sarah to help her bear the loss of her father, her despair grew and grew. She began to long for death, to join her parents in heaven. Living was too hard, too painful.

Now she sat in the cart, staring at familiar landmarks without seeing them. A voice penetrated her consciousness, someone was calling her name. Peering around, she caught sight of Helen waving to her from the street. It was only half-past five in the morning and still dark. She must have got up especially, to see her off, defying the curfew. What a good, loyal friend she had been. Nora's misery mounted as she realised she may never see Helen again.

'Take care, Nora, and good luck. Try to let me know how you are.'

Tears, never far away, formed at Nora's eyes and she attempted a wave. Her mouth wouldn't form any words. Helen watched as her friend disappeared into the distance, shocked and saddened by the pale, mute figure hunched in the open cart. What had they done to her? She prayed her country assignment would help her get back on her feet. A constable had told Helen when Sarah was due to leave but not her destination.

Nora and the other women shivered together in the cool autumn weather. A pale watery sun rose over the mists of the Derwent River. Across the water ghostly, slumbering trees loomed like giants through the mist. After an hour or so, they arrived at a ferry where the river narrowed. Climbing down from the cart they stamped their frozen feet trying to get the circulation back. A short ferry ride in a flat-bottomed boat took then to the far side of the Derwent, where another cart waited. The journey began anew, this time eastwards up into tree clad hills and then back down towards open farmland. The sun regularly dodged behind large, scudding grey clouds which threatening rain. At noon, they stopped to eat a chunk of bread and cold meat and to drink tepid water from a flask.

'What I wouldn't give for a warming cup of tea' said one of the women. The words flew over Nora's head, making no impression. That she was cold, her body knew, but her mind was closing down.

Grumbling, the women made their way to some bushes to relieve themselves. Nora joined them, before being ordered back on the cart.

Five stops were made in the early afternoon. Each time a woman's name was called. Nora watched, without curiosity, as the woman departed with her new master. In the back of her mind, she knew it would be her turn soon. The remaining women hunched into their shawls as the sun began to sink into the sky, and a fine drizzle began. As dusk fell they arrived at a small town with handsome, brick buildings, before turning right. A little way down the road was a lock-up, their home for the night. Three shivering, damp women were led into the goal, given much needed hot food and left to sleep in an unheated, solitary cell. Huddling together for warmth, they passed an uncomfortable night, their bones sore and aching from being thrown around in the un-sprung cart for ten hours.

How much longer they asked the constable as he hurried them back into the cart the next morning. He told them everyone would be settled by noon. They passed over a handsome arched sandstone bridge as they left the town of Richmond behind. Travelling eastwards once more, the horses clip-clopped through rich farmland, up a slight incline and turned south-east.

The rain passed leaving a bright clear sky and Nora began to find herself interested in her surroundings. Her father would have loved this land. She remembered how he longed for the green land of Ireland, while closeted in his tiny workshop in smoggy London. Nora wished she could write to him and describe it but this upset her again. She sank back into her shawl and closed her eyes and began to doze. She awoke with a start. It was her name being called this time, but she couldn't think where she was. The constable shouted for her to get off the cart and began to tug at her sleeve. Wiping her sleep dribbled mouth on the back of her other sleeve she rose unsteadily and made her way to the back of the cart and climbed off. The constable got on and picked up the box, which confused Nora. It wasn't her box, was it? She still had her tag.

A tallish man dressed in shabby work overalls stood by the cart. She guessed his age to be about thirty-five. His thin, sandy hair caught the light of the sun which was now overhead. His pale blue, almost grey eyes, looked kindly at her. Although numb, she felt relieved to see the hint of a smile under his moustache and beard.

'Are you Nora?' he asked.

She nodded even more confused that he should know her name. He took a piece of paper made his mark on it and handed it back. Then hoisting the box on a broad shoulder gestured at her to follow him. She looked around at the constable and the two remaining women. The constable gestured impatiently at her to follow the man, while the women stared on with blank faces. What did they care where she was going? Mute with resignation she followed him towards a rough looking wooden dwelling where she could see a woman and children waiting. So this was assigned to the country, she sighed. From a smart Westminster address to this poor farm in the back of beyond, the downward spiral continues.

She noticed the woman was in convict dress as she got closer. Oh Lord, servant to a convict, how she's going to enjoy taunting me. Her torment wasn't over by any means. 'Is this God's way of punishing me?' She murmured, reaching into her pocket for her rosary.

All at once the woman started running towards her crying 'Nora.' She recognised the voice but didn't believe it. This woman, now taller than Nora, looked comely and her body, shapely, not whip thin or scrawny. Caught up in her arms, kisses poured onto Nora's face and her hands. The children and the man smiled and laughed and everyone seemed to be patting her and Sarah. Yes, it was Sarah. Nora, overcome with emotion, heard the voices becoming fainter and she stopped being able to focus. Blackness descended before she fell to the ground.

When she came to, she was lying on a flock mattress under a rough woollen blanket, her head on a feather pillow in a room smelling of newly cut wood. There was little in the way of furniture or decoration and the unglazed window just had a piece of canvas clipped back against the log wall. The door opened and Sarah walked in.

'Do you like the room that Henry built for you?'

'Built for me?'

Yes. I always used to sleep in the kitchen out back, but I told Henry that you would expect a proper bedroom. I'm sorry it's so small.'

'I would be happy with the kitchen, as long as you're here. Look I don't understand what's happening. Why am I here?

Sarah smiled and gave a nervous cough. 'You are our new servant, but don't worry about that. If you feel like getting up I have some food prepared.'

'Isn't it me, who should be serving you?'

Nora got out of the bed and followed Sarah through the door. The man, who must be Henry, was sitting at a rough, rustic table with three boys and another older man, a convict to judge by his clothes. The remains of a meal lay on the table but with a clean tin plate for Nora. Introductions were made and then the men and the two older boys made their excuses, saying they had to get back to work, leaving the two friends to get reacquainted.

Sarah sat with Billy on her knee and while Nora ate, she told her of her life on the farm. Nora was shocked to hear of the death of Henry's wife but stunned to hear that Sarah was to marry Henry the following week.

'You look so happy, Sarah. I can see he's a good man. I can't believe that the last time I saw you I wasn't even sure you could survive here. How we have changed, you and I. It's me who now wonders if I will live through this sentence.'

Sarah silently agreed. This Nora was a shadow of the girl on the ship. Sadness had dulled her beautiful green eyes. Her gentle, welcoming smile had disappeared behind a face, gaunt with fatigue and fragility. And her hair, that jaw-dropping coppery hair, hung lifeless and unkempt. Nora reminded her now of herself as a fourteen-year-old. She saw the same vulnerability, the lack of hope. We have got to her just in time, she thought. Silently she thanked Helen for suggesting Nora came here and Henry for making it happen. But life on this farm would cure her ills, of that she had no doubt.

'I am so sorry for your loss Nora. But now you are here your life will change. I will make it so. Come, let me show you around our little home and the farm. We will work together and soon you will come to love it as much as I do.'

Later that same night as Nora helped clear away the meal she began to yawn and Sarah told her to get to bed. As she made her way to the small bedroom, Nora caught sight of Henry watching her. She worried that he was judging her for leaving Sarah to finish the work.

She knelt beside her bed.' Tomorrow', she vowed,' I will work as hard as I can to justify his kindness and Sarah's belief in me. Please give me the strength, dear Lord. Help me repair the mess I have made of my life. I will always be your servant.' She crossed herself and then climbed into bed and slept soundly.

Sarah and Henry peeped in before they went to bed and Sarah could not leave without planting a kiss on Nora's head.

'Thank you, Henry,' she said, turning towards him. 'I believe we have saved her life.' He took her in his arms and kissed her. He had no need for words.

There was so much to do with the wedding only six days away. Apart from all the usual chores, Sarah was making new clothes for the boys out of material she found in a trunk in the bedroom, which she suspected had been Janet's best dress. But she also needed to look at her own dress and lifting it from of the box she smoothed it out. The quality material didn't appear to have suffered much. Yes, it smelt musty and needed a good wash and press but the dress was serviceable if a little plain and old fashioned.

Nora told her to try it on because she suspected it no longer fitted Sarah. Perhaps by reversing her original alterations, it might work. She held out her reddened, scarred fingers which had not held a needle for months.

'Janet had a salve for hands and fingers; let me get you some. You can't sew yet, but maybe in a day or two.' Sarah scurried off to find the ointment.

Nora thought the dress needed a lace collar as decoration but where could they get that? Sarah returned and took her hands, gently applying the ointment.

'Is that Maudie and Peg's bag? Nora pointed to the bottom of the box and Sarah lifted it out. They silently grasped each other's hands sharing a smile.

'Will you be my bridesmaid? The boys are going to be pages but I would love you to be my bridesmaid, Nora.'

Nora looked down at her brown convict dress, trying to imagine the scene in which it could appear normal to be dressed like this and still be a bridesmaid. She laughed wryly.

'Of course, I will but are you sure? Just look at me. I am a mess.'

Sometime later, on the second day of Nora's arrival, she was doing her best to scrabble around in the hen house to find more eggs when she heard a voice above her saying.

'So, you must be Nora.'

Nora got off her knees and faced a smiling woman whose ample girth and short stature made her look as round as she was wide.

'I'm Mrs Daniels from the next farm over yonder.' She pointed towards the south-west.

Nora quickly bobbed her knee.

'Oh goodness! You don't need to bother with that my dear. My father came here the same way you did and the same way as Henry's parents. We're all trying to make a go of it here and it's a better life, I think, than the streets of London?' She looked at Nora, but getting no affirmative nod, continued.

'I hear Sarah wants you for a bridesmaid but you haven't anything else to wear. Is that so?' Nora nodded this time. 'Well, I will send over an old dress of my mother-in-law's. It's good material, and you are about the same size as her, perhaps you can do something with it. I hear you are a wonder at sewing. If that's so I might be able to find you a little extra work. You wouldn't mind earning a bit of money in your free time I don't suppose?' Nora smiled this time and gave her thanks.

Despite the hard physical work involved with helping to run the house and the farm and the painful, extra hours sewing into the middle of the night to get the wedding clothes ready, Nora's cares began to drift away. Suddenly she was useful and valued again. Sarah was solicitous and Henry and the boys welcoming and, most importantly, she felt part of a family. Even 'Old Isaac', as everyone seemed to call him, was friendly, showing her the best way to milk cows and how to gather honey without getting stung.

She breathed in the fresh air and looked north towards the hills, and then towards an inlet which she could just glimpse to the west. Nora realised that her vision of a home was Sarah's reality. However pleasant to share it with Sarah for the moment, one day she wanted her own. Perhaps she would still get to wear her wedding dress. Another George must be out in Van Diemen's Land somewhere. Her spirits lifted and Sarah, seeing her later that morning, knew a corner had been turned.

'There is magic in this place,' she thought.

The morning of the wedding day dawned warmer and sunnier than of late. Henry had gone over to stay with the Daniels the night before and Mr Daniels would drive Nora, her bridesmaid and three pages into Sorell. The boys got into their new clothes laughing excitedly and looking forward to the promised feast.

Nora finished altering her new dress late the night before. The dark navy blue wool flattered her pale skin and she was thankful for the long sleeves should it get chillier later. Dancing was promised that evening. The dress was high-waisted and Nora guessed it dated back to the early years of the Regency. Alas, there was no time to restyle it, but she edged the sleeves and hem with a strip of red material she discovered in the trunk to make it a little more stylish.

After altering Sarah's dress, she had washed and pressed it, still bemoaning the lack of embellishment. Two days before the wedding she plucked up the courage to ask Henry if he would go into Sorell to find a lace collar.

'I was wondering what to get Sarah for a wedding present. Do you think that would do?'

'Yes,' said Nora. 'She would probably ask for a book, but a lace collar will also last for a lifetime.'

Sarah looked a picture. The dove grey of the dress with its delicate lace collar suited her fair colouring. Mrs Daniels had lent her a pretty blue bonnet and Isaac had woven some greenery and dried summer flowers into a posy for her. When Mr Daniels arrived with his cart they were overwhelmed to see the horse's tail had been plaited with red ribbon and the cart decorated with garlands of greenery.

Old Isaac helped Sarah and Nora into the cart with the boys. He and Mr Daniels sat up front and they set off on the three-mile journey to Sorell.

'I feel like a princess,' whispered Sarah.

'And so, you should,' replied Nora, squeezing her arm. They continued to trot down the road and as they came into Sorell people waved to them and wished the bride happiness.

The wedding guests barely took up two rows of pews in the recently consecrated, galleried church, which could happily seat hundreds. Sarah, holding on to Mr Daniels' arm, walked slowly and in silence down the aisle, there being no money for an organist. The boys and Nora followed behind. Sarah stopped beside Henry and Nora gave an involuntary gasp as she recognised the Reverend Garrard from the ship. Sarah grinned as she gave Nora her posy and whispered.

'Sorry I forgot to tell you about him.' She turned back to Henry, who smiled lovingly at her and the service began.

Later, at the wedding breakfast, Sarah tried to describe to Nora what had happened during the service. She and Henry were kneeling and saying their vows to each other when Sarah suddenly became aware of the light. Nora said it must have been the sunlight striking the window bur Sarah said no. The light was not just around them it was in her head and her heart and she heard Mrs Barnard speaking as clearly as Reverend Garrard.

'Search for the light,' she said over and over. I told her I've found it, it's here inside me. Love has found me. But I can't have spoken out loud because no one else heard. Then I noticed this warmth creeping first into my toes and slowly up my body until my fingers tingled and I felt the love of everyone around me and in return I loved them. This feeling hasn't left me since. It is God, isn't it? He has saved me.'

Nora didn't know what to say to Sarah but she was so happy for her. She stood watching the dancing, somewhat forlorn, wondering where was her own love? Still trapped in the depths of the sea or was there someone waiting for her on this island? She scanned the few wedding guests but there was no one young, single or who could measure up to George. Yes, she was happy for Sarah, her life had been turned around by the love of a good man. It just made Nora's own loss more acute. The great emptiness inside her no longer craved strong drink, but oh how she yearned to love again.

Part 3- Chapter 14

December 1827 Hobart

Jenny told Helen at the Sunday service that she had received a letter from Nora. Helen was used to them coming every couple of months or so. From the tone of them, both Nora and Sarah were in good health and enjoying their quiet country life. It gave Helen pleasure to know how she had helped Nora escape the perils of Hobart. Helen despaired of her life in Hobart. As the town grew, so did the availability of drink, gambling and bawdy houses. It reflected the worst excesses of British city life. A new Female Factory was being built at Cascades, way out of town, to house the many women who fell foul of the authorities by their drunken, wanton and impudent behaviour.

Jenny even confided to Helen that women and men came to the back of the hospital for sexual liaisons. The new doctor was complicit and said to be earning extra money with this arrangement. It upset Jenny and she was only too pleased to accept an offer of marriage from a widower. She intended moving out to New Norfolk in the New Year.

Helen steered clear of trouble as much as she could. There had been one other incident when she was caught fighting with another servant at the hotel. The new servant, also off the Henry, was a hardened Glaswegian, who loved a drink and when drunk, would pick a fight with anyone. Helen didn't want to fight but, forced to protect herself, fought with her usual passion and it turned into a right old ding-dong. They were both up before the magistrates again the next morning, Helen, remorseful and terrified at the thought of being unable to see Davy for months, the other woman, Maggie, hung-over but still belligerent. Yet again Mrs Ogilvie had spoken up for Helen and she received a reprimand for her behaviour, Maggie, however, was not seen again at the British Hotel.

Mrs Ogilvie told Helen, on her return, that it was her last chance and she would not speak up for her again. Since then she managed to keep out of trouble.

There was good news this time in Nora's letter. Jenny read that Sarah was in the family way and the child was due to be born in April. There were no health worries and Nora commented on how Sarah was a changed person. No more was she the scared, cowering waif, but a loving wife and mother to her three stepchildren, and serenely confident in her belief that she had been saved by God.

'How I wish you could see her, Helen,' Jenny read. 'She has such gentleness and grace, that make all who meet her love her. She is still shy but has an inner strength which was totally absent before. She almost shimmers when Henry looks at her so adoringly. Even the animals behave for her as they never do for me. I am not sure I am cut out to be a farm servant, so Sarah leaves me to the domestic side and carries on with the chickens, or chucks as they call them here, and the cows and vegetable garden.' Jenny wiped away a tear as she read it. 'Isn't that wonderful,' she said. 'To think how she was so ill, we all despaired of her.'

Helen agreed with Jenny, saying it was a miracle. Later, thinking of the letter, she smiled for the Nora she knew would have no idea what to do with a cow. She, on the other hand, longed to be out of Hobart and working on a farm, as long as Davy was with her. She could imagine how happy and healthy he would be toddling around and helping her with the chores. Still daydreaming in this vein she prepared to serve the Sunday dinner to this week's guests.

By this time, she did not need to think too much about what she was doing. After almost three years of domestic service, she accomplished her duties efficiently and automatically. Set the table with a cleanly laundered cloth and polished silverware, hand out the plates of good prime beef and serve the vegetables. Next, gather up the empty dishes and serve out a hot steamed jam or syrup pudding, nothing too difficult in that.

The clatter of the plate of beef as it hit the floor made heads turn and wonder at Helen's face, with its look of shock and fear, her hand clasped to her mouth, her eyes wild and staring. Whatever was it that had made her so frightened? All were agog, and there was silence as the guests stayed their knives and forks, intent upon what was going to happen next.

'It's Helen, isn't it? Whatever is the matter? It's only me. Surely I am not such a shock that would make you stare so.'

'You are supposed to be dead.' The guests gasped at her words. Here was a drama to recount to their friends. Torn between their hot dinner and this riveting conversation, their knives hovered above their plates. 'Did you not drown? We were told the ship went down.'

'Yes, but all were saved. We were shipwrecked near the shore and there was time to launch a boat. With only the crew and a few passengers we made it to shore in time.'

'Nora supposes you died two years ago. She has been mad with grief.'

'Nora thinks me dead? She has not married another, has she?'

You could hear a pin drop as the diners waited for the answer.

'No, she has not.' A pleasurable sigh rippled around the room. They would have clapped their pleasure at this happy outcome if they could, but now turned back to their beef with a smile of contentment. Helen fell to the floor to clear away the mess. George made a move to help and she whispered that she had received a letter from Nora today.

'May I read it?'

'Do you still want to marry her?'

'Oh yes, if she wants me.'

'She will.' The letter was in her pocket. She fished it out and passed it to George who took it eagerly.

'Why did you not write to her?' she demanded, still upset at the pain Nora had needlessly endured and so angry with that good-for-nothing Jane. She better not come anywhere near Helen again.

'I can barely write my name. I gave her a note when you left the ship, but someone else wrote it. It has taken me longer than I hoped to get back. It was several weeks before we got another ship, and that time was without wages. How long will it take me to get to Sarah's farm?'

'Nora wrote that her journey took a day and a half, it may be quicker by boat.' For the first time, Helen noticed the youth seated next to

George. He reminded her of someone and seemed rapt in her answers but now she needed to replace the plate of beef and get a move on because the other diners wanted their pudding.

Later that night as her mind revolved endlessly around the scene in the dining room she saw the lad once again clearly in her mind and suddenly realised why he looked familiar.

'Oh yes,' she said to herself and turning over in her narrow bed. She smiled and drifted off into a restless sleep.

Part 3- Chapter 15

December 1827 Sorell

It was one of those beautiful summer days, the kind you dream about in the depths of winter; a cloudless blue sky; the heady perfume of flowers; bees busily darting around the flowering plants of the kitchen garden; the joyful sound of children's laughter as they scamper through their chores and pleasantly warm. Not so hot that you feel drained and long for a cool spot to lie down in, but warm enough to enjoy the sun's rays on your body.

Nora was picking the season's first peas and strawberries, as Sarah was too burdened now to crouch amongst the vegetables. Her back giving a little twinge, Nora sat back on her heels for a rest. She arched her back and neck, the mid-morning sun in her eyes now, despite the brim of her bonnet. As she moved her head sideways to stretch it she caught a glimpse of movement. There was a man walking towards her. By the way he walked, it wasn't Henry or Isaac, no this man was younger and taller and clean shaven, he walked with a slight roll. But he had come from the house so it must be her he wanted. She began to be alarmed that he was a constable come to take her back to Hobart. She didn't want to go back. She loved it here, she felt safe and peaceful. He still came towards her. Trembling she got to her feet, wiping her muddy hands on her dress.

'Nora,' he said. 'Nora it's me. See I'm not drowned. I've come back for you.'

For the second time in her life, Nora simply fell senseless to the ground, certain she had seen a ghost.

This time she did not wake on her bed but in George's arms, first aware of his murmuring voice and then the soft stroking of her hair and the salty wetness of tears falling from his eyes onto her upturned face. She did not struggle; thinking maybe she had died and gone straight to heaven, for this was not purgatory, no not at all. But her green eyes flickered open and she glimpsed his face and the love in his eyes, watching as his lips formed her name and bent to hers. At last, she drowned in the caress of those lips staying glued to him for what felt like minutes as her insides melted away. She could not move her lips from his but he, breathlessly lifted her face in his hands, wiping away his own tears and held her so close she felt the beating of his heart against hers.

'We will never be parted again,' he said and once again she drowned in his love.

When she could stand, he said, 'Come with me.' And he led her by the hand back to the house, where Sarah stood waiting at the door, her face lit by happiness and, Nora thought, a somewhat gleeful look. Sarah was bouncing on the balls of her feet she was so excited; her newly round stomach, jiggling up and down. She grabbed Nora's other hand and led her indoors.

'Close your eyes,' George said.

Nora looked up at him and he nodded so she closed her eyes and his hand covered her face.

'Now open them.'

She felt his arm slip around her body holding her in case she should fall again. Whatever next? Wasn't George's return from the dead the best present anyone could give her? Nothing compared with this joy. As his hand left her eyes, she opened them blinking in the gloom of the house and saw before her a boy, or rather a young man, the same height as her. He was grinning and she screamed his name.

'Jimmy. How on earth are you here?' She looked up at George, his face one big grin, and then Jimmy launched himself into his sister's arms. Once again, she was crying but this time laughing at the same time. This was a present she could never even have dreamt of and she mouthed 'thank you' to George, as she spun around the room with her middle brother whom she never thought to see again.

A little later, after Sarah made a pot of tea and they were sitting down at the table, George explained how it all came about.'

'After the shipwreck, I signed on as crew on a ship to South America and sailed around there for nearly eighteen months. But I knew I must get back here for you. First I wanted to go back to England to pick up some savings I left with a friend. When I was in London, I thought I should visit your father and ask his permission to marry you. So, I hung around outside Newgate until I saw that Mrs Barnard, the one who visited the ship before we sailed.' Sarah and Nora both nodded. 'She held both of you in high regard, asking for news of you and sending good wishes for when I saw you next. She gave me your family's address, Nora, and I made directly for it. But when I got there your father was already dead.' George took Nora's hand and kissed it. 'I wish I had been sooner, but then Jimmy wouldn't be here.'

'Your sister Annie was there with her baby boy. She told me that they could not afford to stay in the house and she was packing to leave as her husband had found cheaper lodgings. Your other sister, Mary, was gone into service and John apprenticed to another master tailor, but it had cost all their savings. Jimmy, you tell her the rest.'

'Sis, it was a bad time. We hoped Mary's wages would help and Annie tried to keep us together she really did. But her and Thomas couldn't manage to, not with the new baby and all. Annie found two rooms to rent and said that she would take Patrick, but that left me. I started my apprenticeship with Da two years ago, but there was no money left to buy another one, so I faced being homeless and jobless. Mary would have found me a job in service, but I did not fancy it. We racked our brains and were getting desperate to avoid me going in the workhouse. Then George knocked at the door and hearing the story says, 'The answer is simple he must come to Van Diemen's Land to live with Nora and me.' Well, you never mentioned George in your letters, so we were shocked at first but then I thought about it and I liked the idea. There was no word from you since Da died and we were worried. So, George got me a place on the ship he had signed on for, and here we are.'

'I was in prison after I got your letter. When I read Da had died it upset me so much that I had too much to drink and got caught. I didn't reply until the end of May, and the letter can't have arrived until after you left. I worry they may not have received it at all. George if I didn't love you before I would fall in love you all over again because of this.' She put her hands on his shoulders and kissed him tenderly. 'If we are to be married I need to know what I am to be called for I only know you as George.'

'Clarke, George Clarke and you will be Mrs Clarke.'

'I like that, Mrs George Clarke.'

'Sing for us Nora,' demanded George. He could wait no longer.

Nora whispered to Jimmy and he went to fetch his father's fiddle. The strains of Barbara Allen were soon heard through the window openings. Old Isaac stopped his scything to listen and Henry smiled but carried on working.

They settled on a wedding in May. Nora would complete a year with no bad behaviour. Sarah's baby would be born and George had enough time to find a home for them and a job for him and Jimmy. Jimmy liked the work on board ship. They hoped to find inshore boat work together, and eventually to buy a boat of their own. Nora remembered her box and the wedding dress and prayed it was still inside. She gave George her tag and asked him to retrieve it for her.

'You don't think it bad luck that I have seen it already?'

'Oh no! I have had all the bad luck I am going to have, and it was you who persuaded me to store it in the hold, to keep it safe. You are my good luck. From now on there will be nothing but good luck for us.'

Part 3- Chapter 16

March 1829 Launceston Female Factory

'You're all wanted in the yard. There's a man outside needs a wife.'

The women in Launceston Female Factory waiting for assignment, were handed a piece of white cloth as they trooped outside. Many of the fifteen women were newly arrived from Hobart. Helen had been in Launceston for around three months and now was between masters. Her time at the British Hotel ended upon the death of Mr Ogilvie. His widow, intending to keep the hotel going, had decided to close for a period of mourning.

Davy remained in Hobart and her parting from him, so distressing for both of them, pierced her brain and replayed in her mind constantly. Aged four now, it would be another eighteen months before her sentence ended and she could collect him. What then? She needed a job where he could be with her. She did not want him in that new orphanage in Hobart, for she would never see him.

He watched as the women came through the door and into the yard, but it was difficult to differentiate between them, dressed all alike in their brown dresses and bonneted against the noon sun. He knew what he was looking for. Not a newcomer to the Island but someone who had worked hard and survived without turning to drink, as so many did. You could tell those women from their bloodshot eyes, trembling hands and vacant stare.

He walked amongst them, stopping sometimes to take a closer look, asking a question or two and not satisfied with answers walked away. Stopping before Helen he appraised her and boldly she did the same to him. He was a few inches taller than her, not tall but middling height and solid looking. His hair was dark brown but shot through with grey. The man was a good deal older than her, perhaps forty, maybe older. He had made an effort to tidy himself up before today. She could tell this by his neatly trimmed beard and his clean working clothes, they looked freshly scrubbed, though well worn. He had never been handsome but his hazel eyes held hers for a second or two more.

'How long have you been in Van Diemen's Land?'

'Four years.'

'Have you worked on the land?'

'Yes, before I came here I helped with the harvest and such.'

Hers was a face of determination. He liked that she held his look. A slight Irish accent but she had probably lived in England because it was tempered with the midland accent of his youth.

'I have an allotment of land in Perth, about seven miles south of here, right by the river Esk, one hundred and fifty-two feet of river frontage next to the bridge. I am building a brick house. Now there are three rooms but I want a family, so there's space for more.'

Helen remembered her journey north from Hobart mainly as a journey of misery from leaving Davy behind. But she did remember crossing the river just a few miles south. It was quite shallow in the high summer, the water blue in the sunshine and there were ducks too on the river. She'd suddenly been so homesick, because it reminded her of a carefree time in Ireland when she and her friends played together by a stream, catching tiddlers and poking sticks around in the water.

'I have a son, Davy. He's four going on five and he's in the Hobart nursery. I want him with me.'

He looked at her closely, studying her. She's young enough and she's proved she's fertile. He liked her straightforwardness and made up his mind.

'The day after we marry we will go to Hobart and collect him.'

'Do you swear so?'

'I do.' He smiled and nodded.

'I'll not be beaten,' her final demand.

'I've been beaten enough for the two of us.'

It was her turn to study him which took no longer than a few seconds. She dropped the white cloth at his feet and it was done.

Part 3- Chapter 17

Perth, Tasmania 1838

'We should leave and settle in Port Phillip on the mainland. There are more opportunities for the children there. If we stay what future will they have? They will not get land now unless they can buy it, and with convicts still being sent here by the thousand, there's no paid work. Our crimes will always be a stain on them. If we move, we can register the older children there and make it look as though they were born of free settlers.'

Helen looked at this man she had married. He had proved a good husband and here he stood, now over fifty years old, wanting to uproot them again. Over the last three years, he had been wearing her down with this idea of his. He was becoming ever more determined. Most men of his age would be looking for an easier life, not starting from scratch.

She was proud of her family of five children with Jane, the youngest, nearly two years old and there was still time for more. Thomas was a vigorous man. Could she bear to leave this house and allotment where all but Davy were born? The place, where she watched her children grow, and where she cared for the strip of land which provided much of their food. Thomas still worked as a sawyer which was tough, the wood being so hard that it was a shock to many new settlers who struck a tree with an axe, expecting to see a clean cut through the bark, only to have the axe shiver through their hands right through to their shoulder and scarce a mark on the tree.

'What if I take us all there to have a look and, if you like it, we can leave Davy there to start building us a house while we come back and pack?'

Davy, yes Davy. He had done his best to be a father for him, but it had been difficult. When she collected Davy, he was very withdrawn. He couldn't bear to be out of sight of his mother and cried if Thomas came near. It took a long time before he settled, and then he was either unnaturally quiet or screaming in rage. Helen refused to let Thomas chastise him until the other children came along. Davy was jealous of them and she was sure he didn't mean to hurt them. Although she pleaded with Thomas not to be too harsh, he told her the children must be treated the same if they did wrong. Now Davy was fifteen, almost a man, but still a child in many ways. Perhaps a new start would be good for him.

'Helen, it's for the best. We need to be in at the beginning of the settlement, there are already about five thousand people there now, but it's growing rapidly and we don't want to miss the opportunity. I've been told the land is good and we must think of the children, please Helen, give it a go. This island is just one big prison, where we can't put a foot wrong for fear of more punishment.'

That was true. She had been punished again, after her marriage, when she came across Jane Smith in Launceston. That fight was her last, but how she taught that woman a lesson! It was worth the fine.

But to leave her good brick house and start again in a wooden shack, could she bear it? She looked at his expression. She could tell he was praying for her to say yes and her objections melted away.

'Very well, Thomas, we'll go and look.' She trusted him and that was all that mattered.

Epilogue

Jane

Melbourne, Summer 1929

'Mother, see what I've found. I have been turning out that old cupboard in your bedroom, and putting in fresh lining paper.'

Whatever is she doing, I thought? She cannot leave me in peace to snooze, which is all I want to do in this insufferable heat. She thrust a piece of old newspaper at me.

'Look mother. I took it and out and started to read it because it's so old, from1884, and then this caught my eye.'

She pointed to a tiny paragraph near the bottom of the page. I looked at it briefly and said.

'You read it. My eyesight isn't good enough with that tiny print.' I didn't tell her I still found reading difficult.

'It reads - David Fitzgerald, an old Van Diemonian, was found dead in a tent on the St Kilda Road, where he lived with Ellen Dugmore, aged 80 - That was your mother's name wasn't it? Who was David Fitzgerald, do you know?'

My heart almost stopped in shock. I tried to speak but my mouth was dry. Sophia must have seen how this news affected me because she went to the kitchen and brought me a glass of water, telling me to sip it slowly. When I got my voice back I asked her to bring me a drop of whisky.

She sat there as I drank the whisky, looking expectantly at me, and I did not know what to tell her. All these years I struggled to keep the secret which my own parents didn't tell me. It was David, that good for nothing half-brother of mine, who told me that my parents had been convicts. I remember the shame of it. It was on the morning of my wedding and he had to spoil it, just as he spoiled everything. Mother told me that he had a difficult first few years as she left him to be looked after while she worked. He was thirty when I married and he should have had a home of his own, but still, he lived and sponged off my mother, and she put up with it. My father was dead by then. I know he tried with David but in the end, even he lost patience with him.

My poor mother aged eighty and living in a tent, she who had kept on telling us that she gave up the eight-roomed brick house my father had built, so we could have a better life in Victoria. I lived in a tent on the goldfields and my first four children were born there but I was less than twenty-three years old and could put up with the hardships. I could not bear it now and I couldn't have done so when I was eighty. It doesn't bear thinking of. What happened to her then I wonder? It was probably the pauper home at Hotham.

'Mother.'

What, oh Sophia is waiting for me to speak. 'I have no idea who David Fitzgerald was and my mother was long dead before she was eighty years old. In any case, it says Ellen and my mother's name was Helen.' I have kept the secret from my children for seventy years. It will go with me to my grave. We Australians prefer to forget our convict roots.

'But you seemed so upset when I read it out. Are you sure it wasn't her?' Sophia butted into my thoughts again.

'Yes sure.' I said harshly. My expression told her not to say anything further. I know my children find me hard, but you had to be in the goldfields, and somehow, I never learnt how not to be.

Sophia left to carry on her sorting out of my bedroom and I was left in peace, but I felt restless now as I thought of my family. Oh, Mother if only you could have written to us to tell us you had nowhere to live. But back then none of us could read or write so it was too easy to lose touch. We moved from goldfield to goldfield all through the fifties and sixties. I would love to tell you that I have thirty-five grandchildren and over seventy great-grandchildren and these descendants of yours have helped to build Australia. You and Father should be so proud. Soon it will be time for me to leave this world behind, so perhaps we will meet in heaven and I can tell you all about my life. What a life it has been.

Author's note

When I was researching my husband's Australian forebears, I found 2 female convicts with the same name, Ellen Fitzgerald. They had been transported within 6 years of each other, one from London and one from Nottingham. I was unsure, at first, which was his ancestor. Searching Old Bailey on-line I found that Ellen's (Nora) case was recorded and the only words in her defence were 'I am an apprentice and my friends don't know where I am' which I found so poignant. It was her first offence and she did not get into any further trouble. Her record is clean, so I apologise to her for giving her further offences. However, Ellen from Nottingham (Helen's) record is a matter of record in the Tasmanian archives and I have woven the story around it.

Although I realised Nora was not an ancestor, the idea to put them on the same ship and write a tale of friendship in the face of great adversity appealed to me. They probably never met but there were similarities, both had the same name, both had fathers named James, both moved to Victoria and died there, both were Catholic and both were Irish or of Irish stock. However, one (Helen) had several children, lived to a great age and founded a family of successful colonists. The other (Nora) married a free colonist, George.

A record of David Fitzgerald appears, as reported in the newspaper of 1884. No convict with that name exists, but he was born around the time of Helen's transportation and there are reports of him as a drunkard, albeit, a devout Catholic drunkard.

Sarah's story is not based on any convict, but she insisted her tale was told. Other convicts appearing in the book are also not based on real people, although 2 convicts from Worcester were transported and both did leave 6 children behind. One of them remarried before her husband died in England. This was acceptable to the authorities and occurred frequently.

Henry II set sail in September 1825 with 79 female prisoners and 10 children. There were also 25 free women with 23 children. Smallpox was diagnosed before they left Woolwich and the record of its spread and treatment can be found in the surgeon's journal. Meat and vegetables were brought on board from the Cape Verde Islands, but no fruit. The incident with the surgeon standing guard against sailors trying to break into the women's prison occurred on the Morley in 1820. There is no evidence to suggest that Surgeon Carlyle took many measures to guard the women against sailors. He did get permission to take 2 prisoners on to Sydney and one of them gave birth to a daughter in 1826 with the surgeon named as the father. He did not marry the convict.

The Henry was reported to have foundered off the Torres Straits in October 1825, but no lives were lost.

Women were transported to Van Diemen's Land from 1803 to 1853, when transportation stopped to all but West Australia. In total, nearly 14,000 women were transported to Van Diemen's Land alone. Their contribution to Australian history was not only ignored but denigrated until recently. It is now being recognised and valued, with sterling work done by the Female Convicts Research Group in Tasmania and the Founders and Survivors Project of which I was proud to be a part.

I have attempted to stick closely to historical fact, unless the story demanded a change e.g. the women were most likely assigned straight from the ship at this date and the consecration of the church in Sorell took place a few months later in September 1827, but there are some points where the evidence is lacking, so I apologise for any historical mistakes. They are entirely my own.

Thank you for reading this book

Thank you for taking the time to read this first book in The Currency Girls Saga. The book telling the story of Helen's daughter, Jane, is the next in the series and called The Digger's Daughter.

If you have enjoyed reading this book, please consider writing a short review on Amazon or Good Reads and tell your friends. Word of mouth is an author's best friend and much appreciated.

The Digger's Daughter (the Sequel)

Based on the life of a real Digger's daughter, this fictional account is a dramatic, historical adventure. It follows the life of the early settlers in Victoria, Australia. Bush Fires, Bush Rangers, Gold Diggers, and rebellion all feature in Jane's early life. But she and her husband are driven to succeed against all probability. She is a convict's daughter who manages to escape her background, building a life of relative prosperity for her numerous children. All the time, the threat of bankruptcy haunts her family. One fire, one drought would bring all she has striven for tumbling down.

Jane never talks about the past, hiding her background from everyone. Her son, Joseph, mixed with the great and the good, from Nellie Melba to Sir Sydney Kidman, the cattle baron, but only Jane knows the truth about the family's origins.

Nearing her death, her nurse, Mary, encourages Jane to talk, to tell her stories, to reveal her secrets. Mary nursed in Egypt and on the Western Front and has her own dark past. Sometimes their stories collide. Excitement mingles with the bleakness of disease, war, and poverty. Families sometimes support each other and sometimes tear each other apart, but at last, Jane learns to love and receive forgiveness. Mary wishes she could do the same, but her sin goes too deep.

Selected Bibliography

Ackroyd, P (2000) London: the biography. Chatto & Windus. (London)

Bateson, C (1969) The Convict Ships 1787-1868. Brown & Sons (Glasgow) 2nd edition.

Brooke, A and Brandon, D (2005) Bound for Botany Bay. The National Archives (Kew)

Carlyle, R (1825) Surgeon's Journal of the convict ship Henry. FCRC

Collier, M (1739) The Woman's Labour, an Epistle. J Roberts (London)

Dickens, C (1836) A visit to Newgate. Sketches by Boz. (London)

Dixon, J (1839) Conditions and Capabilities of Van Diemen's Land as a Place of Emigration. Smith Elder & Co. (London)

Female Convicts Research Centre (FCRC) www.femaleconvicts.org.au/

Founders and Survivors; Australian Life Courses in Historical Context 1803-1920 foundersandsurvivors.org

Griffiths, A (1987) The Chronicles of Newgate. Bracken Books (London)

Hammond, J L and Hammond, B (1978) The Village Labourer, 4th ed. Longman (London)

Hoe, S (2010) Tasmania: Women, History, Books and Places. The Women's History Press

Jennings, H (2012) Pandaemonium 1660-1886. Icon Books (London)

Mortlock, J. F. (1965) Experiences of a Convict. Sydney University Press (Sydney) 3rd edition.

Oxley, D, (1996) Convict Maids. Cambridge University Press. (Cambridge)

Shaw, A.G.L (1966) Convicts & the Colonies. Faber & Faber (London)

Staniforth, M and Brand, I (1994) Care and Control: female transportation voyages to Van Diemen's Land 1818-1853 Australian National Maritime Museum

Trove National Library of Australia Newspaper Archive www.trove.nla.gov.au/

West, J (1852) The History of Tasmania Volume 1. Henry Dowling (Launceston)

Lightning Source UK Ltd.
Milton Keynes UK
UKOW01f0621030817
306605UK00001B/110/P